ARCHES ENEMY

ARCHES ENEMY

A National Park Mystery
by Scott Graham

TORREY HOUSE PRESS

SALT LAKE CITY • TORREY

This is a work of fiction set in a real place. All characters in this novel are fictitious. Any resemblance to actual events or persons, living or dead, is entirely coincidental.

First Torrey House Press Edition, June 2019
Copyright © 2019 by Scott Graham

Published by Torrey House Press
Salt Lake City, Utah
www.torreyhouse.org

International Standard Book Number: 978-1-948814-05-8
E-book ISBN: 978-1-948814-06-5
Library of Congress Control Number: 2018952023

Cover design by Kathleen Metcalf
Cover illustration "Delicate Arch" by David Jonason
Interior design by Rachel Davis
Distributed to the trade by Consortium Book Sales and Distribution

ABOUT THE COVER

Acclaimed Southwest landscape artist David Jonason painted "Delicate Arch," a portion of which appears on the cover of *Arches Enemy*.

Combining a keenly observant eye and inspiration drawn from a number of twentieth-century art movements, including Cubism, Futurism, Precisionism, and Art Deco, Jonason achieves a uniquely personal vision through his vivid, dreamlike oil paintings of the American Southwest. Jonason connects on canvas the traditional arts and crafts of the Southwest's native tribes with the intricate patterns in nature known as fractals. "For me as a painter," he says, "it's a reductive and simplifying process of finding the natural geometries in nature, just as Navajo weavers and Pueblo potters portray the natural world through geometric series of zigzags, curves, and other patterns."

"Delicate Arch" (36×36 inches, oil on canvas, 2015) is used by permission of The Jonason Studio, davidjonason.com.

To all those fighting to preserve southern Utah's magnificent Bears Ears and Grand Staircase-Escalante National Monuments

PROLOGUE

Her death was her own damn fault.

He'd done everything right—research, surveillance, charge level, timing. His planning and execution had been perfect, his actions beyond reproach, which was why not a single question would come his way.

He was sure of it.

The notion had come to him when the vibrations first coursed through his body two months ago. He'd been out for a late-summer hike on Behind the Rocks Trail, following its serpentine path through the maze of red sandstone fins jutting skyward south of town, where the tall slabs of rock sliced the landscape into linear strips of windswept dunes separated by shadowed slot canyons.

He knew Utah's politicians had long fed voters the same tired line—that the citizens of the state could sell their souls to the petrochemical industry while still attracting millions of tourists to southern Utah's incomparable canyon country. In recent years, however, young environmentalists from the Wasatch Front had disputed the politicians' claim. Hoisting the torch of Edward Abbey above their heads, the conservation warriors declared that if the oil and gas giants were allowed to continue mauling the land with their bulldozers and excavators, soon nothing would be left of Utah's stunning red rock country but savaged earth.

The tremors from the thumper truck surged along the ground every few seconds during his hike, pulsing upward through his legs and reverberating in his torso. With each mini earthquake came the same question, over and over again. Could he really send a seismic wake-up call to every citizen of Utah? *Thump.* Could he? *Thump.*

In the ensuing weeks, the truck's pulses became a living thing inside him, a thrumming reminder of what he was prepared to do, and why.

He purchased a used laptop from the classifieds, wiped its hard drive clean, and conducted research only through his secret online portal. He made his purchases in cash at gun shops and farm and ranch stores in nearby towns, collecting everything his research told him he needed.

By early November, the cottonwoods along the Colorado River through Moab glowed with late autumn gold, the trees resplendent in the slanted fall sunlight. On the crisp, clear morning the massive thumper truck trundled through town, its passage noted by a handful of sign-waving activists, the brilliant yellow cottonwood leaves snapped free of their branches by the thousands, fluttering to earth in shimmering cascades. The truck turned off the highway twenty miles north of Moab and crawled across public land on a winding two track to Yellow Cat Flat, hard against the northern border of Arches National Park.

A few final leaves clung to the skeletal limbs of the cottonwoods in town when the year's first winter storm drew a bead on southern Utah a week later. He checked the truck's timetable on the O&G Seismic website as the storm bore down, set to bring decreasing temperatures, whipping winds, and icy sleet to canyon country. According to the schedule, the truck would be thumping its way across the broad desert flat just outside the park throughout the storm.

* * *

He checked his drill and tested the detonator and timer batteries. He apportioned the blasting powder with care, making sure his measurements were exact.

The storm crossed into Utah late in the afternoon. Dense clouds gathered over the state as darkness fell, bringing heavy snow to the northern mountains and sleet to the high desert lands in the south. He deleted his secret online account and drove over the Colorado River bridge after nightfall, slowing to toss the laptop into the roiling waters below.

Biting gusts of wind and frigid blasts of sleet struck him when he shouldered his pack and set out on foot, clicking on his headlamp and hiking into the empty desert. He wended his way through sage and rabbitbrush, the bluffs and promontories at the heart of Arches National Park looming above him, black against the overcast sky in the midnight darkness.

He finished hand-drilling the hole in the sandstone arch as the sky lightened with dawn. The arch soared across the desert, connecting humped ridges of slickrock. He tamped the blasting powder into the drill hole, sank the parallel detonation prongs into the charge mixture, and backed away, unspooling the thin detonator cord as he went. He crouched in a shallow pothole two hundred feet from the rock span, plunger in hand.

The first *thump* of the day pulsed through him in his hiding place at 7:30, right on schedule. A second *thump* coursed through him from the north seconds later, then another, and another. Needles of wind-driven sleet gathered on his shoulders as the inexorable beat of the pulses continued. Trembling with anticipation, he wrapped his fingers around the plastic plunger handle, preparing to press it downward.

A light *tap-tap-tapping* noise reached him—the sound of running steps, propelled by the squalling wind. He stiffened and checked his watch: 7:35. He leaned forward, eyes wide and heart pounding.

She appeared a hundred yards beyond the arch, her blue jacket and black tights stark against the gray clouds. She ran through the swirling sleet with the easy gait of a gazelle, crossing the spine of rock high above the desert floor, headed straight for the stone span.

He nearly leapt to his feet and screamed at her to stop. But he had a job to do. He knelt in place, his head ducked, convinced she wouldn't dare venture onto the arch itself.

She slowed and edged down the sloping ridge of stone—and stepped from the solid rock onto the narrow span.

The digital numbers on his watch flicked from 7:35 to 7:36. Timing was critical if his alibi was to hold up. He tightened his fingers around the plunger handle, his breaths coming in strangled gasps.

She extended her arms from her sides and placed one foot directly in front of the other, her pace slow and deliberate. She was fifteen feet out on the arch when, finally, he could contain himself no longer.

He rose from the depression and revealed himself to her, convinced the mist and sleet between them would make it impossible for her to see his face clearly. Surely, having been spotted, she would retreat.

The plunger, forgotten in his hand, slipped from his fingers. Its handle struck his shoe. It depressed little, if any—but a sharp, concussive *crack* sounded from the arch.

The woman dropped her arms, her gaze fixed on the bridge of stone extending through the air in front of her.

The middle of the span cleaved in two. Dark lines shot like black lightning down its entire length. For an instant, the arch maintained its shape, suspended in the sky. Then it fractured into dozens of jagged chunks of stone.

"No!" he cried out.

Too late.

The woman screamed and grabbed at the air with outstretched fingers as she fell with the pieces of the shattered arch to the desert floor five stories below.

PART ONE

"League on league of red cliff and arid tablelands, extending through purple haze over the bulging curve of the planet to the ranges of Colorado—a sea of desert."

—Edward Abbey, describing Arches National Monument, soon to become Arches National Park, in *Desert Solitaire*, 1968

1

Thump.

Chuck Bender quivered from head to toe as the pulsing vibration passed through his body.

He lay awake beside his wife, Janelle Ortega, in their camp trailer. His stepdaughters, Carmelita and Rosie, slept in narrow bunk beds opposite the galley kitchen halfway down the camper's center aisle, their breaths soft and steady.

He didn't need to check his watch to know the time. The O&G Seismic truck had begun its work promptly at 7:30 the previous two mornings. No doubt the crew was on schedule at the start of this day as well.

Chuck pulled back the curtain over the window abutting the double bed at the back of the trailer. Sleet pelted the glass. Dark clouds hung low over the campground. He dropped the curtain back into place. Another *thump* sounded, followed by another rolling vibration, as the seismic truck pounded the earth outside Arches National Park to the north, trolling for underground deposits of oil and natural gas.

He rolled to face Janelle. Her eyes were closed, but her breathing was uneven, wakeful. He drew a line down her smooth olive cheek, tracing the gentle arc of her skin with his fingertip. Her eyes remained shut, but the corner of her mouth twitched.

"Hey, there, *belleza*," he murmured, lifting a lock of her silky black hair away from her face.

She opened her eyes and turned to him, tucking her hands beneath her pointed chin. "*Belleza nadie.* Nobody's beautiful this early in the morning."

"You are. Besides, it's not that early. We slept in."

A powerful gust roared through the campground, tearing at the trailer's aluminum shell.

She raised her eyebrows. "That's some storm."

"As predicted." He gathered her in his arms and pressed his body to hers.

Sheets rustled in the lower bunk. Janelle raised her head to peer down the walkway over Chuck's shoulder. "Look who's awake," she said. *"Buen día, m'hija."*

"Hola, Mamá," eleven-year-old Rosie responded from the bottom bunk in her deep, raspy voice. "You two woke me up with all your lovey-dovey talking. Are you having sex?"

Chuck released Janelle, who slid away from him to her side of the bed. A snort of laughter sounded from behind the drawn curtain that hid thirteen-year-old Carmelita in the top bunk.

Janelle grinned at Chuck as they lay facing each other. She said to Rosie, "No, honey, we're not . . . we're not . . ."

". . . having sex? But you said that's what people do when they love each other."

"There's a time and place for everything, *m'hija.* I can't say this is exactly the right time and place to be asking about that sort of thing, but I guess it's good you're remembering all the stuff we've been talking about."

"The birds and the bees," Rosie confirmed from her bed. "Sex, sex, sex."

Janelle pulled her pillow from beneath her head, pressed it over her face, and issued a heavy sigh from beneath it.

Chuck folded his pillow in half beside her. Settling the back of his head on it, he looked down the center aisle of the trailer as Carmelita drew back the upper-bunk curtain and leaned over the side of her bed. Her long hair, dark and silky like her mother's, hung past her head, hiding her face. Rosie lifted herself on her elbows, looking up at Carmelita. Rosie's hair, also black, was short and kinky and smashed against the side of her skull from her night's sleep.

Carmelita scolded her younger sister. "You're never gonna learn the right time and place for anything."

Rosie flopped back on her mattress and crossed her arms over her thick torso, hands clenched. "Will, too."

"I wouldn't bet on it."

"I would," Chuck said to Carmelita from the rear of the trailer. "Your sister's going to keep on getting smarter and smarter, just like you. I mean, look how wise and all-knowing you've gotten, just in the last few weeks."

Carmelita sat up straight in the bed, her spine rigid. She gathered the top sheet around her waist, slitted her hazel eyes at Chuck, and whipped the curtain back across the bed, closing herself off from view.

Janelle lifted her pillow from her face and whispered to Chuck, "There's no need for that."

"I couldn't help myself," he whispered back. "I can't get used to her, to our new Carmelita."

"We don't have any choice."

Chuck worked his jaw back and forth. Carmelita had been a loving big sister to Rosie and a kindhearted daughter and stepdaughter to Janelle and Chuck until a few weeks ago, when she'd woken one morning with a scowl on her face and a smirk playing at the corners of her mouth. Since then, as if inhabited by an alien being, she had subjected her little sister to incessant teasing, and had responded with little more than monosyllables and grunts of exasperation to all attempts at conversation by Chuck and Janelle.

Chuck knew Carmelita was simply expressing her growing sense of independence as she entered her teen years. But knowing the why of her behavior didn't make dealing with the reality of it any easier.

"You can't be the one going on the attack," Janelle insisted. "You have to control yourself—which is to say, you have to stop channeling your mother."

Chuck recoiled. "Sheila has nothing to do with this."

Janelle rested her hand on his forearm. "She has everything to do with this. Especially now, for the next two weeks."

"Between the two of them, it's like we're surrounded."

"The only way you and I will survive is if we stick together. *Juntos.* And we have to keep on being nice to Carm. Just like we'll be nice to your mother." She tapped his nose with her finger. "Remember, this was all your idea—Sheila, your contract, the four of us crammed together into this teeny tiny trailer for two whole weeks in the middle of winter."

"It's not winter yet. Not quite. Yesterday and the day before were great—sunny, warm. Plus, we've managed to avoid Sheila so far."

"The first two days were the calm before the storm." Janelle lifted the curtain on her side of the bed and peeked out. "Literally."

Chuck stared at the trailer ceiling, close overhead. At eight feet by twenty-eight feet, the camper had seemed palatial when he'd bought it off a used lot in Durango a month ago for their planned stay in Arches. But by the end of their first day in Devil's Garden Campground, in the heart of southern Utah's spectacular red rock country, palatial had become cozy. This morning, with the gale raging outside, the trailer felt hopelessly cramped.

The four of them couldn't possibly stay inside all day, trapped by the storm. They would drive each other nuts. Nor could Chuck avoid Sheila forever. Maybe today was the day—finally, after four years—to introduce Janelle and the girls to his mother.

He tensed, anticipating the next pulsing beat from the O&G Seismic truck. Instead, a sharp *crack* sounded from somewhere just north of the campground, much closer than the truck's location outside the park boundary. A thunderous rumble shook the camper, accompanied by a shock wave that rocked the trailer on its wheels.

Chuck clambered out of bed, smacking his forehead on the cabinetry lining the walkway. Janelle threw off the sheets and grabbed the fitted jeans and black T-shirt she'd worn yesterday from hooks in the center aisle.

Carmelita pulled back her upper-bunk curtain. She and Rosie looked on, their eyes large and round, as Chuck and Janelle tugged on their clothes.

"Wait here," Chuck told them from the trailer doorway. "We'll be right back."

He caught his reflection in the small window set in the door as he bent to tie his boots. His short hair, brown going gray, rose straight up, thatched and unkempt, from his grooved forehead. The wan morning light streaming through the window reflected off his high temples, bared by his receding hairline. Crow's feet cut away from his blue eyes, seared into his leathery skin by the harsh desert sun over the course of his two decades of shovel and trowel work on archaeological digs across the Southwest, tough physical labor that kept him lean and fit.

He pulled on his insulated rain jacket and ducked outside with Janelle. They strode through the campground together. Motor homes the size of city buses loomed out of the mist, backed into numbered sites along the paved driveway. Moisture puddled on the roofs of tow cars parked in front of the massive recreational vehicles. Electric generators hummed at the back of the RVs. Blurry faces peered out from behind the motor homes' tall fogged windshields. No one besides Chuck and Janelle was outside.

"Everybody must think the sound was part of the seismic operations," Chuck said.

"That's what it sounded like to me," Janelle replied.

"It wasn't, though. It was different. Sharper. And closer."

"It came from the direction of your work site, didn't it?"

"That's one of the things I'm worried about."

Janelle glanced back at the trailer. "Will the girls be okay?"

Chuck swept a hand at the watching motor home owners. "We couldn't ask for nosier neighbors. Besides, Carmelita's in charge. She knows everything at this point."

Janelle whirled to face Chuck, the sharp movement sending droplets of melted sleet cascading off the hood of her jacket. "Don't go there." She ticked a finger back and forth at him in warning. "One smart aleck in the family is enough. You can't try to fight her, not in this case. You'll never win." She slipped her hand back in her jacket pocket.

"*Sí, señora mía*," Chuck said. "I promise." Though he wasn't at all sure he had it in him to do as she directed.

The paved parking lot fronting Devil's Garden Trailhead—at the end of the road into Arches from the park entrance town of Moab—was devoid of cars. Like the RV owners in their massive homes on wheels, would-be park visitors clearly were holed up in town this morning, waiting out the storm.

Devil's Garden Trail led north from the parking area. Chuck's foot slipped when he stepped from the pavement onto the dirt trail. He shot out his arms, struggling for balance, his boots sliding like skis in the saturated soil. Janelle giggled behind him as he caught himself and continued on the path, his feet squelching in the untracked mud.

Soon after leaving the parking lot, the trail entered a low-walled sandstone corridor choked with sagebrush. The short corridor opened onto a mile-wide flat, where the trail came to a junction marking the start of the seven-mile Devil's Garden hiking loop. The roughly circular path led to five of the more than one hundred sandstone spans within the park boundaries that gave Arches National Park its name. From the junction, the trail's right-hand branch passed Private Arch on the way to Double O Arch. The left-hand branch led northwest to Landscape Arch, just over half a mile from the parking lot, then to Navajo and Partition arches.

"We should go left," Chuck said as they approached the junction.

A gust of sleet-laden wind whipped across the flat, carrying with it the piney scent of wet sage.

"But your contract site is to the right."

"The more I think about it, the more it seems to me the sound came from one of the arches—and of all the arches in Devil's Garden, Landscape makes the most sense."

Janelle moaned. "Please, no," she said.

"Something made that noise. Besides, the timing's right."

"But it's been there for thousands of years."

"It's by far the longest and skinniest arch in the park—and it's never had a seismic truck pounding away at the ground so close to it before." Chuck hunched his shoulders against the lashing sleet. A gust of wind slapped a wet sage branch against his thigh, soaking his pant leg. "The freeze-thaw cycle is what causes most arches to collapse. The most recent one to fall in the park was Wall Arch, in 2008. It fell in late October, the time of year when temperatures drop below freezing at night and climb back above thirty-two degrees in the daytime." He raised his hand, allowing the icy needles plunging from the sky to wet his palm. "This is the first real cold snap to hit the park this fall. The temperature dropped into the twenties last night, before the clouds came in. That was the freeze part of the cycle. Then came sunrise and the thaw part, with temperatures rising to freezing or a little above—just as the truck started thumping."

"You really think . . . ?"

"Lots of people have been worried about it. That's why they fought the seismic work so close to the park for so long. But the courts finally okayed it. O&G Seismic started pounding the ground outside the park a week ago, just in time for the storm to come along."

Chuck led Janelle down the left branch of the trail. The path angled across the flat and entered a gap between tall cliffs. The sandstone walls fell back after a hundred yards, giving way to a second opening, this one less than a quarter-mile across and dotted with sage, rabbitbrush, and Indian ricegrass. Sandstone bluffs surrounded the desert flat. Wind whistled off the bluffs and across the opening, making the sage and rabbitbrush branches shiver. Ice crystals clung to the bushes' miniature gray-green leaves.

Chuck peered ahead from the edge of the flat. His back muscles drew up tight at what he saw. He stepped aside and pointed. "There."

On the far side of the opening, a pair of sandstone stumps extended outward from rock bluffs a hundred yards apart. The stumps marked the two ends of the place where, until this morning, Landscape Arch had soared through space.

Bile rose in Chuck's stomach, fiery and burning. He'd hiked here from the campground with Janelle, Carmelita, and Rosie just two days ago, their first day in the park. When Carmelita had spied the span, she'd become a little kid again for a few welcome moments, oohing and aahing with Rosie at the spindly rock bridge arcing across the sky. But now the sky was empty, the arch reduced to a line of jagged rocks lying jumbled on the ground between the two sheared shoulders of stone.

Janelle passed Chuck, leading him across the flat, her movements stiff and stilted, to a split-rail fence that kept onlookers from venturing closer. The sandstone stumps protruded from the opposing bluffs fifty feet above their heads. On the ground below, pieces of the shattered span lay amid smashed clumps of sage and ricegrass.

Thump.

The rolling vibration from the seismic truck caused a broken chunk of sandstone the size of a softball to break free from a waist-high block of the broken arch. The small piece of stone fell to the ground, coming to rest in the mud beside something blue extending upward from beneath the larger hunk of rock.

Chuck gripped the top rail of the fence, his fingers cold and white. "See that?" he said to Janelle.

He vaulted the fence and sprinted toward the fallen block of stone. The pungent smell of pulverized sagebrush filled the cold morning air. He drew close to the line of shattered rocks. Another scent mixed with the smell of crushed sage, something metallic.

The scent of blood.

2

Chuck slid to a stop in front of the fallen block of sandstone. A forearm and hand protruded from beneath the edge of the boulder. A thin navy glove sheathed the hand and a sleeve of indigo fleece covered the forearm. The hand was small, that of a woman. The hunk of stone, ten feet long by six feet wide, rose out of the mud to Chuck's beltline. Blood pooled in the wet earth around the forearm and along the base of the jagged segment of rock. In the pallid overcast light, the blood was dark red, almost black.

Chuck shuddered as he stared at the woman's arm and hand extending from beneath the rock. He had unearthed countless ancient skeletal remains without emotional distress while conducting his archaeological digs over the years. But the sight of the forearm, extending from the woman's body crushed beneath the fallen rock just minutes ago, filled him with anguish.

Janelle squatted next to the forearm. Steeled, Chuck supposed, by all she'd seen and experienced on her new job as a part-time paramedic for Durango Fire and Rescue over the last few months—victims of traffic accidents, domestic abuse, bar fights—Janelle took the petite upraised hand in both of hers without hesitation. She peeled off the glove. The hand was purple, its fingers folded inward. Turquoise polish adorned the nails. A gold band and matching jeweled ring encircled the ring finger.

"The skin is cold," she said over her shoulder to Chuck. "No pulse, of course."

"It can't be more than thirty minutes since the collapse."

"Death clearly would have been instantaneous." She fingered the sleeved forearm. "I recognize the fabric. She's wearing a Top Peak Atomizer—the latest thing in cold-weather athletic wear these days. I was thinking of getting one for Carm for her birthday, to use on her after-school runs this winter."

Bending, Chuck put his shoulder to the stone block above the victim's forearm and hand. He dug his boots into the mud for traction and put his full weight into shoving the jagged-edged boulder. The block didn't budge.

Janelle rose and put her shoulder to the stone next to his.

"One, two, three," Chuck counted.

They shoved the rock together, huffing, until their boots lost their grip and slid in the wet earth, leaving long stripes in the viscous mud. Still no movement.

They straightened. Up close, the bitter odor of blood rising from the base of the block enveloped them. Chuck turned his head, his forearm to his mouth.

"Move away if you're going to lose it," Janelle said. "This is a crime scene. I know we've already contaminated it by being here, but there's no need to add to what we've already done."

Her words instantly settled Chuck's stomach. He lowered his arm. "Crime scene? You came to that conclusion awfully fast." He scanned the sandstone promontories encircling the flat. The shadowy depressions in the surrounding rock ridges made for countless hiding places.

Janelle's mouth turned downward. "You don't get it. I'm talking about the truck, the seismic pounding." On cue, another *thump* rumbled across the flat. "That's what brought down the arch, like you said."

"Or the victim brought it down herself." Chuck pointed at the leaden sky overhead, where the span had soared. "She was up there for some reason. She was out on the arch when it collapsed. That's completely against park rules."

"Just because something's against the rules doesn't keep people from doing it. Before we left home, Carmelita showed me videos on her phone of people climbing on arches all around southern Utah. There's footage of people doing handstands on them, practicing yoga, even swinging off them on ropes."

"But Landscape Arch was so long, so narrow. You'd have to be crazy to go out on it."

"That's what scares me. I've been worried Carm might go out on one of the arches to click a selfie to send back to her climbing teammates, just for bragging rights."

"You didn't say anything about that before we came."

"I convinced myself I was just being a freaked-out mom." Janelle's eyes ran along the line of jagged blocks lying in the mud. "Maybe I wasn't."

"Carm's not crazy."

"Given where her hormones are at these days . . ." She let the sentence dangle.

"Speaking of whom, we need to call this in so we can get back to her and Rosie."

Janelle reached for her phone. "I'll do it. I know the lingo."

Shortly after Janelle completed the call—a brief conversation with a 911 dispatcher in rat-a-tat first-responder patter—the thumps from the seismic truck outside the park ceased.

By the time Chuck and Janelle reached Devil's Garden Trailhead on their return hike, sirens wailed from emergency vehicles approaching on the park road. A dozen vehicles streamed into the parking lot. White ranger sedans and park-service pickup trucks slid to a stop on the wet asphalt, along with a pair of local ambulances, a Grand County Sheriff's Department sport utility vehicle, and a hulking short-wheelbase fire truck. The vehicles' sirens died away as they parked.

National Park Service personnel and first responders leapt from the vehicles, a handful of women among mostly men ranging in age from mid-twenties to well over fifty. They greeted one another, their voices grave and their demeanor reserved. A few of the staffers and responders glanced at Chuck and Janelle as they threw on winter jackets and gear packs and slammed the doors to their vehicles. Chuck and Janelle stepped aside, allowing the workers to stride past them and on up the trail.

Another white park-service pickup truck arrived at the end of the road as the park staffers and responders departed on the muddy path. A pair of black bars stenciled on the truck's front doors marked it as that of the park's chief ranger. A large red work truck trailed the pickup into the parking lot. The words "O&G Seismic" and the company's pump-jack logo emblazoned the doors of the work truck.

Chuck glowered at the O&G truck. "Here come the murderers," he muttered.

"Nobody killed anybody," Janelle responded. "I told you, that's not the kind of criminal activity I was talking about."

Chuck spat on the ground. "The shock waves from O&G Seismic's thumper truck caused the arch to fall, and the woman we found is dead as a result. As far as I'm concerned, anybody who works for O&G is an accomplice."

The work truck towed a flatbed trailer with a yellow front-end loader chained to its bed. The truck pulled to a stop, its air brakes hissing. The driver and a passenger, both men, hopped out. The workmen wore heavy leather boots and blue insulated mechanic overalls with O&G Seismic patches on the breast pockets.

One of the men was in his early twenties, Chuck guessed. Vestiges of teenage acne pocked his cheeks. He was slight, his knees knocking around inside the wide legs of his overalls. He settled a hardhat on his head and pulled on a pair of heavy leather work gloves.

The other man looked well past middle age. His salt-and-pepper beard climbed his cheekbones nearly to his eyes and descended below his chin to his collar, swathing his face and neck like a wool balaclava. Gray hair poked from beneath his greasy hardhat.

Arches National Park Chief Ranger Sanford Gibbons climbed out of his white pickup and crossed the pavement to the O&G workers. Leaving Janelle's side, Chuck strode through the falling sleet to the ranger and workmen.

Sanford turned to Chuck and extended his hand. The chief ranger was a head shorter than Chuck and at least thirty pounds heavier, his stomach bulging beneath his rain jacket. A gray mustache and beard covered his upper lip and jaw. Deep creases cordoned the sides of his mouth. Plastic-framed glasses encircled his wide-set green eyes, topped by bushy eyebrows. His face was pale save for small circles of red, high on his cheeks above his beard, growing brighter in the cold.

Rather than shake Sanford's hand, Chuck confronted the two workmen, his arms stiff at his sides. "They sent you to clean up the mess you made, did they?"

Sanford raised his palm to Chuck. "There's no call for that."

Glaring at the two men, Chuck said, "They crushed a woman. They murdered her."

The older of the two workmen threw back his shoulders, his eyes flaring and his facial muscles twitching beneath his beard.

"Please, Chuck," Sanford said. "I asked them to come. I need their help."

"It's a little late for that, isn't it?"

"I haven't been to the site yet. I need these guys to get out there." Sanford took hold of Chuck's arm and tugged him away from the workmen. "Come with me." Leaning close as they walked together across the parking lot, Sanford said in Chuck's ear, "Let it go. That's an order."

Chuck scowled over his shoulder at the two O&G Seismic employees. They glared back, their gloved hands twisted into fists, then set to work unfastening the chains that secured the loader to the trailer.

Chuck turned away and drew deep breaths as he wound with Sanford through the scrum of parked emergency vehicles to Janelle, who shot him a withering look.

"I know," he acknowledged, hanging his head. "I shouldn't have done that."

"You're absolutely right you shouldn't have." She held out a hand to the chief ranger. "You're Sanford, aren't you?" They shook. "I'm Janelle Ortega." She aimed a thumb at Chuck. "I'm married to this hothead."

Sanford tipped his head at Janelle. "I knew what I was getting into when I signed the contract with him. His reputation preceded him, I'm afraid to say."

The chief ranger had selected Chuck's one-person firm, Bender Archaeological, to perform the contract that had brought Chuck to Devil's Garden two days ago with Janelle and the girls.

Janelle admitted, "I had a pretty good sense of what I was getting into when I married him, too."

On the far side of the parking lot, the older of the two workmen climbed into the operator seat of the front-end loader, atop the flatbed trailer, and fired up its engine. A dark cloud of diesel exhaust belched from the stack as the engine coughed to life. The engine settled into a rattly idle and the older man backed the machine, freed of its chains, off the trailer and braked it to a stop. The younger man tossed the loosed chains into the loader's front bucket, then clambered onto the machine and hunkered behind the driver, clutching the metal roll bar for stability. The older man threw the loader into gear with a grinding clank and drove the machine across the parking area. Leaving the pavement, the loader straddled the hiking trail, the machine's oversized rear tires crushing bunch grass, sage, and rabbitbrush into the saturated soil on either side of the path as it trundled northward.

Sanford turned to Chuck, his eyebrows rising behind his glasses to the sleet-speckled brim of his forest green National Park Service ball cap. "You're the one who found her?"

Chuck tilted his head to Janelle. "*We* found her." He explained to Janelle, "As chief ranger, Sanford is in charge of law enforcement in the park."

"In that capacity," Sanford said, "I'll want to check in with both of you as soon as I can get back. But I've got to head out to the site first."

Chuck eyed the twin lines of crushed plants left by the front-end loader as it proceeded up the trail.

Sanford followed Chuck's gaze. "Least of my worries. I made the call. No choice. The clouds were too low to bring in a chopper for an aerial lift."

Chuck said, "The chunk of rock on top of her is pretty big."

"I'm hoping the loader can handle it. The loader can dig under and we can get the body out that way if we have to."

Janelle pooched her lips, studying the departing machine. "I think it'll work."

Sanford dipped his chin to her. "We'll know soon enough." He looked at Chuck and sighed. "As if the contract wasn't enough."

"Along with the collapse of the arch itself," Chuck said, "if it turns out she's a local—and you have to figure she most likely is, or was—then this'll be a bigger deal with everyone around here than anything having to do with the contract."

"In which case I'll be dealing with two big deals." The chief ranger set his mouth in a hard line, his mustache hiding his upper lip. He set off across the pavement after the loader. Turning and walking backward for a few steps as he departed, he said, "Don't go anywhere, either of you. I'll have plenty to ask you about when I get back."

3

Chuck and Janelle crossed the parking lot after Sanford disappeared up the trail.

"I shouldn't have gotten into it with those guys," he said. "Sorry."

"I need more than just another 'sorry' from you. I need an attitude adjustment." She shook her head. "*Dios.* It's like I've got two *loco* teenagers in the family instead of just one."

"I won't do it again. I promise."

"That's the second time today you've said that."

He glanced at the sky. The sleet was letting up as the leading edge of the storm passed, but the cold wind continued out of the north, harsh and stinging. He shoved his hands deep in his jacket pockets. Ahead, a group of more than two dozen elderly campers wearing hooded rain jackets huddled together at the entrance to the campground, the wind pressing their polyester slacks against their legs.

A tall man at the front of the group frowned at Chuck and Janelle as they approached. "What the hell's going on?" he demanded.

The man's jacket hood was pushed back, revealing thinning silver hair dotted with sleet. His shoulders were stooped with age. Even so, he was taller than everyone else around him by several inches. His face was bounded by a cleft jaw, jutting cheekbones, and a high aquiline forehead.

Chuck and Janelle stopped in front of the group. The campers stood in obvious male-female pairs. Most of the couples sported matching insulated raincoats. Some of the women wore their hoods up. The men were bareheaded, like the man who'd spoken.

All the gathered campers were white and all were elderly, ranging in age, as best Chuck could tell, from their late sixties into their eighties. Several of them gripped pairs of telescoping hiking poles with their gloved hands. One man leaned on a sculpted wooden walking stick that rose as high as his head.

Janelle answered the tall man. "That's what the first responders are here to find out."

A woman standing next to the man asked, "Is it safe?"

The woman's face was heavily lined, her mouth turned down in what appeared to be a perpetual pout. Wire-rimmed glasses high on the bridge of her nose framed her watery blue eyes. She was taller than the other women standing around her, but still several inches shorter than the man beside her.

The tall man rolled his eyes at the woman. "Martha," he carped. "Get a grip, would you?"

Martha lowered her head until her hood hid her face.

The tall man focused his ire on Janelle. "That's not much of an answer, young lady."

Janelle's voice remained calm when she responded to Martha. "If there was any danger, I'm sure they'd have warned us by now."

"That rumbling we heard earlier," another man asked. "What was that all about?"

This man was short and round. His navy jacket draped like a skirt from his broad waistline. A thin strip of gray hair rimmed his otherwise bald head. His brown eyes glistened behind thick glasses speckled with water.

"Quite right, Frank," said a woman next to him. "And now, all the bump-bump-bumping has stopped."

Frank turned to the woman. "Why, you're right, Nora. The bumping noise has gone away, hasn't it?"

Nora nodded. Her face, caked with makeup, was shrouded

by the hood of her navy jacket, the same style and color as the one worn by Frank. She peered at Janelle from beneath her hood, her brown eyes as large as those of an owl. "Miss?"

"Maybe they'll tell us when they come back," Janelle said.

The tall man with silver hair thrust out his chest. "They'd damn well better. We deserve an explanation. They've got us trapped here." He aimed an accusatory finger at the emergency vehicles abandoned haphazardly in the parking lot. "I couldn't get my Country Rambler through that mess if I tried."

"There, there, Harold," Martha said, patting his arm. "We've got our tow-behind. We could squeeze right through with it if we needed to. But it's not as if we're planning to go anywhere today."

Harold harrumphed and jerked his arm away from her. "That's not the point, Martha. The point is, I can't leave, we can't leave, even if we wanted to. It's just what you'd expect from the government, taking advantage of the little guy." Harold turned to the bald man, looming over him. "Isn't that right, Frank?"

Frank nodded his round head vigorously. "You got that right, Harold. We're just pawns to them."

"That's how it always is." Harold swung his hand in an arc, indicating the vehicles arrayed in the parking lot. "It's you and me, Frank, who paid for all of those things." His eyes flicked from one man in the group to the next. "All of us hardworking guys did."

Frank ticked his rubbery chin up and down. "Don't you know it, Harold," he said. "Don't you just know it."

The other men nodded along with Frank, their arms cordoned across their chests.

Harold continued his tirade. "We cough up the taxes they demand of us so they can buy their fancy fire trucks and ambulances. But do they even know we exist? Do they care? Of course not."

Frank and the other men in the group kept their eyes on Harold, while Martha, Nora, and the other women at the men's sides gazed into the distance, stone-faced.

Chuck and Janelle slipped past the group and on into the campground. When they were out of earshot of the elderly campers, he said, "You set a good example for me back there, keeping your cool with that guy."

"Imagine that."

"I'm learning," Chuck said. "I'll do better."

She snorted. "Sure you will."

They passed the massive motor homes one by one. The coaches, polished to a high sheen, lined both sides of the campground drive. Droplets of melted sleet beaded the roofs and clung to the windows and sides of the recreational vehicles, glittering like jewels beneath the overcast sky.

"Those things cost hundreds of thousands of dollars each," Chuck said of the RVs. "For all that guy's complaints, I'll bet his accountant keeps him from paying much, if anything, in the way of taxes."

In front of each motor home sat a miniature sport utility vehicle, detached from its tow position behind the RV and parked in front for day-to-day use.

Janelle tipped her head at the coaches and mini SUVs. "They can afford their expensive toys, but they sure love to whine about the cost of their emergency services. You should hear them if we show up at their homes in our ambulance more than five minutes after they call. 'Where have you been?' 'What took you so long?' They go bonkers."

Chuck counted more than twenty motor homes lining the drive, taking up most of the sites in the campground. Besides the spot occupied by his and Janelle's hard-sided trailer, a handful of pup tents and small, pop-up, canvas-walled trailers occupied the few remaining campsites.

"I thought we'd have the place pretty much to ourselves this late in the year," Chuck said.

"The motor home people are obviously some sort of organized group," Janelle mused.

"The guys appear to be the ones in charge."

"They *think* they're in charge, anyway."

"Especially the tall one, Harold."

Janelle flicked her hand behind her, in Harold's direction, as if shooing a fly. "He's all bark and no bite. I'd bet money on it."

The one-ton Bender Archaeological crew-cab pickup was parked in front of the trailer, facing the campground driveway. They passed the pickup and entered the trailer, stripping off their wet jackets in the doorway. The heater fan purred inside, blowing warm air down the center aisle. Halfway down the aisle, Carmelita's bed curtain remained closed. Below Carmelita's bed, Rosie's lower bunk was empty, as was the built-in dinette table at the front of the trailer and the double bed in back.

"Hello?" Chuck called down the walkway.

Carmelita drew back her curtain. She sat propped against her pillow, wearing the oversized tie-dye T-shirt she'd recently adopted as her sleeping attire. She cradled her phone in her hands between her bare legs, her thumbs poised over its screen. In the shadowed bunk, the glow of the phone tinted her face blue. "Uh, yeah?"

"Where's your sister?"

"How am I supposed to know?"

Chuck pressed his lips together, remembering his vow to Janelle.

He strode down the walkway to the tiny bathroom and rapped on the closed door. "Rosie?" he asked, gripping the recessed handle.

No answer. He opened the door. The bathroom was empty.

He turned a quick circle in the aisle and wound up facing Janelle, who stood next to the dinette table at the front of the trailer. A blast of wind rocked the camper.

"Rosie's not here," he said.

4

Chuck turned to Carmelita, who sat head-high to him in her bunk. Worry showed in her eyes, though whether her concern had to do with her younger sister's whereabouts or her own culpability in Rosie's disappearance, he couldn't be sure.

"Stay here," he said, his tone harsher than he'd intended. "Someone needs to be at the trailer when Rosie comes back. And stay off your phone. I want you ready to respond right away if we need you." He strode down the walkway to the front of the trailer and spun to face Carmelita as he shoved his arm into the sleeve of his jacket. "Call us the instant Rosie comes back."

Carmelita pushed herself higher in the bed, her back against her pillow. "Why don't you call her yourself?"

Chuck froze, his arm halfway up his sleeve. "What'd you just say?" he snapped, before he recognized her sincere tone.

"Call her phone," Carmelita explained. "She'll tell you where she is. Then you can yell at her all you want for not asking to go somewhere all by herself. She's probably having hot chocolate in one of the old people's motor homes. She's the only little kid in the whole campground. They all love her to death."

Chuck sucked in the corner of his mouth. "Good idea," he admitted.

Janelle yanked out her phone. Her fingers flew across its face. She brought it to her ear just as the cricket-chirp ringtone of Rosie's phone sounded from the lower bunk. Chuck reached the bed in two steps. He rooted in the rumpled sheets until he uncovered Rosie's phone. Sheathed in its hot pink protective cover, the phone chirped to announce Janelle's incoming call.

In the upper bunk, Carmelita raised her shoulders to her ears in an exaggerated shrug. "She always forgets that thing."

Chuck punched off the incoming call and pressed Rosie's phone to his chin. Nearly three dozen campers had been gathered at the campground entrance. That number accounted for the owners of virtually all the motor homes in the campground—and didn't leave many who could be hosting Rosie for hot chocolate and cookies.

Despite Carmelita's display of nonchalance, her eyes continued to gleam with worry. A hard nugget of concern burrowed its way into Chuck's gut as well. How many times had he and Janelle emphasized to Rosie the importance of asking permission before setting off somewhere on her own? The storm front and the worst of the sleet had passed, but it was still bone-chillingly cold outside—not the sort of weather a child should be wandering around in alone.

Chuck and Janelle returned to the gaggle of RV owners at the front of the campground. None of the campers reported any sightings of Rosie. Next, he and Janelle knocked on motor home after motor home along the campground driveway. Only four couples answered their knocks. Rosie wasn't sipping hot cocoa in any of the coaches, nor did the RV owners report having seen her outside through their front-facing windshields.

The other campsites were occupied by a mixture of twenty-something couples and solo campers, all weathering the storm in their sites. Those in pop-up trailers cracked their doors a few inches, retaining the heat inside, and reported no sightings of Rosie. Those with pup tents sat marooned in tiny cars with rental company stickers on the rear bumpers, the windows heavily fogged from within. When Chuck and Janelle knocked on the cars, the storm-bound campers rolled down their windows and peered out with forlorn expressions on their faces.

They, too, said they hadn't seen Rosie—though they couldn't see much of anything through the obscured glass of their vehicles.

The tent camper in the site at the end of the campground rolled down his driver's window in response to a knock from Janelle and asked in a heavy German accent how long the storm would last. His wavy blond hair and broad shoulders took up much of the interior of the compact rental sedan. Janelle and Chuck stood together at his window.

"It'll move out fast," Chuck assured the German camper. "Storms always do in the desert."

"But the desert is supposed to be hot," the camper groused through the thick golden beard covering his face.

"In the summer, sure." Chuck gave the curved roof of the small sedan an encouraging tap. "Hang in there. The weather'll get better soon."

The German grunted. In answer to a query from Janelle, he reported he hadn't seen Rosie and rolled up his window.

"I don't think he understands how a calendar works," Chuck said to Janelle as they turned away.

"I'm not worried about him. I'm worried about Rosie."

"The same thing I told him goes for her, too—the storm will move out fast. The day is already getting warmer. We don't need to be too worried. Not yet, at least," Chuck said, seeking to reassure Janelle as well as himself. "It's just like Rosie to wander off somewhere without telling us, even in weather like this. She took her jacket with her. That's a good thing. And it's still morning; it's a long time till dark."

"Could she have followed us out to the arch?"

"I wouldn't put it past her. But she wouldn't have gotten by us without our seeing her."

"Unless she got lost on the way. Maybe she took the right-hand trail at the start of the loop, toward your work site. She's been wanting to see it."

"That's one possibility." Chuck scratched the bristles on his unshaved jaw with his thumb. Then he snapped to attention.

"What are you thinking?" Janelle asked.

His eyes went to the canted ridge of sandstone that framed the west side of Devil's Garden Campground. The gently sloping ridge, seventy-five feet high, served as a natural sound and visual barrier between the campground and the final stretch of road into the park.

He scratched the air with his fingers. "Meow," he said. "It's those damn cats. I'm sure of it."

"God, I hope you're right," Janelle said, out of breath, as she and Chuck strode up the tilted slope of stone toward the top of the ridge. "Why didn't we think of this sooner?"

"I was betting on the lure of hot chocolate."

"I should've thought of it first thing. It would be just like her."

"Even though we warned her not to come up here without checking with us first."

"*Because* we told her not to come up here without letting us know." Janelle paused and circled her mouth with her hands. "Rosie!" she hollered up the angled ridge. "Rooooo-sie!"

The wind muffled her voice and tossed her words back at her.

"Rosie!" Chuck bellowed. "Rosalita *mía*!"

They waited. No reply.

Janelle set off again up the stone ramp. Chuck climbed after her, huffing.

He'd been a runner all his adult life, putting in countless miles on the backcountry trails around Durango, his mountainous hometown in the southwest corner of Colorado. Janelle had taken up running after her move with the girls to Durango from Albuquerque, New Mexico, upon marrying Chuck four years ago. She'd run with him for a few weeks, until, as her fitness level increased, the decade-and-a-half age difference between them grew increasingly apparent, and she sped ahead of him on her own. Carmelita had taken up the sport a few months ago on the advice of her rock-climbing coach. Her runs added an aerobic element to the strength workouts provided by the competitive climbing she practiced with her teammates after school at the local indoor climbing gym three afternoons a week.

Janelle crested the ridge. Wind coursed over the spine of rock, spinning long strands of her hair around her neck. She pulled the strands past her shoulder and into place with both hands.

Chuck reached the top of the ridge and glanced past Janelle, his eyes darting. As forecast by the weather report he'd checked on his phone last night, sleet no longer fell from the clouds surging by close overhead. A lone patch of blue sky showed between broken cloud banks to the north.

The ridge was a quarter-mile long, sloping to the campground on one side and to the two-lane park road on the other. The road extended north fifteen miles from the park entrance to the campground and, immediately outside the campground entrance, the parking lot at the Devil's Garden Trailhead.

An immense flat of sage and rabbitbrush spread beyond the road, running up against distant red sandstone bluffs and towers that rose to the scudding clouds. Light green patches in the flat denoted the rabbitbrush plants, also known as chamisa, among the darker sage. Swatches of brown at the ends of the rabbit-brush branches were the last seed hulls still clinging to the plants as winter approached.

Shallow arroyos cut across the high-desert flat, gathering what little moisture fell in the park and delivering it to the primary drainage through the southern half of the national park, Courthouse Wash. From Chuck's viewpoint atop the ridge, piñons and junipers were distant spots of dark green. The trees grew in the arroyos and close against sandstone bluffs to take advantage of precipitation trickling off the walls of rock and gathering in the drainages on rare stormy days like today. Far to the north, the sandstone monolith known as Island in the Sky loomed half a vertical mile above Arches, its sheer rock prow piercing the clouds.

At the base of the ridge opposite the park road, the elderly campers' motor homes lined the campground drive, the coaches' rooftop air conditioners and television satellite dishes plainly visible from the ridgetop. Beyond the line of RVs, three matching sandstone bluffs stood like frozen ocean waves, bounding the campground to the north. Each of the three bluffs ended in a vertical west-facing wall fifty feet high.

Other than the campground and deserted road, the only sign of civilization visible from the ridgetop was the line of rangers and first responders snaking across the mile-wide flat north of the trailhead. The front-end loader bounced across the flat a hundred feet behind the emergency workers, the deep rumble of its engine just reaching Chuck's ears.

Janelle cupped her mouth and hollered, "Rosie!"

Only the whistling wind greeted her cry.

"Rosie!" she screeched again.

Over countless centuries, wind and rain had created a series of shallow depressions and stubby stone projections along the spine of the ridge. Rosie's head popped up from behind a short plug of stone fifty feet down the ridgetop.

"¡Mamá!" she cried. Her sandpapery voice, filled with joy, rode the gusting wind. "Look what I found!"

5

Rosie rounded the stone projection as Chuck and Janelle ran to her. She cradled a gray house cat with bright yellow eyes in her arms.

"Her name is Pasta Alfredo," she announced. "I made it up all by myself."

Janelle hugged Rosie, cat and all.

"Careful," Chuck warned. "It's feral."

Janelle stepped back, eyeing the creature.

A black collar encircled the cat's neck, resting deep in its matted fur. The feline, decidedly chubby, purred in Rosie's arms, making no attempt to flee.

"It doesn't look very wild to me," Janelle said.

"It does seem pretty content," Chuck conceded.

"She's not an it," Rosie corrected them. "She's a she."

Janelle traced the cat's collar with her fingers. "No identification tags." She lifted Rosie's chin. "You shouldn't have come up here without telling us."

Rosie pressed Janelle's fingers downward with her chin and gazed at the cat. "I know." She looked up at her mother. "But you were gone for sooo long."

Chuck rested his hand on the back of Rosie's neck, his fingers in her curly hair. "It's good you didn't go far."

He, Janelle, Carmelita, and Rosie had spent the day before last, their first day in the park, settling into the trailer and hiking to Landscape Arch. He'd made his way to the contract site yesterday, based on directions supplied by Sanford. After putting in a solid day of work at the secret site, he'd returned in the evening to the campground and a buoyant Rosie.

"Guess what, guess what, guess what!" she had announced breathlessly, grabbing his hand and swinging in a circle around him before he had a chance to take off his gear pack. "We found a cat. Cats. Kitty cats. More than one. Maybe three. Up in the rocks above the campground. Can I have one? Can we keep them?"

"Hold on just a minute there," Chuck had said, loosing himself from Rosie's grip. He shucked his pack from his shoulders and dropped it in the bed of the truck. "Cats? As in house cats? That's not exactly what we came here for."

Rosie again took his hand in hers and dragged him toward the trailer. "You made me come here. I didn't want to. You're making me miss a whole week of school with my friends, plus all of Thanksgiving week, where I don't get to be with my friends either. That's mean. You're mean." She looked up at him with pleading eyes. "You should give me a cat to make up for it."

Chuck laughed. "You've got it all figured out, haven't you?"

"I already asked *Mamá*."

"What'd she say?"

"That she'd have to talk to you."

"I wouldn't get your hopes up."

"But they're so cute, cute, cutie cute cute."

Janelle met them at the trailer door.

Chuck asked her, "Rosie found some cats up on the ridge?"

At his side, Rosie nodded vehemently, her entire body rocking back and forth along with her head.

"I surfed the Net about it," Janelle said. "Turns out pets are abandoned in national parks all the time, as if people think they'll return to the wild or something."

"That's right," Chuck said. "It's a pain for the park service. A lot of times, dogs and cats run off from campsites, and people just leave them behind."

Shoving out her jaw, Rosie declared, "They're assholes."

"*Rosalita*," Janelle admonished. "You know better than that."

"But my friends say it all the time."

"Maybe you need some different friends."

Rosie stomped her foot and crossed her arms over her chest. "The people who leave their pets behind are *total jerks* then."

Chuck crossed his arms in solidarity with her. "Anyone who would abandon a pet is awfully selfish, that's for sure."

"I only saw kitties up there, no doggies," Rosie said.

"That's because lost dogs tend to wander along roads and get picked up and taken to shelters right away," Chuck explained. "But cats are skittish. They know they'll get eaten by coyotes and foxes and other predators, so they hide. Pretty soon, they go feral. The ones that manage to survive may have been somebody's pets at one time, but not after a while. Plus, there's plenty of food for cats in national parks—mice and birds and baby rabbits."

Blood drained from Rosie's face. "Baby rabbits?"

"Afraid so. Cats hunt whatever's small enough for them to sink their teeth into. House cats kill millions of birds every year all across the country. So far, bird populations in places away from cities and towns, like national parks, are doing okay. But if too many cats get left behind in the national parks, you can probably guess what'll happen."

"The birdies will get wiped out in the parks, too!" Rosie clasped her hands in front of her. "Then there would be no birdies left anywhere. Or baby rabbits." She looked at the sandstone ridge rising beyond the trailer, her brows arched. "We have to catch the cats up there. We *have* to."

"How about this?" Janelle offered. "You can chase the cats around up there in the rocks all you want while we're here. Just make sure you tell us you're going up there first."

"Yay!" Rosie cheered. She thrust a fist in the air. "Cat, cat, kitty cats!"

Janelle turned to Chuck. "What do you think?"

He swept the ridge with his eyes. It climbed gently to the top along its entire length. "It looks pretty safe," he said to Rosie. "But if you come to any steep places up there, you have to stay away from them, okay?" He turned to Janelle. "I bet none of the cats will let her anywhere near them anyway. In fact, I guarantee it."

Now, atop the ridge, Chuck squeezed the back of Rosie's neck as she held the gray cat in her arms.

So much for his guarantee.

He let go of Rosie's neck and stroked the cat's matted fur. The feline laid its head against Rosie's chest and closed its eyes, purring.

"This one doesn't seem the least bit wild." His hand came away from the cat's fur gritty with sand. He wiped it on the leg of his work jeans. "Not yet, anyway."

Rosie nuzzled the cat's back with her chin, coating her jaw with a film of red dust. "That's why we have to take this one with us. She's not very wild yet, like you said. She probably just got left behind a little while ago. But if we leave her here, she'll get fer—, fer—"

"Feral," Chuck finished for her. "How do you know she's a she, anyway?"

"I checked. She let me. She doesn't have a penis, not even a little one. I've been learning about all that stuff from *Mamá*."

"Oh, you have, have you?" He cast a sidelong glance at Janelle.

"So, Rosie," Janelle said, ignoring Chuck, "you've found a girl cat named Pasta Alfredo."

Chuck eyed the furry creature in Rosie's arms. "Maybe she's been reported lost within the last day or so. Maybe she's even owned by one of the campers staying here in the campground right now."

"That means we *have* to keep her," Rosie proclaimed.

"Only until we can find her owner," Janelle said. She asked Chuck, "Right?"

Rosie begged, "Pleeeeease."

Chuck groaned.

Janelle cocked an eyebrow at him. "You promised none of the cats would let her near them. This is all your fault."

"No, *Mamá*," Rosie said. She puffed her chest with obvious pride. "It's all *my* fault!"

Rosie skipped down the sloped rock leading to the campground ahead of Janelle and Chuck, the cat clutched to her chest. Janelle descended behind her.

Just as Chuck turned away from the crest of the ridge to follow them, a flash of movement caught his eye.

6

He studied the stone plugs and rolling undulations of slick-rock atop the ridge.

Nothing moved.

He watched, unblinking.

Still nothing.

Janelle stopped and called up to him from below. "What are you waiting for?"

"I thought I saw something," he hollered back down to her over the howl of the wind, his eyes on the spine of the ridge.

"Probably one of the cats."

"Maybe," he replied, though whatever movement he'd seen definitely had been caused by something larger than a cat—and he *had* seen something, he was sure of it.

When nothing more revealed itself, he descended to Janelle. A rush of wind buffeted them as they trailed Rosie down the long stone ramp.

"She won us over pretty easy," Janelle said.

"This whole thing with the girls getting lives of their own, I'm not sure I like it very much," Chuck replied. "We can't even say no to Rosie anymore, much less Carmelita."

"Rosie's way more of a handful than Carm was at her age. I dread when her teen years come along. Carm is just acting a little self-centered these days. Who knows what Rosie will get herself up to."

"Rosie? Are you serious?"

"Believe me, you have no idea."

"You're speaking from experience, aren't you?"

"No teen ever in the history of the world was as stubborn as I was. I still don't know where it came from. But there was no way I was going to let my parents tell me what to do about anything, no matter what it was. Any advice they tried to give me, I was determined to do exactly the opposite—which, in the South Valley, was just a bad idea waiting to happen."

In her teen years, Janelle had abandoned her family in Albuquerque's rough South Valley neighborhood to take up with a seedy local drug dealer, the girls' father, now deceased.

"Except . . ." Chuck urged, knowing the happy ending to come.

"Except I got Carm and Rosie out of the deal." Janelle slung her arm around Chuck's waist. "And, eventually, you."

He snugged her to his side. "I got you and the girls out of the deal, too."

"Compared to what I put my parents through, there's a lot to be said for the fact that, pissy as Carm has been of late, her biggest complaint isn't that big of a deal. The main thing she's upset with us about is that we keep insisting on dropping her off and picking her up from the climbing gym, instead of letting her catch rides with the older girls."

"She's two years younger than anyone else on the senior climbing team," Chuck said. "It's bad enough imagining the things the older girls are filling her ears with while they're at the gym. I don't want her hanging with them any more than I can help it."

Janelle squeezed his waist as they descended the sloping stone together. "Which is all on you. You're the one who introduced her to climbing—to *your* sport."

In his twenties, Chuck had dedicated his every spare moment to scaling vertical walls of stone. During time off between his contracted archaeological digs, he'd climbed in Yosemite Valley in California, Red Rock Canyon in Nevada,

Rifle Mountain Park in Colorado—wherever perpendicular faces of granite, sandstone, limestone, or any other kind of rock offered the intense challenges he and his fellow climbing devotees sought. Two decades later, witnessing Carmelita's climbing prowess on safe indoor climbing walls filled him with unaccustomed fatherly pride.

"We've both agreed," he said. "The fact that she's so talented is all to the good for her."

Until Carmelita had taken up climbing a year ago, she'd been shy and insecure, with only a handful of friends. But since establishing herself as the star of the youth climbing scene in Durango, she'd gained confidence and numerous new companions. Too many, perhaps—particularly of the older variety. But, as Chuck and Janelle repeatedly told each other, too many friends was a better problem for a teenager to have than too few.

Back at the trailer, Chuck crowded into the front entry with Janelle, Rosie, and the cat. At the sight of the feline in Rosie's arms, Carmelita set her phone aside and hopped down from her bunk.

Rosie introduced Pasta Alfredo to her sister. "She's a she. I checked."

"Let's call her Fredo for short," Carmelita suggested.

"Okay," Rosie agreed instantly. "Want to hold her?"

"Not yet. We have to figure out how to take care of her first."

Carmelita grabbed her phone from the upper bunk and set to work, her fingers tapping the screen.

"We should get her some milk," Rosie suggested. "That's what all cats want."

"Good idea," Chuck said, reaching for the refrigerator handle.

"Nope," Carmelita said, her eyes on her phone. "It says here milk is only for kittens. It gives full-grown cats diarrhea."

"Yuck," Rosie said.

Chuck dropped his hand from the refrigerator.

"It says canned tuna fish is okay in place of cat food," Carmelita continued.

"We've got that." Janelle slipped past Chuck and opened the food cabinet.

"Plus some water," Carmelita said.

"Will do." Janelle pulled a can of tuna from the cupboard and turned to the sink.

"What about a bed?" Rosie asked, cradling the cat. "I bet she's really tired from being outside and running away from all the foxes and coyotes so she wouldn't get eaten up."

Carmelita slid her fingertip down her phone, scrolling. "It says a towel would be okay for a pad, but a fleece blanket is best. And that they like to sleep up off the ground."

"Oh, oh, oh!" Rosie crowed. "She can have the fleece blanket on my bed. And she can lay on my bed, too. It's above the floor." She turned to Janelle. "Okay, *Mamá*?"

"I guess," said Janelle. "She has to sleep somewhere." She set out two bowls on the counter next to the sink.

Carmelita tugged the red pile blanket from Rosie's lower bunk, folded it in quarters, and arranged it on the foot of the bed. As Carmelita stepped away from the layered blanket, Pasta Alfredo leapt from Rosie's arms.

"Wow!" Rosie stumbled backward. "She can fly!"

The cat landed on the blanket and immediately began ripping at the fleece with her front claws.

Chuck moaned. "She's tearing it apart."

Janelle said, "With purpose, though. It looks like she knows what she's doing."

"Yeah," Rosie said. "See? She's making a round spot."

Sure enough, the cat created a perfect circle of raised pile with her claws, then settled atop it.

"You're right," Chuck admitted grudgingly. "She made her bed and now she's lying in it, too."

Janelle opened the can of tuna. The trailer filled with the smell of fish.

Chuck squeezed his nostrils between thumb and finger. "Ugh," he said to the girls.

"It's just fishiness." Rosie gave him a shove. "Geez."

On the blanket, Pasta Alfredo settled her head on her paws and closed her eyes.

Rosie took Chuck's hand and whispered, "She's more tired than she is hungry."

Chuck nodded. "It does seem like she's happy to be indoors."

Carmelita looked up from her phone. "She'll need a litter box. It says we can use a cardboard box and tear some paper into strips until we get some real kitty litter."

Chuck said to Rosie, beside him, "We'll have to check with everyone in the campground to find out if anybody's missing her—the sooner the better."

His phone buzzed in his pocket. He checked the number on its screen.

"It's Sanford," he told Janelle.

As he put the phone to his ear, the vision of the dead woman's hand and forearm, protruding from beneath toppled Landscape Arch, came flooding back to him.

7

Chuck and Janelle met the chief ranger at Devil's Garden Trailhead, outside the entrance to the campground. Three hours had passed since Janelle's phoned-in report that Landscape Arch had collapsed, taking a woman to her death along with it. Other than the national park and emergency vehicles, the Devil's Garden parking lot was empty.

Sanford stamped mud from his black leather boots onto the wet pavement and eyed the quiet parking area. "I've closed the park, at least for the next few hours."

He ran Chuck and Janelle through a series of chronological questions. In response, they described the sound they'd heard while in the trailer, and what they'd encountered when they tracked the source of the sound to the collapsed arch.

When the chief ranger completed his questioning, Chuck asked, "Did the loader manage to lift the rock?"

"Barely."

"And?"

Sanford pushed his glasses up his nose. "The body was crushed beyond recognition. *Her* body, that is. Gender is clear enough, along with the fact that she is—or was—a runner. Caucasian. Slight build. Young. Brown hair, no gray. No identification on her, not even a phone. Out for a morning jog, apparently."

Janelle's brow furrowed. "In the middle of the storm?"

"You know Moabites. They have to get their workouts in no matter what."

Chuck asked, "She's a local, then?"

"She almost certainly is, or was. She didn't drive into the park. She probably left her car along the highway, outside the park boundary to the west. She would have taken one of the unofficial trails leading into the park from there. I've got a couple of people retracing her route. Should be easy to follow in the mud."

"Seems she knew where she was headed."

"To the arch? I'd expect so."

"She'd have been early enough to go out onto it before any tourists showed up on Devil's Garden Trail and spotted her doing it."

"I wouldn't be surprised if she was a regular at it. More and more people are sneaking onto the arches these days. They claim they feel special energy or something when they're prancing around on them."

"She didn't take the thumper truck into account, though."

"Based on the location of her body, she was fifteen or twenty feet out on the arch from its north end, at the very narrowest part, when it collapsed."

Janelle said, "She was looking for the right kind of energy, but the wrong kind took her down." She noted to Sanford, "The truck stopped thumping after I called in what we found."

"That was me," the chief ranger responded. "Doesn't take a rocket scientist to figure out what happened—the vibrations from the truck, the cold snap from the storm, the woman's weight on the skinniest part of the arch. I called George Epson, regional operations manager for O&G Seismic, right away. He's sick about it."

Chuck muttered, "Sure he is."

The corners of Sanford's eyes constricted. "George is the guy you wanted to punch in the parking lot. The older one. He came out here with the front-end loader the instant I asked."

"He doesn't look much like a manager."

"He was a heavy machinery operator for a lot of years before they moved him up. He still spends a lot of time in the field. He's a good enough guy. He had his share of misgivings about the decision to move the truck to Yellow Cat Flat and pound so close to the arches."

Chuck grunted. "But he did it anyway, didn't he?"

"Easy for you to say. You work for yourself; you can decide which contracts to bid on and which to pass up. George is a life-long local, one of the few left in Moab these days. He was raised here in the years after the uranium mines closed and before all the tourists showed up, when the town almost dried up and blew away. He's made something of himself with O&G, keeping on with what put Moab on the map in the first place."

"I don't get it. The contract you hired me for is aimed at keeping southern Utah from being destroyed by oil and gas development, but you're standing here defending the guy who's doing the destroying."

The chief ranger filled his cheeks with air and huffed. "I'm not going to get into this with you right now, Chuck. I came back here to get your story. I need to return to the site. I've still got a dead body to identify."

"You mean," Chuck said, holding Sanford's gaze, "you've got a crime scene to investigate."

"What are you saying?"

"I'm merely stating the obvious. O&G Seismic killed that woman. In fact, your guy George Epson killed her. He's the boss, you said so yourself."

Sanford's eyes flared, the red spots on his cheeks growing brighter. "When it comes to crimes, you have to have intent, as in *criminal* intent. From what I saw out there, if anyone had any criminal intent, it wasn't O&G Seismic, it was the jogger herself. She's the one who went out onto that arch, against every regulation in the book."

"Try telling that to her family, or to the people of Moab."

"She snuck into the park and went out onto the arch. She was a lawbreaker, willingly and with forethought." Sanford stabbed the air with his finger for emphasis. "Now *that's* what I call criminal intent."

Janelle said, "The locals around here might consider her something else. They might consider her a martyr."

Sanford stuck out his chest, looking like a stuffed penguin. "You honestly think she might have been out there on purpose, in the middle of the storm, waiting for the truck to start?"

"For all I know, she might've jumped up and down on the arch to try to make it break after the truck started thumping. You're the one who said she was on the narrowest part when it fell."

Sanford lifted his cap and ran his fingers through his gray hair. "I . . . I can't believe . . ." he sputtered.

Chuck said, "If the O&G guy, George, was uncomfortable with the thumper truck's work outside the park boundary, I have to figure pretty much everyone else in town has been concerned about it, too."

"True," Sanford admitted. He returned his cap to his head, pulling its bill down until it met his glasses.

"People react to stimuli in odd ways," Chuck went on. "You just talked about people feeling special energy or whatever when they go out on the arches. For some of them, moving on from there to martyrdom might not be much of a stretch."

Beneath the brim of his hat, a hard glint entered Sanford's eyes. "Which brings us to one of the reasons you're here."

Chuck held his breath as the chief ranger continued.

"You told me you were interested in the contract because of a specific newcomer to Moab, someone who's all about special energy—or, I should say, truly enlightened energy."

Chuck grabbed the legs of his work jeans, his fingers digging into the thick cotton fabric. Sanford's phone chimed. He pulled it from a Velcro-fastened holster at his waist and put it to his ear, raising a finger to Chuck and Janelle. As he listened, his hand, holding the phone, began to tremble.

"Okay, yes, thanks," he said, ending the call. He lowered the phone, his hand still shaking, and looked up the trail toward the toppled arch.

"Bad news?" Chuck asked.

Sanford returned his phone to its holster and knotted his fingers in front of him. "Can't say."

"Can't say or won't say?"

"Either. Both."

"Sounds like you got an ID on the woman."

"A probable," the chief ranger agreed.

"Who was she?"

"You know I can't tell you that. But . . ."

"But what?"

"You're going find out soon enough. She was a friend of you know who."

Just before the call, Sanford had mentioned a specific new-comer to Moab, one who was all about truly enlightened energy. Chuck shivered. The chief ranger had been referring to Sheila.

8

Two months ago in Durango, over pints at Steamworks, Janelle's kid brother Clarence had posed a series of questions to Chuck concerning the Arches contract.

Clarence had followed Janelle to southwest Colorado a year earlier from Albuquerque. A graduate of the University of New Mexico School of Anthropology, Clarence tended bar at Steamworks between stints with Bender Archaeological and other contract archaeology firms in the region, making use of his degree when Chuck or other area companies needed an extra hand on a dig or site survey.

Tourists and locals alike flocked to Steamworks, Durango's largest brewpub, housed in a 1920s-era former automobile showroom a block off Main Avenue. Chalk drawings by children covered the polished concrete floor. Muted televisions aired basketball and football games from walls shorn of plaster to reveal the building's brick walls and ornate iron-lattice framework. Stainless steel air ducts webbed the high ceiling.

At twenty-eight, Clarence was three years younger than Janelle. He wore a checked flannel shirt over his sizable belly. His shoulder-length black hair, as lustrous as Janelle's, was tucked behind his ears, revealing large silver studs glittering in both lobes. Deep laugh lines cupped his mouth, enhancing his bright white teeth. His brown eyes glittered almost constantly with mischief.

"I don't trust it," Clarence said to Chuck, his tone unusually serious. "This guy Sanford you're telling me about, he's in too much of a hurry."

"He says he doesn't have any choice," Chuck replied. He took a swallow of his beer. The hazy wheat lager left a tart aftertaste at the back of his throat as he continued. "The Utah legislature convenes in January. The national monuments will be the first thing on the agenda."

"I don't see what that has to do with your contract at this secret site you're so fired up about."

"A coalition of tribes first proposed the monuments in southern Utah. They wanted to protect the sacred lands of their ancestors from bulldozing and drilling. But as soon as the feds created the monuments, Utah's politicians pushed back, hard, on behalf of their Big Oil masters. They got the size of the monuments reduced by ninety percent. Now they're talking about wiping out the monuments entirely. They care a lot more about easy oil money than they do about preserving the tribes' ancestral lands."

Clarence aimed a thumb at his face. "*Digame, jefe.* I already know a lot of them politician types got a problem with me 'cause of my brown skin and my *inmigrante* parents. It's the same with them Indian folks, huh?"

"Well, the 'Indian folks'—" Chuck made air quotes with his fingers "—sure as hell aren't immigrants. But as long as there's money to be made keeping them in their place, politicians will be willing to do it."

"Keepin' 'em down on the rez."

Chuck took another sip from his pint and plopped it on the scarred wooden tabletop with a foam-raising thud. "Under thumb and under gun, as the tribes have been saying, ever since the white man showed up out here in the West a hundred and fifty years ago. Which is why, right after the monuments were created, Utah's politicians had no problem getting the monument borders cut back to practically nothing, indigenous peoples be damned."

Clarence tipped his glass on its cardboard coaster in front of him. Bubbles streamed from the bottom of the tumbler in curling lines. He straightened the pint and studied Chuck across the top of it. "And now, you're saying this discovery in Arches could reverse that?"

"It's a long shot, but yes, that's Sanford's idea. The tribes and environmentalists have been working together to get the monuments returned to their original size. Petitions, court cases, protest marches—nothing has worked. Then, a few weeks ago, a twelve-year-old girl from New York wandered off the trail in Devil's Garden and, boom, Sanford saw opportunity knocking."

Clarence plucked an unshelled peanut from a wicker basket on the table. He'd filled the basket from a large wooden barrel of the unshelled nuts at the back of the restaurant. The peanuts were offered free by the brewpub to all its patrons. Clarence had worked his way through the basket since returning to the table, cracking open the nuts and dropping the empty shells on the floor beside him.

"That may be all well and good for him, Chuck, but I gotta be honest—this contract doesn't sound like you," Clarence said, opening the shell and tossing the nuts into his mouth. "You always keep your head down. You work your digs and come home to Durango and write up your reports. Then you bid for your next contract and repeat the process, nice and quiet and steady. This thing's different, though. All the secrecy with this discovery you're talking about—I mean, it has politics written all over it. It could blow up in your face, big time."

A boy of about six walked toward them, a basket of peanuts held chin-high before him in both hands, returning from the barrel in the back of the brewpub. As the youngster passed, Clarence plucked one of the unshelled nuts from the upraised basket.

"Hey!" The boy turned to face Clarence. His head barely

reached the bar-height table at which Clarence and Chuck sat.

Clarence stuck the pilfered nut behind his ear. Leaning forward from his tall chair, he peered imperiously down at the youngster and held out his empty hands. "Hey what?"

The boy stared at the peanut, plainly visible between the top of Clarence's ear and his head. "Give it back."

Clarence plucked two peanuts from his basket on the table and dropped them on top of the pile of nuts in the boy's basket. "Two for one. How's that?"

The youngster looked with wide eyes from the newly added nuts to Clarence. "Um, okay, I guess." He shifted his weight from one foot to the other.

"Sounds like we got us a deal, then," Clarence told him. "You're good now." He shooed the boy away with both hands. "You can skedaddle. Vamoose. *Sayonara. Adiós.*"

Chuck grinned and shook his head at Clarence as the boy returned to his family's table. "I'm supposed to take advice from the likes of you?"

Clarence reached over his shoulder and patted himself on the back. "I'm your counselor of all counselors, *primo*." He pulled the stolen peanut from behind his ear, cracked it open, and offered Chuck the nuts inside.

Chuck waved them off and attempted to get the conversation back on track. "The political stuff is for Sanford to deal with," he said. "I'll just be doing the grunt work. It's a simple one-man contract. Two weeks, tops."

"I dunno," Clarence countered. "Sounds like this one could turn out to be a real headache for you. Seems it could cost you down the line—it could cost your *bottom* line—is all I'm saying."

Chuck spread his hands on either side of his glass. "I've been doing this kind of work for a lot of years, Clarence. Most of my contracts have had ancestral findings associated with them in one way or another, which means I've been making the bulk of my living for more than twenty years digging up and cataloguing all the stuff left behind by the ancient ones who lived all around here a thousand years ago. Now, finally, I have the chance to offer a little payback to them and to their modern-day descendants." He turned his palms up. "So that's what I'm going to do."

Clarence popped the stolen nuts in his mouth and raised his pint to Chuck. "Respect, man," he said. He chewed and swallowed. "That's why I call you *jefe, jefe.* 'Cause you're da boss."

Chuck considered Clarence's warning as he watched Sanford slog back up the muddy trail from the Devil's Garden parking lot.

The chief ranger disappeared between the low walls of sandstone flanking the sides of the trail fifty yards north of the trailhead, returning to the collapsed arch.

Chuck sighed and said to Janelle beside him, "I guess it's time."

Taking out his phone, he dialed Sheila's number. Since moving from Los Angeles to Moab six months ago and reestablishing contact with Chuck after years of silence, Sheila had answered a number of his calls. This morning, however, he reached her voicemail.

A few bars of classical harp music played. The music died away and Sheila's voice, soft and muted like the music that preceded it, invited "all seekers of truly enlightened energy" to describe to her their "desires for fulfillment, whether personal, emotional, or—" her tone grew husky "—physical."

Chuck gulped. Sanford's familiarity with Sheila's "enlightened energy" voicemail pitch meant that since arriving in Moab in the spring, her marketing efforts had reached all the way to park headquarters.

Her voice fell to a whisper as she ended her recorded message with the promise to provide "complete satisfaction" to all those who reached out to her.

"It's me," Chuck said when the message ended. "Chuck. We're all settled at Devil's Garden." No need to mention that they'd been settled in the park for three days now. "I've got a break in my work schedule and wanted to see if today might be a good time for us to swing by and say hello."

He ended the call and drummed his phone against his leg. Why hadn't she answered? Did she really know the woman crushed beneath the arch, as Sanford had indicated?

"Okay, the wheels are in motion," he said to Janelle.

She eyed his phone as he tapped it against his thigh. "You're nervous."

He returned his phone to his pocket. "I should be. It's been a long time."

"Which is all her fault, you say."

"All those years, she never called. She wouldn't return my calls, either. She wanted to be forgotten after she moved to California, and she wanted to forget me, too, as near as I could tell."

"Until she came to Moab, just a couple hours' drive from Durango . . ."

". . . and all of a sudden she decided to pick up the phone and dial my number. That was the first chance I'd had to tell her about you and the girls."

"She's been in touch pretty regularly since."

"Almost every week," Chuck agreed. "She's been asking me all sorts of questions about you and Carm and Rosie the last few months—which is what makes me nervous about your meeting her."

"The girls and I will be fine. It's you I'm worried about."

"She has this way about her."

"Which you've brought up, what, a million times now?"

"She uses people. She used *me*." Chuck blinked, angered at the tears welling suddenly in his eyes. He was a grown man, for Christ's sake, in his mid-forties.

Janelle gave his arm a squeeze. "I get it," she said gently. "She had responsibilities to you as your mother that you don't feel she kept."

"She *didn't* keep them."

"I know what you've told me, Chuck. She drank, she partied, she slept around. I get that she was troubled. But you've said she always kept a roof over your head."

"Depends on what you call a roof. A boyfriend's dumpy apartment, a crappy motel room, a falling-down trailer."

Janelle's lips curled upward. "You've got us living in a trailer right now ourselves."

"That's not what I'm talking about."

"I was a single mom, too."

He pulled her close. "I know that," he said in her ear, his lips to her hair. He leaned back, his hands at her waist. "But you stood by your girls. When they came along, you made them the center of your world. You were, you *are*, the best mom Carm and Rosie could ever have asked for. Sheila, on the other hand, barely acknowledged my existence the whole time I was growing up. She made it clear I was a mistake, like I was some sort of penalty she was paying. She never beat me, I'll grant her that. But that's about the best I can say for her."

"People can change, Chuck."

"You were a good mom from day one, and you've stayed a good mom."

"I'm not talking about me."

"I know."

"It's been five years since you saw her last, right? I remember you telling me she came through Durango the year before you and I met."

"She called out of the blue, looking for a place to stay. I happened to be in town between contracts."

"You told me you got her a motel room."

"If I had let her stay with me, she'd probably still be there on my couch."

Janelle smiled as she looked up at him. "At least, if that was the case, the girls and I would have gotten to know her long before now."

Chuck tightened his grip on Janelle's waist and rocked her back and forth. "I admit it sounds like she may finally be getting her act together. And I know it's time you met her."

"I guess we can thank Sanford for making it happen."

He dropped his hands from her sides. "Speaking of whom, I'd like to go check on the site, seeing's how we've got a little time since Sheila didn't answer."

Janelle's dark brows drew together. "You honestly think the collapsed arch and your contract might be related somehow?"

"I just want to make sure everything's okay. It'll take less than an hour. The girls will be fine."

"That's what you said earlier."

"They've got the cat now. They won't go anywhere till we get back."

Janelle glanced toward the trailer. "Less than an hour?"

"Forty-five minutes. I promise."

She rolled her eyes. "You and your promises."

Chuck and Janelle paused where the path branched at the start of the loop. Boot marks pocked the muddy left fork between lines of plants flattened by the front-end loader. Chuck turned right, away from the collapsed arch, leading Janelle along the saturated path on a winding route across the open desert.

He pointed out a thick black mat covering an expanse of ground. "That's why I gave Sanford the look I did when he let the backhoe drive to the arch."

"What is that stuff?" Janelle asked, inspecting the knobby

substance. "It looks like the ugliest hunk of shag carpeting I've ever seen."

"It's called biological soil crust. It takes years to recover when someone steps on it—or drives a front-end loader across it—because it's alive. It's not really soil at all."

"What is it, then?"

"It's a web of lichen and mosses held together by cyanobacteria, one of the oldest forms of life on the planet. Way back at the start of things, cyanobacteria created a thick layer across all the land masses. Every other plant form developed off of it. Cyanobacteria are really good at converting carbon dioxide—that is, greenhouse gases—into oxygen, too. They're so good at it, in fact, that biologists are looking into growing them to help stop global warming."

"The stuff is a real hero, sounds like."

"Especially here in Arches. The crust isn't much to look at, but it absorbs every bit of precipitation that falls on it, like today's sleet. It controls erosion, which in turn sets the stage for all the other plants around here to grow and do their pretty flowery thing."

"I'll never set foot on the stuff," Janelle declared.

"It's easy enough to avoid when you're walking across the desert," Chuck said, "but not when you're driving a front-end loader across it."

At the far end of the flat, the trail passed behind a stone column and alongside a sandstone wall. Chuck led Janelle to a V-shaped notch in the wall. He kicked mud from his boots and preceded her into the notch. Their boots left no marks on the bare rock as they passed through the break in the thirty-foot-high barrier.

The notch gave way to an expanse of brush and scattered boulders out of sight of the trail. Two months ago, an adolescent girl visiting the park with her parents from upstate New York had wandered through the break in the wall. She turned left at the end of the opening and made her way along the far side of the stone barrier until she came to a head-high patch of sagebrush that grew close against the wall and blocked her passage.

Rather than walk around the obstruction as adult logic would have suggested, the youngster slid between the sandstone and stiff branches. According to Sanford, the girl reported she'd expected to squeeze past the sage branches and continue along the base of the wall. Instead, she entered an opening a dozen feet across, surrounded on three sides by encircling sagebrush and on the fourth by the sandstone wall itself. The head-high plants hid a ten-foot length of the wall's base from outside view.

Now, as Chuck retraced the girl's steps with Janelle, he imagined the excitement that must have suffused the girl's voice when she'd cried out to her parents to come see what she'd discovered in the hidden opening.

Eight weeks after the girl had made her discovery, the sage branches still pressed close against the stone wall, hiding the opening beyond. Chuck squirmed past the stiff branches, as he had on his first visit to the site yesterday, then held them aside for Janelle. In the opening, he turned with her to face the short stretch of rock hidden from prying eyes by the surrounding patch of brush.

"*Ahí está*," Chuck said. "There it is."

Janelle gasped. "*Dios mío.*"

9

A dark cavern mouth, five feet wide and less than half again as high, opened into the base of the stone wall.

"It's real," Janelle whispered.

According to Sanford, the girl from New York had shimmied into the cavern at the bottom of the wall and shone her cell phone light around inside. What she saw, as reported by her parents after they returned from their hike, had set Arches National Park staffers abuzz. When word of the girl's find reached members of the Southwest archaeological community, Chuck knew the news would set his fellow archaeologists on fire with wonder and speculation as well. Sanford had explained to Chuck that he was counting on a similar reaction from the public in January, at the start of the Utah legislative session. For now, however, the chief ranger had sworn the family from New York to secrecy, along with the close-knit members of his Arches staff, while enlisting Chuck to perform the hurry-up contract, with the contract's completion mandated by year's end.

The chief ranger planned to release the results of Chuck's report in a coordinated blitz after the first of the year to as wide an audience as possible: state legislators in Salt Lake City, National Park Service brass in Washington, local and national media, and indigenous rights, environmental awareness, and social justice groups nationwide. Capitalizing on the synchronized release, Sanford expected advocacy groups to use the discovery, as detailed in Chuck's preliminary findings, as a potent new weapon in their crusade to return the state's eviscerated national monuments to their original size.

When Sanford first had discussed the contract with Chuck on the phone, the chief ranger had admitted he knew he would face reprimand, perhaps even demotion, for his decision to hide the news of the discovery from his superiors.

"But if I let anyone at headquarters in Washington know what the girl found, word would get out in a matter of days, if not hours," Sanford explained to Chuck. "I'm close to the end of my run. I can retire tomorrow if I want, so I'm safe and secure. But you know who's not? You know who's under siege?" He answered himself: "My wife, Elsie, and her people."

"Her people?" Chuck asked.

"She's *Diné*. Navajo. From Chinle in northern Arizona. We met when I was posted at Canyon de Chelly at the start of my career. She's moved with me from one posting to the next ever since. It's been tough on her, leaving her family behind. I've been assigned to every national park in Utah—Bryce, Zion, Canyonlands, Capitol Reef, and now, for the last ten years, Arches. Through her eyes, I've seen how Native Americans are regarded in this state too much of the time—as if they don't exist. With their mix of ancient spiritual customs and mainline, non-Mormon Christianity, Navajo people in Utah often are considered outsiders by the Mormon Church, and it's the Mormon Church that controls so many levers of power in the state. In the past, that kind of power led to out-and-out racism in parts of Utah like San Juan County, south of Moab, the only county in the state where Navajo tribal members outnumber whites. For more than thirty years, not a single Navajo was ever called to serve on a jury in county court there."

"Sheesh," said Chuck. "That's hard to believe."

"It's the truth, though. Or, it was. Lawsuits by human rights organizations finally changed things for the better in San Juan County. But the state still tends to treat Navajo people as second-class citizens if there's money to be made by doing so.

For me, the last straw was the Utah legislature's support of the decimation of the new national monuments. Elsie fought for years alongside her *Diné* people and members of other tribes for the protection of the ancestral lands included in the initial monument boundaries. Working together for a common cause was a new thing for the Navajo people and the other tribes—Hopi, Zuni, Ute, Ute Mountain Ute. Elsie was so proud of the creation of the monuments, and of what the preservation of those lands meant to her people and to the other tribes."

"I don't see what all that has to do with the discovery you've been telling me about, and the work you want me to do," Chuck said.

Sanford explained. "Another piece of the puzzle is Moab and the way the town is changing. You're probably aware of the fight that's been going on around here. Lots of locals are convinced Moab is getting too big and too overrun with mountain bikers and Jeepers and, most of all, tourists flooding into town to visit Arches. The park road is approaching gridlock. We're almost to the point of having to limit the number of visitors allowed in each day. The old-timers in Moab are convinced the boom is bad for the town and the surrounding desert."

"But you're not?"

"Well, I understand four-wheelers and all-terrain vehicles are ripping the hell out of the unprotected public lands of southern Utah. But that's nothing compared to what full-scale oil and gas development would do. Until now, Utah's canyon country has been spared because of the high costs to drill around here. But the advancement of fracking has changed all that. When you get ten times more production from every well you drill by fracturing the rock deep underneath it, you can afford to blast and bulldoze roads and put in drill pads pretty much everywhere. Doing that would destroy canyon country forever. The politicians reduced the size of the new national monuments specifically to open the way for fracking. In January, the Utah legislature is planning to go even further. They're going to push for the elimination of the monuments altogether."

Over the phone, Sanford's words crackled with emotion.

"We've already lost the easy-to-get-to places to oil and gas development in most of the state. The national monuments provided the opportunity to save the lands of southern Utah from destruction now that fracking has made them a target."

Chuck said, "Which brings us back to your wife and her people, the *Diné*."

"You're a quick study, Chuck. I appreciate that. The people I talked to recommended you without hesitation. I'm beginning to see why. And yes, it all comes back to Elsie and her Navajo people and all the others who fought to create the monuments. As you know, southern Utah was the land of the Ancestral Puebloans. The national monuments were created to preserve the final resting places of those people, the ancestors of today's indigenous peoples."

"Your wife must be heartbroken at how the monuments have been cut back."

"She's pissed off, is what she is. She's a real firecracker, Chuck. You'd like her. She's everything to me. *Everything*. The little girl's discovery is my chance to do something for her in return for all the years she's followed me around Utah. Plus, the discovery gives me the chance to do something for local Moabites as well. Everybody in town has chosen Moab, specifically, as the place they're spending their lives. They may be different from one another in all sorts of ways, from environmental activists to mountain bikers and hikers to off-roaders and dirt motorcyclists, but they all came here because they fell in love with the town and the red rock lands that surround it. They don't want those lands destroyed by fracking. Given the chance, I'm betting they'll come together and join the fight to return the monuments to their original size—as long as, with your help, I can give them a weapon to fight with."

Now, a month and a half since Chuck's initial conversation with Sanford, wind gusts from the passing storm roared over the top of the sandstone wall while Janelle ogled the dark hole at the wall's base. Grains of sand rode the wind over the rock barrier and settled on her hair and shoulders.

She glanced around the hidden opening and wondered aloud, "Why this particular cave?"

"Sanford thinks it's because there are so many arches around here so close together," Chuck replied.

"Are you saying he seriously believes ancient people from centuries ago were as crazy about the arches as people are these days?"

"Ancient people*s*," Chuck said, emphasizing the *s*. "And not just those who lived nearby." He pointed at the cave mouth in the base of the wall. "What's in there suggests that this area may have been a central meeting point for peoples living hundreds of miles from here in all directions."

"*No entiendo.*"

"It'll be easier for you to understand after you have a look."

"*Bueno.*" She tucked her long hair inside her jacket, pulled up her hood, and lay on her back in the damp sand in front of the opening. "Here goes." Turning on her phone light, she wiggled headfirst into the hole, leaving a line in the sand like that of a slithering snake. She paused with three-quarters of her body inside the opening, her legs visible to Chuck from her knees down.

"*¡No puedo creer esto!*" she exclaimed, her words echoing from the cavern mouth.

Chuck settled on his haunches next to her lower legs. "I couldn't believe it either." He rested his hand on one of her protruding boots and spoke into the cavern opening. "I still can't."

"When word of this gets out . . ." Janelle said from inside the rock wall.

"Now you see why Sanford is in such a hurry for me to do my work. And why he's so bent on a coordinated release in January." He tapped her boot. "Move over, would you? I'll squeeze in with you."

"It's pretty claustrophobic in here."

"It's about to get worse."

She scooted sideways in the opening. Setting his ball cap aside, Chuck pulled his headlamp from his jacket pocket and centered the lamp on his forehead. He squirmed into the hole on his back until he lay beside Janelle, their heads even. The beam of his headlamp illuminated the cavern, a low-ceilinged chamber ten feet across. The small grotto, three feet high at its center, tapered to the sandy floor on all sides save for the cavern's tunnel-like entrance.

"This is . . ." Janelle said, staring at the ceiling. "This is . . . it's . . . it's . . . unbelievable."

10

Yesterday, on his initial visit to the cavern, Chuck had wriggled inside on his back and stared upward, overwhelmed by what he was seeing. Today, the sight of what he beheld as he lay beside Janelle astounded him all over again.

"Unbelievable is right," he said to her. "Even with everything Sanford told me, this is way beyond what I imagined."

Painted in thin black lines on a light gray background over every square inch of the cavern's ceiling and sloping walls was, in simplest terms, a map—though the painting was, in fact, a thousand times more than that. Rendered on the interior ceiling and walls were clear depictions of specific places and peoples across the Four Corners region, encompassing southern Utah and Colorado, and northern Arizona and New Mexico. The depictions provided a mapped representation of the area and its ancestral peoples so detailed and extensive as to be hardly fathomable.

The courses of the Green and Colorado rivers formed a large Y across the cavern ceiling, from their mountainous sources in the north, to their confluence in southern Utah, and on into Arizona as the continuing Colorado River. The courses of the two primary waterways through the Four Corners region served as the pictographic map's framing device, running diagonally from the floor of the cavern up and over the ceiling to the opposite side, with the confluence of the two rivers directly overhead. According to a compass reading Chuck had taken yesterday, the rivers were painted on the cavern interior in perfect relation to their actual courses.

Upstream from the Green River's confluence with the Colorado, famed Bowknot Bend—where the Green curled back to within a hundred yards of itself over the course of seven torturous miles—was painted on the ceiling of the grotto in precise relation to where the river actually corkscrewed back on itself east of Moab. Also depicted in its correct location on the cavern ceiling map was the abrupt change in the course of the Colorado River as the river struck Vishnu schist, the oldest exposed rock on the planet, at the bottom of the Grand Canyon and was forced west for dozens of miles before turning south once more on its long journey to the Gulf of California. The San Juan River was painted in true correlation with its westward journey to its junction with the Colorado River, with each of the San Juan's seven source tributaries extending correctly northward into the rugged San Juan Mountains.

In addition to the rivers, dozens of clearly recognizable geologic and cultural sites throughout the region were depicted on the cavern ceiling. Upheaval Dome, a massive stone uplift encircled by a deep syncline north of Bowknot Bend, was painted in intricate detail. Petrified Forest, a sprawling expanse of high desert dotted with tens of thousands of fossilized logs, was correctly placed near the Mogollon Rim in present-day northern Arizona. The famed Mesa Verde cliff dwellings, stone-and-mortar apartment complexes protected beneath overhanging cliffs, were depicted at the foot of the San Juan Mountains. The dwellings were painted in such exquisite detail that individual Mesa Verde complexes were easily identifiable, including Cliff Palace, Balcony House, and Spruce Tree House.

Hundreds of paintings of people and animals covered the ceiling and walls of the cave as well. Each figure was barely an inch high and rendered in meticulous detail. Hunters brandished spears, bows and arrows, and dart-hurtling atlatls. Gatherers bore maize-filled baskets from fields. Animals were discernible by type—desert bighorns high on cliffs, mule deer with branched antlers along creeks, ravens wheeling in flight, and caged turkeys among the human figures. Some game animals were shown as slain, their carcasses slung from poles carried by hunters across flatlands of sage and bunch grass and through stands of juniper and piñon.

"To me," Chuck said, gazing at the cavern ceiling with Janelle, "more than anything else I can think of, the work in here resembles the ancient paintings in underground tombs along the Nile River in Egypt. But the Egyptian paintings were dedicated almost entirely to battles and conflict, while these show only peaceful interactions between members of the various ancient Southwest cultures—the Ancestral Puebloans, or Anasazi,the Fremont to the north, and the Mogollon to the south."

"Isn't the term 'Anasazi' going out of use?"

"They're almost entirely known as Ancestral Puebloans these days. They were an ancient people—ancestral—who built and lived in permanent homes—pueblos."

"The term 'Anasazi' has some negative connotation to it, doesn't it?"

Chuck nodded, causing sand from the floor of the cavern to work its way into his hair at the back of his head. "You know almost as much about my work as I do these days. And yes, you're right. In the Navajo language, *Anasazi* means 'ancient enemies,' which is why the Navajo people don't like the term. But they don't necessarily like the 'Puebloan' part of Ancestral Puebloan either, because the word is Spanish—from the language of the Spaniards who subjugated the Navajo people in the 1500s and 1600s. Even so, 'Ancestral Puebloan' is widely used nowadays for the Anasazi culture."

Chuck allowed his eyes to roam across the cavern ceiling, lit by his headlamp, as he continued.

"The ancient Southwest cultures were similar in lots of ways. Over several centuries, they progressed from semi-nomadic hunting and gathering to sedentary lifestyles, with communal homes and irrigated farm plots. Their housing structures improved over the same time period from simple pit houses to large stone-and-mortar structures. Then, a decades-long drought hit the Southwest in the early 1200s that led—almost everyone agrees these days—to the dispersal of the cultures. We can't know for sure exactly when the painting in here was done, but I can pretty well guarantee it was painted at the height of the ancient cultures, in the late 1100s or early 1200s, just before the drought years."

"How can you tell?"

"By how the cultures are depicted on the map, as distinct entities from one another, each in their own style."

"What do you mean, their own style?"

"The ancient cultures had particular forms of ceramic decoration and, at the height of their societies, particular writing styles, too."

"I thought they didn't leave behind any sort of written history."

"In the way you and I think of writing today, they didn't. But don't try to tell that to the descendants of the ancient cultures, like today's Navajo and Hopi people. Modern indigenous people believe their ancestors were just as much storytellers—that is, writers—as we are today with our words and letters. It's just that the ancient peoples used pictures to tell their stories—pictographs painted on stone, like we're looking at here, or petroglyphs chipped into rock."

"You mean, the rock art that's found all over the Southwest?"

"That's right. Modern indigenous people call what their ancestors did rock *writing*—essentially, storytelling. The ancient cultures of the Southwest might not have developed a written alphabet, but their pictographs and petroglyphs tell distinct stories of their lives—the animals they hunted, the crops they grew, the kinds of clothing and personal ornamentation they wore. There's even a big slab of stone south of here known as Newspaper Rock. Dozens of picture messages were chipped into it over the course of centuries. For all its pictures, though, Newspaper Rock is nothing compared to what we're looking at in here. This pictograph is far and away the most detailed example ever discovered—and the story it tells is beyond incredible."

11

Chuck shifted his shoulder blades on the floor of the cavern. "As the ancient cultures grew and prospered across the region, the groups developed their own ceramic and pictographic styles," he explained to Janelle. "In the south, the Mogollon perfected coiled brown-paste pottery. To the north and east, the Ancestral Puebloans used the clays in their area to create smooth-walled pottery featuring stark black geometric patterns on white-slipped backgrounds. Members of the Fremont culture north of here made coiled pottery, like the Mogollon culture, but in the gray color of the northern and central Utah soils."

Chuck's voice reverberated inside the cavern.

"All of the ancient cultures used rock walls as canvases for depicting their daily lives, but each did so in its own way. The members of the Mogollon culture in the arid south did far more rock-wall chipping than painting, much of it related to celestial observations. The Ancestral Puebloans, in their more verdant region watered by rivers and streams, developed an elaborate pictographic and petroglyphic style that featured anthropomorphic figures with broad shoulders shaped like inverted pyramids. The Ancestral Puebloan figures were topped by round heads and thick necks adorned with earrings, necklaces, and dangling pendants. The Fremont culture, meanwhile, developed a style as artistically advanced and distinctive as any style of art produced today. Fremont storytellers painted on rock walls with beautifully curved strokes and powerfully blunt lines—a style eerily similar to the cubist school of art made famous in the early 1900s by Pablo Picasso and Georges Braque. The best known example of the Fremont style is the Great Gallery panel west of the Green River in Horseshoe Canyon. But if you ask me, I'd say the most striking example is the Four Faces panel, a line of human portraits painted in red on tan stone, with squared-off heads, heavily ornamented upper bodies, and haunting eyes gazing out across the remote desert landscape in Canyonlands National Park just a few miles from here."

Chuck pointed at the cavern ceiling, close overhead.

"Until now, each of the ancient cultures' pictographic styles has been found only in the areas inhabited by that particular society. But all three styles are evident here, indicating that supremely talented painters from each of the cultures worked in this cavern, in close collaboration, to create what we're looking at. The most astonishing thing about this map is that it clearly shows the various ancient cultures thriving together across the Four Corners region. There's some debatable archaeological evidence of the ancient peoples warring with one another at times, but this pictograph depicts only peaceful gatherings between members of the ancient Southwest societies."

He aimed his finger down and to the right, at a depiction low on the cavern wall of humans in the distinct cultural styles of the Mogollon, Ancestral Puebloan, and Fremont dancing together on the bank of a stream.

"See there? That looks to me like some sort of ceremonial dance involving members from the different cultures gathered along the lower San Juan River near today's border between Utah and Arizona."

He pointed up and left, where members of the cultures exchanged baskets of goods on Cedar Mesa, south of the twin Bears Ears buttes.

"That's another scene of peace."

He ticked his finger to the left, at a depiction of a coordinated group hunt. In the painting, Fremonts walked in a line across the landscape, driving a herd of deer toward waiting Ancestral Puebloan and Mogollon archers in the remote Henry Mountains west of the confluence of the Green and Colorado rivers.

"There, too—they're even hunting together."

"The detail, the quality," Janelle said. "It's like those caves in France, only more so."

"You know about the Lascaux caves?"

"I read about them when I was studying up on you online after we first met."

"You checked me out? You never told me that before."

"I liked you. I wanted to know what I was getting myself into. I'd made a bad choice in men once, and I didn't want to do it again."

"Did you?"

"Did I what?"

"Did you make a bad second choice?"

"I'm still deciding."

Chuck smiled. "I'm not." He took Janelle's hand in his as they lay on the floor of the cavern. "You probably remember that only animals are painted on the walls of the Lascaux caves. Those paintings are beautifully rendered in full color, but they don't include humans, which means they don't convey much in the way of cultural information. Whereas, it's the renderings of the human stories that make what's in here so fascinating. Sanford thinks the quality of the work, combined with the depictions of all the ancient cultures coexisting across the region, will serve as a catalyst in the fight to return the national monuments to their original size."

"That seems a bit of a stretch."

"I tend to agree with you. But in today's age of social media campaigns, he may be onto something. It was big news when the national monuments were reduced in size to almost nothing. Sanford wants to hit back at the boundary reductions before what was done fades from the public's memory."

Chuck shook his head, flickering the beam of his headlamp across the pictograph.

"This is what he wants to use. The original monument boundaries protected much of the area shown on this map—almost two million acres of desert wilderness around the confluence of the Green and Colorado rivers. The modern tribes won the initial fight to create the monuments by setting aside conflicts and working peacefully together. This map shows that their ancestors worked together in peace, too. It demonstrates what today's tribes long have maintained, that their ancestors a thousand years ago were real human beings whose activities and societal growth led directly to the cultural traditions of the Ute and Zuni and Hopi and Ute Mountain Ute and Navajo people of today—to the modern tribes' peace-oriented powwows and rain ceremonies and healing rituals."

"What, exactly, does Sanford want you to do for him?"

"The contract calls for me to photograph and measure the cavern interior, and then use the pictures and measurements to create a digitized representation of the pictograph. The representation will be presented to the legislature and shared via social media as part of the public release in January."

"What made Sanford reach out to you? It's not like you were friends with him."

"We had run across each other at conferences a time or two, and he knew of the different discoveries I've made over the years. He also knew I'd done work involving all the ancient cultures represented here. I've led digs in Nine Mile Canyon, at the heart of Fremont culture in central Utah. I've conducted plenty of archaeological assessments over the years in Arizona and southern New Mexico, where the Mogollon people lived. I

SCOTT GRAHAM

created a spatial map of the road system built by the Chacoan people, part of the Ancestral Puebloan culture, in northern New Mexico. And, of course, I've worked all sorts of contracts close to Durango, in and around Mesa Verde in southwest Colorado, the heartland of the Ancestral Puebloan people. Plus, Sanford knew that I haven't been afraid to write up my reports based on what I find, even when my findings go against accepted trends."

"My smart-guy husband," Janelle said, squeezing Chuck's hand.

Then she hoisted herself on an elbow and looked past him at the base of the cavern wall. She lifted her eyebrows, crinkling her forehead, obviously baffled.

12

Janelle gazed past Chuck at the point where the pictograph met the floor of the cave. "I don't get it," she said. "It looks like the painting continues right down into the ground."

"Sanford agrees with you," Chuck replied. "So do I. There's definitely more of the pictograph hidden beneath the sand floor of the cavern, maybe lots more. That would explain how the painters were able to do such detailed painting in here, particularly without obscuring their renderings with smoke stains from fires to provide light while they worked."

"But they'd have needed light from somewhere."

"The mouth of the cavern is directly beneath a cut in the top of the sandstone wall above it. I'm not sure if you noticed, but grains of sand fell on you when a gust of wind blew over the top of the wall while we were outside. The sand gathers on the windward side of the stone barrier the same way snow gathers behind snow fences next to highways. The cut in the top of the wall above the cave mouth acts as a funnel, so even more sand falls to the ground in front of the cavern than anywhere else. That accounts for the opening in the sagebrush in front of the cave—so much sand gathers below the cut in the wall that no plant growth can get started before it's covered up."

Janelle settled back on the sandy floor beside Chuck. "So the cave was a lot bigger when it was painted?"

"The concept is that, over time, the cave has filled in with sand swirling into its mouth, almost like a sand dune on the move. The cave might've been so big back when the pictograph was created that the painters were able to stand up in here while they did their work. If so, sunlight would have come inside, with no need to paint by sooty firelight. That would explain the crisp clean lines of the pictograph."

"The fact that the sand filled the cave almost to the roof would explain why no one ever spotted it, too, wouldn't it?"

"Yep. Until the little girl came along a couple months ago."

They wiggled out of the cavern and stood in the opening, surrounded by the head-high sage plants.

Janelle slapped sand from the seat of her jeans, her eyes on the low cave mouth at the base of the wall. "When news of the pictograph becomes public," she said, "every vandal on the planet will be drawn here."

Chuck rubbed his palms together, sending grains of sand cascading to the ground. "They had to bar the entrances to the Lascaux caves in France. They built a replica of the caves nearby for tourists to visit. I could see something like that happening here."

Janelle folded her arms around her waist, frowning. "It'd be like Disneyland, contrived and fake."

"Sometimes that's what it takes. Arches National Park provides an easy way, right outside Moab, for more than a million people each year to drive on a paved road and see Utah's incredible red rock country from the comfort of their air-conditioned cars."

Janelle loosened her arms from her torso and pushed back the hood of her jacket. "They don't exactly experience the real desert that way."

"It's true they don't get down and dirty with all the grit and scorpions and rattlesnakes. But the hope is they come away from visiting Arches with an appreciation for canyon country that leads them to support efforts like returning the national monuments to their original size. Besides, any land preservation is good preservation, Arches included, as far as I'm concerned. The cave and pictograph have been right here—undiscovered, a couple hundred feet from Devil's Garden Trail—while millions of visitors have streamed through the park over the last few decades. Who knows what's still out there in more remote parts of the park? Artifacts and pictographs and petroglyphs that, because they're inside the park boundary and therefore off limits to drilling and development, are safe from being bulldozed and destroyed."

Chuck's phone buzzed in his pocket. He checked it, finding a text from Sheila: *Wonderful to hear your voice! I'm ready for you anytime today!!*

He groaned as he showed the text to Janelle. "I guess the time has come."

"You've put off meeting her long enough," Janelle said. "Besides, I want to find out what she knows about the woman who died beneath Landscape Arch."

The front-end loader approached Chuck and Janelle from the direction of the toppled span when they reached the trail junction at the start of the loop trail. They waited as the machine bounced across the flat toward them. Exhaust belched from the loader's stack, dissipating in the stiff wind. The front bucket cradled a black body bag bulging with the shape of a human body inside it.

The two O&G Seismic workmen rode the front-end loader as before, the manager, George, driving, and the younger workman squatting behind him. Sanford trailed the loader on foot. The rangers and first responders trudged down the muddy path behind him, their packs low on their backs and their heads bowed.

George braked the loader to a stop at the trail junction and glowered at Chuck from the driver's seat. The machine swayed on its shocks, its engine rumbling. Sanford halted next to the loader.

George said to the chief ranger out of the corner of his mouth, "I thought you cleared the trail of visitors."

"I cleared the whole park," Sanford told George. "We closed the road at the entrance station. We couldn't empty out the campground, though."

George tilted his hardhat at Chuck. "This guy shouldn't be out here." George's eyes went to the bucket at the front of the machine, his jaw trembling. He threw the front-end loader into gear and accelerated past Chuck and Janelle toward the parking lot with a jouncing burst of speed.

Without speaking to Chuck, Sanford led the rangers and first responders down the trail behind the loader.

Janelle spoke after everyone passed. "He looked pretty upset."

"The O&G guy, George?" Chuck asked. "He killed that woman."

"He didn't kill her. His company did."

"Corporations don't kill people. The people who work for corporations do."

"You saw his chin shaking. He knows what he did." She took Chuck's hands in hers. "You shouldn't be so upset with him. He's just doing his job. It's the same with Carmelita. She can't help how she's acting. Your backtalk only makes matters worse." She massaged his knuckles with her thumbs. "You have to be able to accept these things, Chuck."

"I agree with you when it comes to Carmelita. But George? I'll have to give that one a lot of thought."

13

Over chips and sandwiches at the dinette table in the trailer, Chuck and Janelle described the events of the morning to Carmelita and Rosie—the collapse of Landscape Arch, the death of the woman beneath it, and the critical importance that the girls stay well away from all the other arches in the area. After lunch, Chuck headed to the pickup truck in front of the trailer with Janelle and the girls, leaving Fredo curled on the fleece blanket on Rosie's bunk, the bowls of tuna and water on the floor beside the bed.

Chuck drove away from the trailer, Janelle opposite him in the front seat, the girls in back. He eased the pickup to a stop at the campground entrance, facing the Devil's Garden parking area. The paved lot was empty of vehicles, the rangers, first responders, and O&G Seismic workmen gone, along with the body of the dead woman.

"That was fast," Janelle said, looking through the windshield.

"Unlike you and me, they don't see the toppled arch as a crime scene," Chuck said. "They just grabbed the body and left."

"I'm not sure what else they could have done."

"Sanford should have brought investigators to the site to examine how the arch fell and look for any indication that the thumper truck was the cause. They should be taking measurements, performing a geological assessment, trying to dig something up."

"Spoken like a true archaeologist."

"Damn straight."

"*Mamá*," Rosie piped up from the back seat. "Chuck just cussed."

"*Darn* straight." Chuck caught Rosie's eye in the rearview mirror. "Okay?"

Rosie grinned back at him. "Damn straight."

Opposite Rosie on the rear bench seat, Carmelita muttered to her sister without looking up from her phone, "You think you're so funny."

"Damn straight, I do," Rosie declared.

"*M'hija*," Janelle cautioned.

Carmelita asked her mother, "Why do I have to be cooped up in here with her? I should have gotten to stay in the trailer with Fredo. I have a bunch of schoolwork I have to do."

"You know where we're headed," Janelle said.

Carmelita scowled and sing-songed, "To Grandma's."

Chuck glanced at her in the mirror. "You might not want to call Sheila that to her face."

"Because you don't even call her Mom yourself?"

"Well, yes. She never really considered herself the mom type. I'm guessing it'll be the same with her and—" he ticked his fingers in front of the mirror, making quotation marks "—'Grandma.'"

"What should we call her, then?"

He returned his hands to the steering wheel. "Sheila, I guess, like I do."

Letting his foot off the brake, Chuck eased the truck through the deserted trailhead parking area and accelerated down the two-lane road toward the park entrance and Moab. In the back seat, Carmelita returned to her phone while Rosie stared out her side window at the passing desert.

Chuck dug his thumbnails into the steering wheel as he drove. It was really happening—his wife and stepdaughters were about to meet his mother.

A blast of wind rocked the truck at the beginning of the descent into Courthouse Wash. The road ahead, normally chockablock with cars and motor homes, was devoid of traffic. Halfway down the mile-long descent into the wash, they passed the empty parking lot at the trailhead to Fiery Furnace, a labyrinth of tight passages between towering sandstone walls popular with day hikers. Two miles farther on, rainbow-shaped Delicate Arch soared above an open rock bench half a mile east of the road. The arch was the most famous in the park, featured on countless greeting cards. It rounded high above its slickrock base, forming a curved window through which the towering La Sal Mountains east of Moab were magnificently framed.

Chuck worked his jaw as he passed the iconic arc of stone. Would it, too, collapse when the seismic truck resumed its work?

He steered the truck up and out of Courthouse Wash, over a sharp ridge of rock, and down a series of tight switchbacks to the park entrance. Upon leaving the park, he crept south with the line of stop-and-go traffic clogging Main Street in downtown Moab.

Despite the cloud-filled sky and the cold breeze whipping through town, crowds of bundled-up tourists trooped along the sidewalks from T-shirt shops and gift emporiums to restaurants and coffee shops. An array of vehicles crawled along the main drag through town along with Chuck, Janelle, and the girls in their crew cab. SUVs topped with mountain bikes trailed big-wheeled pickups towing all-terrain vehicles on flatbed trailers, which followed rusty camper vans bearing twenty-something rock-climber couples, their dreadlocks corralled beneath beanie caps.

Not many years ago, Moab in November had been a ghost town. Back then, the tourists disappeared and businesses shuttered at the first hint of winter's chill. These days, however, the town of a few thousand on the banks of the Colorado River burst with visitors year-round. Dozens of motels stretched along the highway at both ends of the compact central business district, enabling Moab to serve as a perpetual basecamp, no matter the weather, for masses of mountain bikers, all-terrain-vehicle enthusiasts, Jeepers, day hikers, backpackers, and—the largest segment of all—tourists bent on visiting nearby Arches and Canyonlands national parks.

With the growing hordes of visitors in recent years had come new residents as well. The newcomers were drawn to Moab for its generally cloudless skies and its spectacular setting beneath the towering rock walls that surrounded the town. They came for Moab's easy winters, too, with little if any snow, and for the restaurants that had sprung up along Main Street to serve the ever-increasing number of vacationers. Over the preceding decade, newly arrived residents had remodeled formerly rundown houses on the town grid and snapped up condominiums in developments on the edge of town as fast as they could be constructed.

A mile south of Moab's commercial center, Chuck turned at Janelle's direction into one of the town's new condo developments. They passed beneath a concrete entry arch roughplastered to resemble sandstone. Gold letters bolted to the arch spelled out JUNIPER HEIGHTS. Freshly paved streets branched in three directions, leading to walled blocks of singlestory stucco condominiums.

Janelle looked up from a map on her phone screen and pointed down one of the streets. "That way. Two thirty-two Slickrock Lane."

Chuck eased the pickup to a stop halfway down the block and climbed out.

A screech sounded as he reached the front of the truck. "Charlie!"

A thin woman in her early sixties threw open the gate to a brick courtyard in front of number 232. Sheila extended her arms as she ran to Chuck, the wide sleeves of her diaphanous dress floating like wings from her sides. A crimson sash secured her flowing mauve dress around her narrow waist.

Sheila's fiery red hair hung long and loose down her back, the way she'd worn it for as long as Chuck could remember. Her face was just as he recalled, too, narrow and pinched, her powdery blue eyes crowding her slender nose. The slathering of bright red lipstick on her lips didn't conceal the age lines cutting away from her mouth.

She enveloped Chuck in a hug, then held him at arm's length. "Charles," she said. "Charlie. My little, little boy." She took his face in her hands, stroking his temples. "Already going gray—and letting the whole world see it." She swished her long hair behind her, displaying its lustrous red color. The only gray visible in her hair was a narrow undyed strip marking the part on the top of her head. "So sad," she said to Chuck. She suctioned her tongue off the roof of her mouth in a *pop* of disapproval.

Janelle rounded the truck and stood at Chuck's side.

"My, my, my," Sheila cooed. "So this is *her*." She reached for Janelle's lustrous hair. Blue veins showed through the sun-aged skin covering the back of her hand. "You wear your hair down your backside just like I do, free and easy," she observed. She batted her eyelids, painted a shade of light blue that matched her irises. "We have to keep all our sides ready for whatever comes our way, don't we, dear?" She spun a full circle, her arms flung wide, her dress floating away from her body. Stopping, she winked at Janelle. "Back side, front side, top, bottom, whatever it takes."

Janelle took hold of Chuck's hand, drawing it in front of her. "I'm Janelle," she said. "Janelle Ortega."

Sheila pursed her lips. "Oh, I know who you are, sweetie." She smiled, the crease of her mouth stiff and saccharin. "It's plain as day. You're me, through and through. Little Charlie here has married his own mother."

14

Janelle's hand quivered in Chuck's grip.

Sheila continued. "No wonder Charlie wouldn't come see me all these years. He's got a new momma now."

Janelle drew a sharp breath. Chuck gritted his teeth.

The girls clambered out of the truck and stood next to Janelle.

Sheila studied the girls in their fleece tops, jeans, and hiking boots. She raised her penciled eyebrows to the top of her forehead. "Wow. Just wow. You two are the most stunningly beautiful young women I have *ever* had the privilege to lay my eyes on."

She edged sideways until she stood directly in front of Carmelita. "And *you*," she said. "Look at your hair. So long, so beautiful." She reached forward and combed her fingers through Carmelita's long black ponytail. "Wonderful," Sheila whispered. "Just marvelous."

Carmelita closed her eyes and scrunched her mouth as Sheila raised the long tail of hair to her nose and took a deep sniff.

"Ahhh," she breathed, her eyes closed.

Dropping the ponytail and stepping back, she flipped her dyed hair over her shoulder and said to Carmelita, "Your hair is just like mine. It's a man magnet. Tell me the truth—you're already fighting them off, aren't you? I'm sure the boys are on you like bees to honey. That's the way they've always been with me, and certainly the way they were with your mother, I bet, before Charlie came along—" she peered at Janelle with one eye "—and still are today, no doubt."

Janelle's fingernails dug into the back of Chuck's hand. He glanced sideways at her. Her cheeks were pale, a look of obvious horror etched across her face.

Carmelita's fingers went to the bulge of her cell phone in the front pocket of her jeans.

Sheila's eyes glittered. "Of course!" she crowed to Carmelita. "That's how the boys send out their mating calls these days, isn't it? A trill on the phone and a text with little red hearts, professing their true devotion."

She winked at Carmelita, whose face colored as she stared wide-eyed at Chuck's mother.

Sheila stepped forward once more and gave Carmelita's phone a seductive stroke with the palm of her hand. "That's where it *starts*."

Carmelita jerked and backed away, covering her phone with her fingers.

Janelle pressed her nails deeper into Chuck's skin. Chuck gripped her hand. Should he say something, anything, to shield Carmelita from Sheila's comments?

"But where it *ends*," Sheila continued. "That's the most fun part of all, sweetness."

Chuck's stomach lurched. He tugged his hand free from Janelle's grasp. Had Sheila really just called Carmelita "sweetness"? That was *his* term for the girls. He'd imagined he'd come up with it himself. But was the term, instead, from his distant past?

He cleared his throat. Rather than do the right thing and confront Sheila, he did what he'd always done with his mother. He zigged.

"Nice place you've got here," he said, looking past her at the condominium.

The condo's tan stucco facade was unfaded and free of cracks. Clean white trim formed radiant squares around its front windows.

"Why, thank you, Charlie." A gust of wind swirled Sheila's hair, haloing her head. She wrapped her arms around herself, shivering. "Brr. It's freezing out here. Come inside, all of you, please. Come in, come in."

Chuck glanced at Janelle. She shrugged, her shoulders stiff and her face taut.

He drew a bracing breath and trailed Sheila through the front gate. Inside the condo, he gathered with Janelle and the girls in a tile foyer that faced a high-ceilinged living room. French doors at the back of the room framed a small rear terrace. Clay pots lined the terrace, empty of plants this late in the year.

The dark dank dwellings Sheila had inhabited with Chuck when he was young had featured threadbare couches and chairs, scratched end tables, and bare walls pocked with nail holes. In contrast, Sheila's Moab condominium was bright and airy, smelling of fruity air freshener. Sleek Scandinavian-style furniture covered in blaze-orange fabric with blond wood trim filled the living room. Framed pastels of canyon-country sunsets adorned the unblemished white walls. Circles, squares, and triangles in bold primary colors patterned the plush area rug that rested atop the tile living room floor. The granite countertop in the kitchen, separated from the living room by a chest-high bar, shone from vigorous scrubbing.

Turning in the middle of the living room to face the foyer, Sheila observed the look of surprise Chuck knew was spread across his face.

"I've made my way up in the world, Charlie," she said. "Not that you've had any idea."

"I'm here now." He rested his hand on Rosie's shoulder.

"We're here. Isn't that enough?"

"Of course, of course. I'm delighted you came." She smiled, revealing bleached teeth between the scarlet slash of her lips. Waving Chuck and the others to the couch and love seat in the living room, she said, "Please, sit. I'll heat some water."

They arranged themselves on the sofas while Sheila went to the kitchen. Tall stools with chrome legs and black leather seat pads lined the granite-topped bar between the two rooms.

"How long will you be here?" she asked over the bar as she filled an electric teapot at the sink.

Rosie answered in a single burst from her perch on the edge of the orange love seat. "We're here for forever. Two whole weeks. I'm missing a week of school. My teacher's mad, but I have to. Plus Thanksgiving. Do you have any pets? I have a cat. Her name's Pasta Alfredo. I got her today. We're keeping her in our trailer at the campground. Devil's Garden. We call her Fredo for short. That was Carmelita's idea."

Sheila shut off the water and snapped the kettle lid closed. "You got your cat just today? Aren't you the lucky one. You're Rosie, right?"

Rosie nodded and directed a thumb at her sister, seated next to her. "This is Carm."

"That's short for Carmelita, isn't it?" Sheila asked.

"Yep," Rosie answered for her sister. "It means candy. My long name is Rosalita. It means rose, I think."

Sheila placed the electric kettle on its base. "No pets for me." She removed boxes of herbal tea and an assortment of commercial mugs from an upper cabinet. "My new life doesn't leave room for that."

She lined the mugs on the bar. They advertised a variety of local establishments—Moab's independent bookstore, Back of Beyond Books; the town's public radio station, KZMU; even a mug emblazoned with the O&G Seismic pump-jack logo.

"You have a new life?" Rosie asked. "Cool. Like me with my new kitty. I'm a pet person now."

"I'm a seer," Sheila said. "While we wait for the water to heat up, do you want to see?"

She returned to the living room. Behind the bar, the water in the kettle came to life, rumbling as it heated.

Rosie stood up. "What's a seer?"

"Someone who sees." Sheila hooked a finger at Rosie. "Come with me, sweetness, and I'll show you." She crossed the room. "Moab never had one before," she said over her shoulder to Rosie, who followed after her. "But the people here needed me."

She and Rosie entered a hallway leading away from the living room.

Janelle sprang to her feet. Chuck rose beside her.

"I first answered the calling in California," Sheila told Rosie as they disappeared down the hall. "But now, I'm here."

The sound of a door clicking open came from the hallway.

"Wojee mahojees!" Rosie hollered.

15

Janelle led the way across the living room, Chuck and Carmelita close behind. They tracked Rosie's excited voice to the end of the hall, where a doorway opened into gloom.

Chuck looked over Janelle's shoulder from the entry at what first appeared to be a bedroom-sized cave. As his eyes adjusted, he saw that the back room of the condominium was, in fact, exactly what Sheila had indicated to Rosie: the den of a seer.

A military parachute, dark green for night skydives, cloaked the ceiling and draped down all four walls, encasing the room in shadow. The room's sole window was a dull square on the far wall behind the suspended parachute. More than a dozen metaphysical objects representing various religions and cultures hung from the parachute around the room. Among them, Chuck recognized a Native American peace pipe molded of clay, an Andean panpipe fashioned from bamboo shoots, and a set of Maori prayer balls woven from flax fronds.

A daybed festooned with furry pillows sat beneath the far window. A portable massage table stood on extended metal legs at the foot of the bed. A small square card table draped with a blue velvet cloth was positioned in the middle of the room. A thick candle rose from a ceramic base in the middle of the table, and a butane lighter lay on the tabletop along with a scattering of half a dozen clear crystals the size of walnuts. A metal folding chair sat at the near side of the table, while a padded chair with a high wooden back was pushed away from the table's far side. Two carved snakes twisted around one another across the top of the chair's high back. Ruby-red gemstones served as the eyes of the entwined serpents.

Sheila lowered herself into the wooden chair and pulled up to the table. The eyes of the carved snakes glowed above her head, matching her russet hair. She waved Rosie to a seat on the folding chair across from her.

Janelle stepped into the room with Chuck and Carmelita.

"Shut the door, please," Sheila instructed them.

Carmelita pulled the door closed, sealing off the daylight streaming down the hallway and cloaking the room in shadow.

Sheila lit the candle in the center of the table with the lighter. The scent of vanilla filled the air. Light glittered off the crystals on the table and cast a flickering glow around the room.

"I'm not so sure Rosie should—" Janelle began.

But Sheila cut her off with a raised palm and reached across the table, taking Rosie's hands in both of hers, her forearms on either side of the candle. She closed her eyes and drew measured breaths, her elbows resting on the velvet tablecloth.

"I can't believe this," Chuck said to Sheila, breaking the silence. "You've turned yourself into a two-bit fortune teller?"

Sheila opened her eyes and gazed at Rosie as she answered him. "Fortune tellers are frauds, charlatans." She massaged the backs of Rosie's hands with her thumbs.

"That feels good," Rosie said.

"You can feel our connection, can't you?" Sheila asked her.

Chuck groaned. "For God's sake, Sheila."

"Shush," she warned him.

The single word, issued briskly, hurtled him back to his childhood. She'd used the admonition regularly on him when he was young, demanding his silence whenever one or another of her shiftless boyfriends came around.

Rosie wiggled in her chair. "I feel it," she said to Sheila. "It's all tingly."

"That's your chakra—your life force—mingling with mine," Sheila told her. "That's how I'm able to see."

Chuck grunted in exasperation. "All you're able to see is the opportunity to make some easy money."

He crossed the room, wrapped his hands around Rosie's wrists, and pulled her free of Sheila's grasp. The candle wobbled as he drew Rosie to a standing position.

He stood before Sheila, Rosie in front of him, his hands on her shoulders. "It's great to see you," he said to his mother, his voice strained. "I'm glad you're doing well. I really am."

Sheila sat back in the padded chair and folded her hands in her lap. In the shadowy room, the candlelight lent haunting contours to her heavily made-up face. "You needn't be frightened of the new me, Charlie," she said. "I am now who I shall forever be. Everything and everyone I've ever been has led me here, to Moab—" she swept her hand in front of her, the sleeve of her dress trailing from her forearm like the tail of a kite "—and to who I've become."

"I'm glad the new you is capable of paying the rent," Chuck said. "That's certainly a change for the better."

"You're wrong there. I don't pay anything for this place. That's how much the owner appreciates having me here." Sheila's eyes shone like the jeweled orbs of the interwoven snakes on the chair behind her. "He likes what I do for him, and he doesn't mind sharing."

Tightening his grip on Rosie's shoulders, Chuck turned her toward the entry to the dark room. Janelle yanked the door open. She, Chuck, and the girls left the room and proceeded down the hall.

Squinting in the sudden glare of daylight, Chuck ushered Janelle and the girls across the living room and out the front door. He turned back into the apartment, holding the door open, as Sheila entered the living room from the rear hallway.

She stopped between the couch and love seat, her dress settling around her.

Watching her closely, Chuck said, "A woman was crushed to death this morning in the park. She was young, married. One of the arches fell while she was on it."

Sheila put her hands flat to her stomach and looked at him with unblinking eyes.

Try as he might, Chuck could read nothing in her look. "Sanford, the chief ranger for Arches, said you knew her."

"He did, did he?" Sheila's brows formed a sharp *V* at the top of her nose. "Hmm. I have no idea what he's talking about."

"How do you know him?"

"Who?"

"The chief ranger, Sanford."

The *V* disappeared from between her eyes. "I hardly know him at all."

Chuck waited, his hand on the doorknob.

Sheila puckered her lips. "I don't know her either, like I said."

Chuck turned his back on his mother and left the apartment, pulling the door firmly closed behind him. He crossed the patio to Janelle and the girls, who waited at the side of the truck.

"She just lied to me. I'm sure of it," he said to Janelle. "But I have no idea why."

Janelle ushered the girls into the back seat of the crew cab, closed the door, and pivoted to him, her face flushed with anger. "You totally blew it with her."

16

"Why didn't you say anything to her?" Janelle demanded. Chuck stepped back. "You mean, after what she said to Carmelita?"

"That and everything else."

"I got us out of there. I grabbed Rosie and we left."

"Way too late. We never should have gone inside in the first place. You shouldn't have let us. The sleazy things she said to Carmelita, the insinuations she made . . ."

"I know, I know," Chuck said, wagging his head.

"Don't try that with me," Janelle warned him. "Agreeing with me isn't enough. It's your job to protect the girls from that sort of thing, no matter who it is."

"I wanted . . ." Chuck began. "I was hoping . . ." He faltered.

Janelle sighed and took his hand in hers. "I know what you wanted. I know she's your mother. And I know what you wanted." She enfolded his fingers with her own. "I should have been better prepared, too, I guess. You did warn me, that's for sure."

He glanced back at Sheila's condominium. No doubt she was watching them from inside, her eye to a crack in the curtains. He looked again at Janelle. "We survived." He matched her sigh with one of his own. "We did what we had to do. We met with Sheila; we let her meet the girls. Now, we can check her off our list." He tightened his grip of Janelle's hand. "What say we get the hell away from here?"

They stopped for groceries on the way back through town. Janelle pushed a shopping cart up and down the store's crowded aisles in stony silence. Chuck and the girls trailed her. Rosie grabbed a number of generally forbidden items—Fruit Roll-Ups, a box of sugary cereal, star-shaped crackers laden with preservatives—and offered them to Janelle, who dropped them in the cart without comment.

As they headed for the cashier stand, Rosie handed cans of cat food to her mother. "I remembered because I'm the one who found Fredo," she told Carmelita, who nodded without looking up from her phone.

Chuck's phone buzzed in his pocket with an incoming call from Sanford while they waited in the checkout line. He headed outside as he answered.

Sanford explained that his wife, Elsie, wanted to meet Chuck.

"Now?" Chuck asked.

"That's right. She said to bring your wife and kids."

"She knows I'm in town?"

"She talked to your mother."

Chuck pressed the phone to his ear, flattening it against his skull. "She did, did she? How do they know each other?"

"It's probably best if I let her explain."

Sanford provided directions, and Chuck waited for him to sign off.

Instead, after a pause, the chief ranger said, "Could you do me a favor? Could you not mention anything to Elsie about what happened this morning? She hasn't heard about it yet, and I'd rather give her the news myself."

They drove to the address provided by Sanford, pulling up in front of a tidy yellow clapboard house with a garage in back. The house sat beneath a towering cottonwood on a large lot in the network of city blocks emanating from downtown Moab.

As in all old Mormon towns, each residential street in Moab was named for the distance in city blocks and the compass-point direction corresponding to the distance and direction of the street from the original Mormon church building constructed at the center of the townsite. The home of the chief ranger and his wife was several blocks east and south of the center of town, and two blocks from the sandstone cliffs rising at the edge of the flat Colorado River bottoms on which Moab had been established in the mid-1800s.

Chuck peered up as he climbed out of the truck. Mountain bikers lined the edge of the cliffs overlooking town, their bikes at their sides. The bikers stood at viewpoints along the Slickrock Trail, the renowned mountain-biking route that looped across miles of undulating sandstone immediately east of Moab. Originally developed by motorcyclists, the trail was overtaken by mountain bikers after the invention of the sturdy off-road style of bicycle.

The influx of mountain bikers intent on riding the Slickrock Trail changed Moab's trajectory almost overnight. In the 1990s, Moab was transformed from a dying uranium mining town to the world's first mountain-biking mecca. Thanks to the dozens of miles of biking trails constructed on public lands around town in the years since, Moab continued to hold the title as the most popular mountain-biking destination on the planet.

Chuck joined Janelle and the girls on the sidewalk. They surveyed the street, an expanse of asphalt stretching more than a hundred feet wide from curb to curb. Brown leaves skittered up the broad avenue, driven by the frigid afternoon breeze.

"That has to be the widest street I've ever seen," Janelle said.

"You can thank the Mormons for that," Chuck told her. "They built every neighborhood street in every town they settled in Utah wide enough to swing a U-turn with a full team of oxen wherever they wanted without—in the words of their leader, Brigham Young—'resorting to profanity.'"

"Yoo-hoo!" came a call from behind them. "Hello-ooo!"

A Native American woman in a blocky blazer and long skirt stood in the entry to the house, holding the front door open. "You're going to catch your death out there," she called to them.

Inside, the home was warm and smelled of cinnamon and melted butter. A pair of overstuffed easy chairs and a well-used leather couch filled the small living room at the front of the house. Drums fashioned from sections of hollowed-out cottonwood trunks served as the room's coffee table and end tables. A worn Navajo rug covered the hardwood floor. More rugs, in pristine condition—finely woven with versions of the primary Navajo art forms—hung from the walls. Chuck recognized the geometric pattern of Two Grey Hills, the strong red background of a Ganado, the soft vegetal tones of the Burntwater style, and the powerful lines of a Chief rug. A dozen masked Kachina dolls, the artistic specialty of Hopi artisans whose reservation in northern Arizona was enveloped by the sprawling Navajo reservation, topped a piano on one side of the room.

Next to the piano, a glass-fronted display case exhibited Navajo jewelry fashioned from silver and turquoise, including necklaces, bracelets, rings, and bolo ties. In addition to the jewelry, arranged on the shelves were samples of pottery—bowls and urns and a Navajo wedding vase with its peculiar double spouts—along with an intricately beaded belt and headband.

Sanford's wife introduced herself. Thick silver bracelets jangled on her wrists as she shook their hands. A colorfully beaded hairpiece secured her hair, black striped with gray, at the back of her neck.

Elsie lowered herself into one of the easy chairs. Chuck took the other, and the girls settled next to Janelle on the sofa.

Janelle's gaze roved around the room, lingering on the jewelry-filled display case. "You have amazing taste in artwork."

"Why, thank you," Elsie replied. "I find it comforting to have the art of my people around me. It seems every time I visit my family in Arizona, I return with something more."

She spoke in the formal tone familiar to Chuck from his years of contract work on the Navajo reservation.

"I think I'd do the same," Janelle said.

Elsie slapped her knees and stood. "Where are my manners?" She faced the girls. "Would you like some cookies?"

"Yes, please," said Rosie without hesitation. "Yum!"

"What kind are they?" asked Carmelita.

Rosie said, "I smell cinnamon."

Elsie clasped her hands in front of her. "Right you are." She said to Carmelita, "They are cinnamon swirl, fresh from the oven."

"I guess I'll try one," Carmelita said. "Thank you."

"I'll take three," Rosie said. At a nudge from Janelle, she added, "Um, please."

Elsie left the room, returning with a platter of cookies. Both girls helped themselves. Elsie sat again and smiled at them. She said to Chuck, still smiling, "I asked you here to thank you in person." She shifted in her chair, addressing the girls and Janelle as well. "All of you. I am grateful that you have chosen to help my husband and me."

"I'm honored," Chuck said. "We're honored. The pictograph is like nothing I've ever witnessed."

"I saw it this morning for the first time," Janelle confided to Elsie.

Chuck sucked a quick breath through his teeth, worried Sanford's wife might be offended that he'd shared the hidden find with Janelle.

But Elsie beamed at her. "I'm so pleased that you did."

"It's incredible," Janelle said.

Rosie protested, spitting cookie crumbs. "They won't let me and Carm see it. Chuck said it's too breakable." She thrust out her jaw in an exaggerated pout.

Carmelita knocked Rosie's leg with hers and asked Elsie, "Is it pretty cool?"

Elsie straightened in her seat, holding her knees with her hands. "It's *very* cool. It tells the stories of my ancestors, from the north, south, east, and west. It is a thing of magic and wonder."

Chuck said to her, "Sanford told me you worked really hard to get the national monuments created, only to see them reduced in size to almost nothing."

A shadow passed across Elsie's dark brown eyes. "The taking of the monuments has been a real blow to the effort by the *Diné* and so many others to protect the lands that are sacred to us."

Janelle said, "I understand you know Chuck's mother, Sheila. What does she see for the future of the monuments?"

Elsie smoothed her skirt over her legs. "I asked her that very question, but she explained to me that she sees for people, not places or things."

"Did she see good things for you, then?"

Elsie smiled. "I tried that with her, too. But it did not work. Sheila merely helps me imagine the things I want for myself. It is up to me to make them real."

Chuck asked, "Is that why you and Sanford want to use the pictograph in your work for the national monuments?"

Elsie nodded. "Anything I can do, I will do—with my husband's help, in this case. And yours."

Chuck asked the question he'd been itching to ask since arriving. "Do you know why Sheila called you to tell you we were in town?"

"Oh, she didn't call me," said Elsie. "I called her. We speak most days for a few minutes. It helps me."

"My mother helps you?"

"That is what she does. When she mentioned to me that you had just left her home, I called Sanford and asked him to contact you. I know that you have been at the campground for the last few days, and now I can thank you in person."

"Do you have any suggestions for me as I complete the contract?"

"I ask only that you understand the significance of all that you are working on—just as your mother does."

Chuck sat back in surprise.

17

"Sheila knows about the cavern?" Chuck asked Elsie.

"We have spoken about it many times," she replied. "I have told her of its value to the *Diné*, and to me personally. She has been a strong supporter."

Chuck picked up a cookie and took a bite, attempting to cover his bewilderment. How could Sheila possibly have any sense of the pictograph's cultural significance, or its value to Elsie and Sanford and their effort on behalf of the national monuments?

Rosie pushed the cookie platter back from the edge of the coffee table, clearing a portion of the leather drum skin stretched across the tabletop and fastened at the sides with sinew. She wiped her hands on her pant legs and pounded the drum furiously with her fingers, bopping her head like a punk rocker in time with her blistering beat.

"Rosie!" Chuck and Janelle admonished simultaneously.

She paused with her hands poised above the drumhead. "I was just trying it out. I guess it was louder than I thought."

Elsie slid from her chair to her knees in front of the drum-cum-coffee table. Facing Rosie, Elsie raised her hands above her side of the drumhead, matching Rosie's upraised hands. "Three, two, one," Elsie counted.

She and Rosie drummed the leather skin together. Gradually, Elsie slowed the cadence of her beat. Encouraged by a smile from Elsie, Rosie slowed her beat, too. Soon, they drummed the taut leather skin together in a slow, powerful beat.

Elsie lightened her stroke. Rosie did the same. The two

tapped the head of the drum gently with their fingers, grinning at one another.

Elsie led Rosie for the next five minutes, increasing and decreasing the cadence of their drumming fingers and the force with which they struck the head of the drum. The drumbeats calmed Chuck, enabling him to relax, if only slightly, for the first time since finding the body of the woman beneath the arch.

"I like Elsie," Janelle said to Chuck when they were settled in the truck and headed back through town, the girls seated behind them. "Your mother, on the other hand . . ."

They crawled with the slow-moving traffic back through town and entered the park, now reopened, joining a line of cars switchbacking up and over the initial ridge and down into Courthouse Wash. Oblivious of Chuck and Janelle in the front seat, the girls discussed what they would do with Fredo when they got back to the trailer.

"We have to comb her hair," said Rosie.

"A comb won't work," Carmelita replied. "Her fur is too dirty. We'll need a brush."

"We'll use *Mamá's* big brush. It'll work great on the tangles."

Janelle showed no sign of having heard Rosie's plan. She stared ahead from the passenger seat, mentally replaying, Chuck presumed, their unsavory visit with Sheila. Overhead, the clouds were clearing, the gray sky giving way to Arches' customary cerulean blue.

The road was closed at a turnaround point a mile from Devil's Garden. A ranger sat in a white park-service sedan next to traffic cones blocking both lanes of traffic. She climbed out of her car when, rather than turn around, Chuck nosed the truck up to the line of cones.

He told the ranger they were guests in the campground. She checked his driver's license against a printout on her clipboard and explained that the park would close overnight and reopen in the morning. She removed a cone from the road to clear the way and waved them onward.

Inside Devil's Garden Campground, Chuck swung the pickup around the same group of elderly campers who had gathered in the morning at the edge of the parking lot. The campers now walked single file along the campground drive. As Chuck eased the truck past them, they turned one by one into a campsite, gathering at the side of a tall motor home in front of Harold, the tall angry man from earlier in the day. Frank, the bald man who'd acted so obsequiously toward Harold, carried a folding stepladder under one arm and trailed the group into the site.

Chuck parked and toted shopping bags into the trailer along with Janelle and the girls. Fredo lay on Rosie's bed on the folded blanket. The bowl of tuna was empty.

As Carmelita and Rosie cooed over the cat, Janelle caught Chuck's eye and pointed at the edge of the padded dinette seat facing the trailer's center aisle. The seat's brown synthetic cover was clawed through to its foam core in half a dozen places.

Chuck glowered at Fredo. The cat looked back at him, blinked her yellow eyes, and yawned. She rolled to her side as the girls scratched the top of her head.

"I'm beginning to see why we've never had pets," Chuck said.

"Fredo's not a pet. She's a wildcat. A wild flying cat," said Rosie.

"In zoos, they keep wildcats in cages," Chuck told her. "We might have to do the same with Fredo."

"Never!" Rosie cried, her fingers in the cat's fur. "Anyways, she's not *that* wild. She's more of a wild flying house cat."

"Whatever that's supposed to mean."

"It means she's wild *and* she flies *and* she's friendly."

"Gotcha."

Chuck touched Janelle's shoulder and tipped his head

toward the door. Outside, he led her to the campsite picnic table, set on a concrete base beneath the outstretched arms of a gnarled piñon tree behind the trailer. He sat on the damp top of the table, his feet on its bench seat, and scooted sideways for her to join him.

"I figure we're not quite done talking about the elephant in the room," he said when Janelle was seated beside him.

"You mean, the pit viper?" She pressed her hands between her legs. "She's . . . she's *awful*."

"I'm hoping Carmelita didn't pick up on what she was insinuating."

"Oh, no. Carm picked up on it, all right. You must have seen the look in her eyes. She knew exactly what your mother was talking about, and she was completely bewitched by it."

"But Carm's smart. She knows hogwash when she hears it."

"Sure, she's smart, as in straight-A smart. But she's hormonally challenged these days. She doesn't need any of that hogwash—if that's what you want to call it—from your mother. I'm sure she gets more than enough of that sort of thing from those climbing teammates of hers." Janelle jetted a stream of air through her lips. "And that's not even the half of it. There's the whole fortune-telling bit your mother pulled with Rosie." She took a hiccuping breath. "The only thing missing was a freaking crystal ball."

"Which is why I got us out of there."

"Too late," she said, repeating her earlier assertion. "But yeah, you did. Thank you for that."

"It was an easy enough call to make."

"She's just . . . she's just so . . ."

Chuck nodded. Then he shook his head. "This new Sheila is someone I've never met before."

"I've never met anyone like her."

"A seer, you mean?"

"No. I mean, whatever it is she is."

"She's as different from your parents, and you, as it's possible to be."

"Not according to her. She said she and I are the same, remember?" Janelle shuddered. "She said you married her when you married me."

"She hasn't got a clue who you are—or how lucky I am."

Janelle took one of his hands in both of hers. "How'd you turn out so different?"

"Easy. It was just the two of us when I was a kid. Or just her, really, stuck with me. She lived in her own world, I just took up space in it. She was hardly ever around, and when she was, she was only there for herself. The good thing about that was I got to make myself into whoever I wanted to be. I knew from day one I didn't want to be anything like her, so I worked to become everything she wasn't."

"You succeeded."

"Thanks. I think." He turned to Janelle. The afternoon sun broke from the clouds and streamed through the piñon branches, lighting her face. "I was alone for a long time. I was convinced, all those years, that the way not to be like my mother was to keep to myself. I didn't want anything to do with the kind of relationships she had—all the screaming and yelling and throwing things. Even when I was in a relationship, which was hardly ever, I kept myself walled off. It was Clarence who first made me realize I didn't have to spend the rest of my life like that."

Her eyes twinkled. "It wasn't me?"

He smiled at her. "You were a close second. Before I met you, though, when I first hired Clarence and he came piling into my world with all his grins and jokes, he made the walls I'd worked so hard to build inside me start to crumble. He never stopped talking about how great you were. When he finally rigged it so we could meet, I was ready for you, and for the girls, too." He traced the spots of sunlight speckling the tabletop beside him with the tip of his finger. "But I sure wasn't ready for the new Sheila we just met."

"How different is she from what you remember?"

"Well, the manipulative part we saw today, that's her all the way. When I was a kid, she burned through boyfriends like a brush fire. She'd take them for whatever they had—drugs, money, a place to crash—and move on to the next. There was always someone or something better, just over the horizon."

"Is that what took her to California?"

"There was this guy, Derrick something-or-other, who convinced her to move out there with him. That was more than twenty years ago. I was on my own, working my way through college. Sheila and Derrick had worked every angle they could in Durango by then—signing up for disability payments, doctor-shopping for pain meds to sell. They even dealt pot, back when it was illegal. I was in high school at the time. I stayed in the mountains around town as much as I could, hunting and fishing and keeping my distance. They made me hide their stash for them up in the woods. They'd send me to get whatever they needed. They said it'd be okay if I got busted since I was still a minor."

He chuckled ruefully.

"That went on for about a year. I was happy enough to do it. It was the most stable home life I'd ever had. She and Derrick got this beat-up one-bedroom apartment—a converted room in an old motel. I got the couch, my own place to sleep. The apartment came with a storage locker in back. I kept my rifle and fishing gear in it. That was the first time I ever had anything like that for my own stuff. They fought constantly, of course."

"You sound so matter-of-fact about it."

"Police radios were the background music to my life. Whenever things got out of hand with Sheila's boyfriends when I was little, I'd pull a blanket over my head and pretend nothing was happening. But the lights of the police cars still made it through, flick, flick, flick. By the time Derrick came along, I was old enough that I could get out of there until things cooled down."

"You've never told me all this before."

"I've hinted at it. Plenty."

"Not with so much detail."

"You just experienced Sheila. You deserve to know."

"It's hard to reconcile the Sheila you're talking about with the woman I just met."

"You and me both."

"Her condo—I mean, it's a nice place. Compared to your old life with her, you must be shocked at what you just saw."

"I numbed myself to her over the years. That way I could keep anything from surprising me. It was the easiest way to deal with her—keep her at arm's length, avoid her at all costs."

"Your own mother."

"My own—" Chuck ticked the air with his fingers "—'mother.'"

"She looked pretty good, considering the life you've described for her. I was expecting some shriveled-up old shrew." A light wind blew Janelle's hair back from her face.

"When I was born, she wasn't much older than you were when you had Carm. Sixteen, seventeen maybe?"

Janelle drew in the corner of her mouth. "I still want to know what her connection is to the woman who died under the arch."

"I asked her about it after you went outside with the girls. She said she had no idea who I was talking about."

"But you didn't believe her."

Chuck let out a harsh chuckle. "I haven't believed a word she said since I was five years—"

A few campsites away, the anguished scream of a woman sliced the air.

PART TWO

"A civilization which destroys what little remains of the wild, the spare, the original, is cutting itself off from its origins and betraying the principle of civilization itself."

—Edward Abbey, *Desert Solitaire*

18

Janelle leapt off the picnic table and sprinted past the trailer and truck with Chuck close behind. Nora, the woman who'd stood with Frank at the campground entrance earlier in the day, stood in the middle of the driveway three campsites up, waving Janelle toward her. Janelle reached the woman and passed with her around the bus-sized motor home beside which the campers had assembled a few minutes ago.

Chuck galloped past the RV behind Janelle and Nora. He came to a sliding stop on loose gravel spread across the paved parking space. The campers stood in a semi-circle next to the motor home, their backs to Chuck, Janelle, and Nora. Beyond the gathered campers, the aluminum ladder Frank had been carrying lay on the pavement next to the RV. Harold was sprawled on his back beside the ladder, his eyes closed. He was motionless save for his chest, which rose and fell as he breathed.

A man in his early twenties squatted at Harold's head. A bushy unkempt beard covered the man's jaw. His dark brown hair, more clumped and tangled than Fredo's fur, hung past his sun-burnished face. Despite the post-storm chill of the day, the young man wore only a long-sleeved flannel shirt and light-weight khaki slacks. Threads dangled from the worn wrists of his shirt. Its plaid shoulders were faded by the sun. Stains streaked the thighs of his slacks. His shirt and pants hung loose from his emaciated frame, and his wrists extended from his shirtsleeves, skinny as reeds. Worn running shoes clad his feet, with bare skin showing through gaping holes in the fabric.

The man pressed his hands to both sides of Harold's skull, assuring Harold did not harm his spinal column by moving his head. The man's protective head-hold mirrored the one Janelle had practiced with the girls on the living room floor in Durango, her textbooks strewn around her, while studying for her paramedic certification exam a year ago.

As Chuck took in the scene, the young bearded man rocked back on his heels and peered up at the crowd of campers circled around him. His hair fell away from his face, revealing a blistered forehead and dark brown eyes filled with fear. He squeezed his eyes shut, his cheeks drawing in upon themselves. His hands shook, causing Harold's head to shake as well.

Janelle slipped through the onlooking campers and reached to still the emaciated man's quaking hands. The instant her fingers touched his skin, however, the man jerked his hands away from her and tumbled backward to the ground. He sprang to his feet and backed away, his face blanched. He turned and ran past the motor home and out the back of the campsite, disappearing among the piñons and junipers at the base of the bluffs girdling the campground.

Janelle took the man's place, kneeling at Harold's head. She steadied Harold's skull, her hands pressed to his ears, her knees on either side of his head. She looked up at one of the men gathered with the campers, a cell phone holstered in an embossed leather case at his waist. "Call 911," she directed him. "Now."

The man stepped away, digging out his phone.

Janelle addressed the other campers. "I need two towels, rolled tight, for stabilization."

"Got it." A woman peeled away from the group and jogged toward a neighboring coach.

Frank stood among the onlookers. "My God," he whimpered to no one in particular. "He was up there because of me." He glanced around the group, wringing his hands. "It's all my fault."

A man standing next to Frank rubbed his arm in reassurance. "Harold'll be okay."

Frank said falteringly, "He's gotta be."

A thin stream of blood trickled from beneath Harold's head and puddled on the pavement. Harold's eyes remained closed and his arms lay loose on the ground at his sides, but his chest continued its rhythmic rise and fall.

Martha, the woman with the pouting face, collapsed to her knees on the wet pavement at Harold's feet. She sobbed, her hands clutched to her chest. "Talk to me, Harold," she begged. "Wake up. Please. Wake up!"

Another woman stepped forward and patted Martha's back. "There, there," the woman soothed, bending forward. "He'll be all right. He's going to be all right."

Martha rocked back and forth, sobbing. "Harold," she cried. "Harold!"

Chuck edged his way through the campers. "What can I do?" he asked Janelle.

"Call Sanford on his direct number. He may be able to get help here faster than through the 911 system."

The woman who'd left the scene at Janelle's instruction returned with matching rolled towels. Janelle wedged them on either side of Harold's head and began checking his ABCs—airway, breathing, and circulation—just as Chuck had watched her practice on the girls a year ago. She propped Harold's mouth open and turned her ear to his lips to assure breath was passing in and out of his lungs, and she pressed her forefingers to his limp wrist to gauge his pulse.

Leaving her to perform her assessment, Chuck pulled out his phone and turned away from the sight of the towels absorbing Harold's blood.

* * *

Chuck and Janelle stood in front of the motor home an hour and a half later. Harold, still unconscious, an intubation tube down his throat, had departed by ambulance for Moab fifteen minutes ago. A uniformed paramedic, positioned beside Harold in the back of the ambulance, had been adjusting the straps that secured Harold's body in place on a gurney as the vehicle pulled away. Martha had been seated at Harold's head.

Sanford had arrived at the campground forty-five minutes ago, shortly after the ambulance and paramedics. In the quarter of an hour since the ambulance's departure, the chief ranger had questioned the gathered campers about the incident. A few minutes ago, Sanford had allowed all the campers except Frank and Nora to return to their motor homes.

Now, Sanford spoke quietly with Nora beside the coach, standing at the spot where Harold had fallen. At Sanford's nod, Frank picked up the stepladder from the pavement and toted it past Chuck and Janelle, headed toward his and Nora's RV.

Nora beckoned Janelle to her side with a fluttering hand. When Janelle reached her, the woman clung to Janelle's arm and turned again to Sanford. Chuck approached to a few steps away and leaned against the RV, listening.

"You were there when Harold fell from the ladder?" Sanford asked Nora.

"All of us were. He's Martha's husband, Harold Meyers," Nora replied, her voice quavering.

"All of you?"

"We're a team. We say we're joined at the hip. It wasn't always that way, of course." Nora's cadence was quick, almost frantic, in the aftermath of the accident. "We're from Phoenix. We did the usual retiree things. We got together for potlucks, to play bridge, go for walks. Then Harold and Martha bought this." She tapped the side of the motor home with trembling fingers. "They drove all over the place in it. They came back and told the rest of us what a great time they had. One thing led to another and, before long, we all got them."

Nora spoke with a Southern accent and a slight lisp, as if her teeth—dentures, perhaps—were loose in her mouth. She swung her sun-spotted hand toward the massive motor homes in the surrounding sites.

"As you can see, we bought some really nice, well, 'rigs' is what Frank, my husband, calls them. Several of us sold our homes to be able to afford what we really wanted. That's what Frank and I did." Nora's words spilled over one another. "We took to the road full time and never looked back. We do things as a team, all of us together, like I said. We move north in the summer and south in the winter in a big group. We came to Canyon Country RV Park in Moab in the middle of the summer. Moab is so nice that we just stayed and stayed, right on into fall. We moved to Devil's Garden last week, when the campground here in the park started to empty out with winter coming on. We'll head back to Arizona for the cold months. It'll be up to the group, of course, to decide if we should—"

"Whoa, whoa, whoa." Sanford lifted a hand. "I'm clear enough on all that, thanks. What I need to know is what happened with the ladder and Harold. You said you were all here, next to the motor home . . ."

"Oh. Yes, sir, that's right. We were all together in the morning, too, watching y'all in the parking lot." Her words still tumbled from her mouth in a torrent. "It was devilishly cold, though, and we went back inside. When the storm broke up, Frank sent out a group text on the phones. That's his newest thing. He can call everyone together with the touch of a button. He's very sophisticated, my Frank. He and Harold decided to send out the group text. Something about the wind and the sleet, and how the seals on the big windows of the rigs might be leaking. Harold wanted to show everyone what to look out for, since he and Martha have had their motor home the longest."

She pressed her hand to the RV.

"Frank grabbed the ladder he keeps in our lower storage compartment and carried it over here. He feels awful, just terrible, about what happened."

Her eyes filled with tears.

"He wanted to use ours, not Harold's, so he could practice with it. He hasn't used a ladder very much. He was an accountant and, well, he's a bit clumsy, is all."

A curtain of loose skin wobbled beneath her chin.

"Frank was going to climb up the ladder, but Harold insisted that he go first, then Frank could go next. So Harold climbed on up the ladder and pushed and prodded at the seal, just there—" she pointed at the top of the large window on the side of the RV, ten feet off the ground "—to show how it could crack and come loose and water could get through. Frank stood right here where I am now. All he and Harold wanted to do was show everyone what to look out for."

Nora sniffled. She plucked a wadded tissue from the sleeve of her jacket at her wrist and pressed it to her nose.

Sanford asked, "So Harold was up on the ladder and Frank was down below?"

"Yes. Harold was pushing at the seal, and then, all of a sudden, he wasn't." She dabbed the corners of her eyes with the tissue. "I'm sorry," she said, taking a shaky breath. "Nothing like this has ever happened before, not to any of us, in all the time we've been together."

"Did you see what happened? I mean, did you see how he fell?"

"From the ladder. He fell from the ladder." Nora tucked the tissue back in her sleeve. "That's very common, you know. It's never happened to any of us, as I said, but it could have. All of us have ladders in our storage compartments, along with tools and such. You need them for cleaning. It's the only way we keep our rigs looking as good as we do." She caressed the gleaming aluminum side of the motor home. "We take great pride in it. Y'all should know that. Great, great pride."

"Yes, I can see," Sanford said, with a note of irritation. "But did you see what *caused* him to fall? Did you see what made the ladder slip?"

"He slipped?" Nora asked wonderingly. "Did the ladder slip?"

Sanford's jaw tightened. "Your friend Harold slipped and fell, remember?"

Nora's eyes grew beady. "Of course, I remember. I was there. I saw it all. The ladder slid out from under him and he went down with it. It must have been because of the gravel." She kicked at the small stones spread on the pavement. "There was nothing we could do," she said plaintively, looking from Sanford to Janelle.

Janelle patted Nora's hand. "What about the young man? Where did he come from?"

"Ohhh," the woman exclaimed. "I do remember *him*."

Sanford turned to Janelle. "What are you talking about?"

Janelle explained, "A young man—in his early twenties, I'd say—was stabilizing the patient when I arrived."

Sanford spread his arms, looking around the campground. "Where is this mystery man?"

"He ran off." Janelle pointed past the motor home, at the back of the campsite. "He took off into the trees, that way."

The chief ranger turned to Nora. "Did this young man have anything to do with the fall?"

"No, of course not. He came to help. After."

"From where?"

The woman looked around, seemingly confused. "Well, I'm not sure. The others might know, though."

"I'll be sure to ask." Sanford bowed his head to Nora. "Thank you for your help." He extended an open hand toward the front of the campsite and said to Janelle and Chuck, "Would you please join me?"

19

Sanford, Chuck, and Janelle huddled in front of the motor home. Nora passed them on her way to rejoin Frank, who waited outside their coach.

"This mystery man, what did he look like?" Sanford asked.

"He was gaunt," Janelle said. "Like he was starving. His clothes were rags, falling off him. Everything he wore had holes, even his shoes. He looked like some homeless guy from a big city, but he was out here in the desert, in the middle of the park. He just ran away."

"Huh." The chief ranger hooked his thumbs over his belt. "What do you make of him?"

"National parks are becoming home to strays more and more these days, just like in cities."

Nora reached Frank and they disappeared together into their RV.

"Strays?" Janelle asked.

Chuck noted, "Like cats."

Sanford nodded. "We're especially seeing it in parks near metropolitan areas—Rocky Mountain, in the mountains above Denver; Zion, north of Las Vegas; and, of course, Yosemite, close to all the northern California hubbub."

"That's the first I've ever heard of this," Chuck said.

Janelle pointed out, "Arches is a long way from Salt Lake City or Phoenix."

"True," said Sanford. "But Moab is right outside the park entrance, and the weather in the park is fairly mild year-round."

He tilted his head at the clearing sky. "Look how fast today's storm rolled through."

"You really think the man is a homeless guy staying out here in the park?" Chuck asked.

"Sounds like it. Everybody knows about the problem of homelessness in America nowadays. Nobody wants to deal with the real issues—drug addiction, mental illness—so people end up on the streets in cities. More and more, they're finding their way into national parks, too. A lot of these folks, with their mental and emotional challenges, appreciate the freedom of the outdoors offered by parks, which, at the same time, offer them some basic infrastructure—a safety net of sorts. As America's national parks have become more popular over the years, they've attracted visitors by the millions and, like it or not, homeless people, too."

"His timing was unbelievable," Janelle said. "He got to the victim before Chuck and me, and we were only a few campsites away."

"Homeless people are on the margins of society, but they're not completely removed from the world. In the national parks, they hang out near roads and commercial centers and—" Sanford glanced at the line of motor homes along the drive "—campgrounds."

Janelle's eyes widened. "Our two daughters are staying here with us."

"These are lost souls we're talking about. They're not predators."

"Well," Janelle admitted, "if anyone fits the description of a lost soul, it would be the guy who showed up to help Harold. But where would he be staying? How would he eat?"

"Moab is close enough to get provisions, and the park back-country offers plenty of places to hole up. There are enough caves and alcoves around here for dozens of homeless people to hide out in. There's a certain mythology to this place, too. Ed Abbey talked up the idea of disappearing into the wilderness when he stayed here way back in the 1950s as a seasonal ranger. His job was to keep an eye on things when Arches was a national monument, before it was a national park, and hardly anybody came this far into the desert from town. At the time, Abbey wouldn't have been much older than the man you described."

Sanford pointed south.

"His trailer was next to Balanced Rock, on the way back toward town, with just tumbleweeds and lizards and rattle-snakes around it. The road was dirt back then. Abbey was a city kid from back East who stumbled into the ranger job—which changed him forever. He wrote about the wonder of this place and how the desert air and sky and light made a person whole."

"Didn't he have an edge to him?" Janelle asked. "Didn't he argue that people shouldn't be allowed to drive into national parks, that they should only be allowed to walk?"

"That's the label that's been applied to him—that he was against any and all development of public lands, national parks included." The chief ranger's eyes took on a faraway look. "'You can't see anything from a car,'" he recited. "That's from *Desert Solitaire*, the book Abbey wrote about his experiences as a seasonal ranger out here in 1956 and '57."

Sanford closed his eyes and continued his recitation, a smile playing at the corners of his mouth. "'You've got to get out of the goddamned contraption and walk, better yet crawl, on hands and knees, over the sandstone and through the thorn brush and cactus. When traces of blood begin to mark your trail you'll see something, maybe. Probably not.'"

The chief ranger opened his eyes and his smile disappeared.

"Ed was known for being a pretty abrasive bastard. But the truth is a lot grayer than that. He fought to protect public lands out West his whole life, but he made good use of public lands, too, including driving through them on paved highways in the gas-guzzling Cadillac he owned and loved. He was a living contradiction—like all of us, really—and he wrote truthfully about his contradictions. After *Desert Solitaire*, he wrote *The Monkey Wrench Gang*, which was unlike anything anyone had ever written about wilderness preservation and the environment. It was laugh-out-loud funny, and it poked fun at environmentalists and their often narrow-minded ways almost as much as it did developers. For all that, though, the book was a full-throated defense of everything wild and undeveloped. It coined the phrase 'monkey-wrenching' for sabotaging development projects on public lands. Between it and *Desert Solitaire*, Abbey lit a fire under the environmental movement that burns red hot to this day."

Sanford's eyes went to the surrounding bluffs, etched against the clearing sky.

"He certainly lit a fire under me. All the time Elsie and I bounced around southern Utah, from Bryce to Zion to Capitol Reef, Arches called out to me because of him. I bet I've read *Desert Solitaire* a dozen times over the years."

"Me, too," said Chuck.

"That's another point in your favor," Sanford responded. "When the chief ranger job opened up here, I jumped at it. And now, finally, I've got the chance to do something old Ed would be proud of. I get to help Elsie and her people and the wilderness of southern Utah that Abbey loved so much." He faced north, toward fallen Landscape Arch. "Except . . ."

Chuck assured Sanford, "Nothing has changed as far as my work on the contract is concerned. We're still on track."

"Good. I'll be assembling a Serious Accident Investigation Team for the collapse of the arch," Sanford said. "That's standard procedure. They'll study the collapse in a few days, once they're all brought in and briefed. I'm closing the park again overnight so I can lead a preliminary investigation tomorrow morning, with my people from here in the park, while the site is fresh. We'll collect any perishable data for the SAIT."

"I assume you'll be looking into the cause of the collapse?"

"That'll be the primary concern of everyone—my group tomorrow and the full accident team when it does its work. The accident team will be multi-faceted. I've got a number of people in mind, from here in the park and other nearby parks—geologists, structural engineers, those sorts of people. The honchos in DC will make the final call on who to assign after I offer my recommendations. The team will be thorough. The collapse, along with the death, no doubt will be national news."

"What about the thumper truck?" Chuck asked.

"There'll be no more seismic surveying anywhere near the park for the time being. I'll make sure of that."

Janelle glanced down the campground drive at the trailer and the girls inside. "And the homeless guy?"

"I bet you'll never see him again."

"He's not supposed to be living in the park backcountry, is he? Aren't people required to have permits for that?"

"I wouldn't be too concerned if I were you. People love the idea of coming out here and making themselves at home in the desert wilderness, but they don't last for long. Even homeless people get bored and lonely, so they head back to town or wherever they came from."

Janelle wrapped her arms around herself. "I hope you're right."

Sanford's phone buzzed. He plucked it from the nylon holster at his waist and put it to his ear. As he listened, his hand began to tremble.

He ended the call and turned to Chuck and Janelle. "Harold, the man who fell from the ladder, was just declared dead."

20

Janelle covered her mouth with the back of her hand. "But he was breathing. His pulse was strong."

Sanford returned his phone to its pouch. "I'm sorry. They said he went into convulsions on the way to town."

"It must have been an internal head bleed. That's the only thing that would have made him go so fast." Janelle trembled.

Chuck gripped her arm and said to Sanford, "Two deaths now, in one day."

The chief ranger shook his head. "Maybe I deserve this." His tone was muted. He looked at his feet. "This whole idea of using the pictograph to make a big statement—I'm not sure what I was thinking."

"Don't go there," Chuck cautioned. "The pictograph is entirely separate."

Janelle added, "As for people falling from ladders, Nora was right. It's one of the most common household injuries of all."

"The cave is still secret," Chuck said. "I'll keep working on the contract. Nothing about that has changed. The guy on the ladder was an accident, like Janelle said. Which leaves you with the collapsed arch."

Sanford raised his head, meeting Chuck's eyes. "And Megan."

"Megan?"

"You talked to your mother, didn't you?"

Chuck gave a reluctant nod. "She denied knowing anything about what happened this morning."

"So you still don't know who Megan is, or was?"

"I take it she's the woman who was crushed beneath the arch."

"That's right. She was your mother's best friend, too. Your mom has made quite an impact in town. Megan was a large part of it. I called your mother as soon as we lifted the boulder and got an idea of who it was. Sheila helped confirm the ID."

Chuck arched his eyebrows. Sheila's best friend in Moab had just died, and Sheila had known about it—yet she had acted as if the death hadn't happened when she'd hosted Chuck, Janelle, and the girls at her home, and she'd gone on to deny any knowledge of the death to Chuck as well.

"What sort of impact?" Chuck asked Sanford, though the velvet-covered table in the darkened room at the end of the hall in Sheila's condominium gave him a good indication.

"Your mother started out calling herself a massage therapist when she moved to town a few months ago. But it turns out she's a lot more than that. She put up posters around town announcing her arrival. She was forced to take them down, of course, but not before everybody saw them. People went to her. They told others. Pretty soon, there was a steady stream of folks headed to her condo."

Janelle asked dubiously, "For massages?"

"That's apparently what got the first round of people in the door. But she's a talker, mostly. She figures out what people want to hear, and she tells them in a blunt way that really works."

"She calls herself a seer," Janelle said. "That's what she told us this morning."

Chuck said to Sanford, "You quoted her voicemail message to me word for word, where she pitches herself to 'seekers of truly enlightened energy.' What's up with that?"

"Elsie," the chief ranger said by way of explanation. "She was one of the first to go to your mother. After a couple of sessions, she made me go to her, too."

Chuck shook his head, incredulous. "When we were at your house, Elsie told us she talks to Sheila nearly every day. I find that hard enough to believe. But you, too?"

"Your mother's not so bad as it sounds like you think she is. Besides, I wasn't alone. By the time I went, Sheila had been in town for about a month, and it was already tough to get an appointment."

"She was fully booked?"

"She said she was, anyway. It added to her mystique, if nothing else."

"So you went to see her?"

Sanford avoided Chuck's gaze. "She offered to squeeze me in, on account of Elsie. I was pretty doubtful. But it was about what I expected. Tough love, mostly."

"Tough love?" Chuck put his fingertips to his temples and shook his head. Was Sanford really talking about the woman who hadn't shown Chuck an ounce of love his entire childhood? He lowered his hands. "What about the massage part?"

"I never would've let her lay her hands on me. I'm not a massage kind of guy. What Sheila offers—what has made her so popular around town so quickly—goes far beyond that sort of thing."

Chuck exhaled, forcing air through his nose. Sheila's voice-mail message urged callers to describe to her their "desires for fulfillment," concluding with her promise to provide "complete satisfaction" to those who reached out to her.

Sanford continued. "I imagine she still does massages, if that's what people want. But what she's really known for around town is tearing into people verbally. That's her game, and I'm telling you, it works."

"On you?"

"Not so much on me, to be honest. I went because of Elsie. She was convinced whatever your mom was doing for her really helped. I think she was right; Elsie has a spring to her step after her sessions with Sheila that I haven't seen in a long time. So I went, too. I played along."

"Your wife seemed to be doing fine today. She'd just baked cookies when we got there. She played with the girls. She's quite the drummer."

"She drummed while you were there?"

"On the coffee table," Janelle said. "It's beautiful, by the way. All the artwork you have in your home is gorgeous."

"That's all thanks to Elsie. She's got a real feel for that sort of thing."

"She cares," said Janelle. "That much was evident. It was sweet of her to have us over just to thank Chuck for being here."

"That's just like Elsie—and why I'm not looking forward to telling her about the arch and Megan." The chief ranger sighed, his cheeks sagging. "Elsie knew her, of course. Everybody knew Megan."

Chuck said, "I can't believe I'm saying this, but maybe that's where Sheila can help."

"Maybe. Sheila might already have broken the news to Elsie, for all I know. They've grown remarkably close."

Janelle asked, "When you went to see Sheila, did she light the candle in the back room, take your hands in hers, that whole bit?"

Sanford nodded. "She said she could see what needed fixing inside me. She fed me a few lines about believing in myself—the sort of mumbo jumbo that plays well with newcomers in town, and with Elsie, too, for that matter. I went a couple of times. That was enough. But Elsie has continued to go to her, so I've kept tabs on what she's been up to. Sheila is focused mostly on folks her age, all the retirees moving to town. They hike and bike and volunteer for cleanup days along the river. They've got plenty of money. That's something I'm sure she's fully aware of."

Chuck said, "The money part, at least, sounds like the Sheila I've known all my life."

"She's good at up-charging," Sanford said. "People show up for massages, and she works them into talk sessions, with the candle and hand-holding. She's been encouraging Elsie to come to her more than once a week, but I've been pushing back from my end. So far, at least, Sheila hasn't been charging for the phone calls between them." He rubbed his beard with his thumb and forefinger and said to Chuck, "She's not cheap, your mother."

"What about Megan? You said they were best friends. Was she one of Sheila's customers, too?"

"Just the opposite. Megan sent customers to your mother. I'm sure she was getting a referral fee of some sort. Megan was a sponsored outdoor athlete, a rock climber and canyoneer. We always have a few of them based here in town. They make money using gear and wearing clothes of various outdoor companies and posting about it online. They get by, but they don't get rich off it, that's for sure. Their whole game is networking. Megan was good at it. She joined clubs, went to events. She took over as director of the Moab Counts 10K. That's the citizen's race along the river every spring. I don't know who'll take it over now. It's the combined fundraiser for all the local nonprofit organizations. Thousands of people show up for it. Being in charge of Moab Counts put Megan in the middle of everything in town, and got her to know just about everyone on a first-name basis. As near as I could tell, Megan recommended Sheila's services to almost everybody she knew, too. She was your mom's fixer, I guess you could say."

"Why would Megan have gone out on the arch like she did today?" Chuck asked.

"That would have been just like her. She had to post stuff online all the time, for her sponsors, about everything she was doing—her daily runs, her stretching routine, her camping trips in the desert—even when it wasn't extreme rock climbing or canyoneering. That's how she made her living, along with the little bit she got for organizing Moab Counts, and whatever your mother may have been giving her."

"She was married," Janelle noted. "She had a wedding ring on her finger."

"That just happened at the end of the summer. She and a guy named Paul Johnson. He's a rock climber, too. Ex-military, crew cut, tightly wound. Quite the beefcake. He and Megan got hitched up on top of the cliff overlooking Castleton Tower in Castle Valley at sunset a few weeks ago, after climbing up there with a bunch of their friends. They posted pictures of it all over social media. You couldn't miss it. They even put their picture and announcement in the *Moab Times-Independent*, the old-fashioned way. Paul is a good enough guy. The sheriff's office made the call to him this morning, after we verified the ID through Sheila. I followed up with a call of my own. He's devastated."

"Just like George Epson," Chuck muttered.

Sanford shot him a sharp look. "If we're back to that, then it sounds like we're about done here."

"Agreed," Chuck replied. "I'll stay on top of the contract for you, like I said. That, at least, you won't have to worry about."

Chuck set out alone from Devil's Garden Trailhead half an hour later, ostensibly headed back to the cavern to maintain his contracted work schedule despite the late-afternoon hour. He had another plan in mind, however, one he wasn't ready to share with Janelle until he answered a few questions on his own.

He left the trail beyond the walled corridor north of the trailhead, out of sight of the parking lot, and worked his way southward, angling back across the open desert toward Devil's Garden Campground. He kept his eyes down, casting for sign in the drying soil.

A few hundred yards from the campground, he spotted what he sought—a set of footprints. He bent over the prints. They were pressed lightly into the soil. The soles were those of running shoes, the heels rounded from heavy use.

The footprints undoubtedly were those of the emaciated man who'd fled the campground after coming to Harold's aid. The tracks headed north, away from the campground, across an open expanse of sage and rabbitbrush and on through a stand of piñons and junipers. Chuck followed them, hidden from the campsites by the three sandstone bluffs that rose side by side north of the campground. The matching vertical walls at the end of the three bluffs towered above the desert like giant tombstones.

The last of the storm clouds had passed. The late-day sun cast long shadows across the damp earth. A red-tailed hawk circled above Chuck's head. Sparrows chirped in the trees. From the safety of a rock crevice came the descending bell-like call, tonal and liquid, of a canyon wren, a close cousin of the Sonoran Desert's noisy cactus wren.

The tracks neared the loop trail's right-hand branch—the portion of the loop that passed near the hidden cavern. Chuck's gut churned. Did the homeless man somehow know about the pictograph? Had he followed Chuck and Janelle to the site earlier today?

The tracks veered west, away from the cavern. Chuck exhaled with relief.

The man's stride, revealed by his footprints, was long and purposeful as he crossed the mile-wide sagebrush flat north of the trail junction, away from the hidden cavern—and straight toward the toppled remains of Landscape Arch.

The tracks detoured where required by low rock outcrops or shallow water drainages, then returned immediately to their fixed westward route. Halfway across the flat, Chuck paused and put his hand to his forehead, shielding his eyes from the sun. He saw no signs of movement ahead. He shifted his shoulders, adjusting his gear pack on his back, and resumed trailing the footprints.

He again came to a halt where the young man, too, had halted, his footprints planted side by side, facing west, upon encountering the left branch of the loop trail on the far side of the flat.

Chuck stood where the young man had stood. What had brought him here? What had he sought?

After the stop, the footprints continued, now following the trail, the tracks imprinted over those of the emergency responders who'd trod through the mud earlier in the day. Chuck followed the tracks into the cliff-walled passage leading from the broad flat to the arch.

The man's strides remained long and steady; he had made no effort to conceal himself as he approached the toppled arch. Chuck, however, slowed as he proceeded through the passage, peering ahead. He'd started out following the homeless man to convince himself the girls were safe; he wanted to be able to report back to Janelle that the man had fled far from the campground. But the man's trek to the toppled arch baffled Chuck, which in turn set his nerves thrumming. He put his back to one of the facing cliff walls, edging sideways up the last of the passageway. Each sidelong step brought him closer to the end of the corridor, affording him a wider view of the small open area beyond.

Chuck stopped where the cliff walls opened onto the flat. The trail extended across the desert to the wooden fence at the arch viewpoint. Beyond the fence, the toppled blocks of stone that had comprised the span lay in an uneven row, silent testimony to the morning's collapse and Megan's death.

Nothing moved among the blocks. In the post-storm quiet

of the waning afternoon, the trail and viewpoint were deserted as well.

Chuck put a palm to the cliff wall at his back, preparing to leave the passageway and cross the opening. He pushed himself away from the stone just as a gunshot rang out.

21

A bullet pierced the air beside Chuck's ear, striking the cliff wall beside his head, mere inches from his skull. The bullet ricocheted into the soil of the corridor, burying itself with a muted *whoomp*.

Chuck threw himself backward to the ground, flipped to his stomach, and scrabbled on hands and knees away from the opening.

The shot had come from somewhere high on the bluffs on the far side of the flat where, until today, the arch had soared. From such a commanding position, the shooter would have had Chuck as an easy target. But the bullet had missed him.

That didn't matter, however, because the passageway extended straight from the flat for more than a hundred feet, offering no protection. As Chuck retreated down the corridor, he remained fully exposed to the shooter, who had plenty of time to line up another shot.

Instead, a male voice yelled, "Stop!"

Chuck flattened himself to the ground.

"I don't want to hurt you," the man called, his words echoing into the passage. "I just want to talk."

Chuck pressed his cheek to the dirt. Could the shooter possibly be the homeless man?

"I've got my crosshairs on your back," the voice cried out.

Chuck dug his fingers into the sandy soil. Why was the shooter offering a truce?

"I don't want to shoot you, but I will." The man's voice broke as he continued. "As God is my witness, I'll kill you if I have to."

Chuck lay shaking. He had only two options. He could trust what the man said, or he could jump to his feet and make a run for it.

Considering the certitude in the man's voice, however, option two almost certainly would end as the shooter promised—with Chuck's death.

He had only one option, really.

He lifted his head from the soil. "Okay," he called over his shoulder. "You win. I'm getting up."

He climbed to his knees, then to a standing position, his hands extended above his head. He turned to face the opening, the late, low sun blinding him.

"Stay on the trail where I can see you," the man called. "Keep your hands up. Come to the fence. I'll meet you there."

Chuck crossed the flat with his hands raised, his pace slow and deliberate.

A broad-shouldered man appeared from behind the hump of rock that had supported the south end of Landscape Arch. He strode down a sandstone ramp to the opening, a hunting rifle in one hand.

Chuck waited at the fence, facing the collapsed arch, as the shooter approached from the line of fallen blocks. He was about thirty, Janelle's age, several years older than the homeless man, and heavily muscled. The shooter's biceps bulged beneath a black poly-fleece top that hugged his flat stomach. His quads filled gray climber pants reinforced with shiny black nylon patches at the knees. He wore lightweight leather boots cinched with vibrant yellow laces. A black wool beanie cap covered his skull, cutting a straight line across his forehead.

The shooter halted ten feet from Chuck. He slung his rifle over the crook of his arm, its barrel pointed at the ground. He had an angular face, with pronounced cheekbones and a square jaw. He was clean shaven, his cheeks sallow and sunken, his gray eyes awash with grief.

"You're Paul Johnson, aren't you?" Chuck said.

The shooter raised the arm holding his gun, lifting the barrel a few inches, until it pointed threateningly at Chuck's legs. "Do I know you?"

"No. But you could've picked a better way to introduce yourself."

"I missed on purpose."

"That's supposed to make me feel better?"

"You're alive, aren't you?"

"For now."

Paul narrowed his eyes at Chuck. "Tell me what I want to hear and you'll stay that way."

"All you had to do was ask."

"I put you to ground. I couldn't risk having you run off. I had the opportunity and I took it."

"You're ex-military," Chuck said, a statement, not a question, affirming what Sanford had said of Paul.

"That's right."

"From the sound of you, I'd say you're the Hayduke type. You've gone rogue, haven't you?"

"Hayduke?"

"The ex-Green Beret in Edward Abbey's *The Monkey Wrench Gang*. George Washington Hayduke—always on the verge of going postal . . . like you, it would seem."

Paul stepped back. "Guns are legal in national parks. I have every right to be doing what I'm doing."

"No one ever has the right to shoot at someone else."

Paul lifted his arm and the barrel of his gun another few inches. "No one had any right to kill my wife, either."

Chuck pointed at Paul's gun. "Take it easy with that thing. I think we're both on the same side. My name is Chuck. Chuck Bender."

Paul lowered his gun, again directing it at the ground. "What do you know about Megan's death?"

"My wife and I found your wife after the arch fell this morning. We're the ones who reported it."

"You were with her?"

"No. We heard the sound of the collapse from the campground. We were the first ones here. There was nothing we could do for her. I'm sorry."

Paul's face fell. "They told me she died instantly. They said they're coming back tomorrow to take a closer look at what happened. I wanted to get out here first."

Chuck nodded toward the hunting rifle. "You've got some suspicions, I take it."

Paul raised his head, his jaw jutting. "We just got married, but we were together for years. We were talking about starting a family." He choked back a sob. "And then . . . and then Megan got all tied up with this woman who came to town."

Chuck's heart drummed behind his ribcage but he kept his expression neutral, waiting for Paul to continue.

"Sheila," Paul said. "That's the woman's name. She considers herself some sort of truth teller or something, but she's got a real edge to her. More than anything, that's what hooked Megan, I think. They would get together at Sheila's place. Afterward, when Megan would come home, she'd be on fire."

"On fire?" Chuck asked.

Paul looked into the distance. "Sheila was Megan's spiritual guide, into this world Megan never had experienced. It was all about touch and feel, using her senses."

"Sheila is a seer," Chuck said, testing the word on Paul.

"That's what she calls herself. I met her a couple of times." Paul shook himself, as if purging himself of the memory. "Her whole shtick gave me the heebie-jeebies. But Megan couldn't get enough of it. She started sending other people to Sheila, too."

"I was told Megan was Sheila's fixer."

"That's pretty harsh but . . . yeah, okay, that's kind of what she was. Sheila was in charge, there's no doubt about that. I tried to get Megan to back off some. It was all too much. But she wouldn't hear of it, until . . ." Paul lifted his eyes to the sky, where the arch had been.

"This morning?"

"Yeah, this morning and everything that led up to it. According to what Megan told me, Sheila had changed her focus the last few weeks. When she first came to town, it was all about how much money she could make off her clients. Then, lately, it was more and more about the environment."

Chuck gawked at Paul. "I don't believe that. Sheila was turning into an *environmentalist*?"

"That's what Megan said. She was really happy about it. Megan and I have been in the movement for a long time. It's part of what she does for her sponsors—fighting the good fight and posting about it all the time. We're totally sincere about it, too. All you've got to do is look around." Paul swung the barrel of his gun in a low arc at the surrounding cirque of stone. "The need to preserve all this is easy to understand, and even easier to fight for."

"Was it Megan who brought Sheila over to the whole environmentalist thing?"

Paul's eyebrows came together. "Hmm. I hadn't really considered it."

"Maybe Sheila was playing along with Megan to make her feel good."

"From what I know of Sheila, she isn't the type to do anything for anyone but herself."

"She gives advice to others, to help them."

"But she does it for money. It's all still for herself."

"You're here with a rifle, shooting at people, for some reason, too. What is it?"

Paul ticked the barrel of his gun upward. "I want to know why *you're* here."

"You're the one who shot at me. I deserve to hear your story first, then I'll tell you mine. You said you think someone killed your wife this morning . . ."

"Not someone." Paul's voice trembled with unconcealed rage. "Sheila. She's the one who sent Megan out here to the arch."

22

Paul explained, his tone calming as he continued, "Megan told me it was supposed to be some sort of spiritual quest. She was supposed to do her runs while the seismic truck did its thing just over the hill, to send the right kind of vibes toward the truck or something. Sheila suggested Landscape Arch because it was the longest and most dramatic out here at this end of the park, where the truck was working. Megan was to time her runs so she was on the arch when the thumper truck started its work each day. She'd been doing it every morning since the truck moved to Yellow Cat Flat last week."

"She went out on the arch every single morning?" Chuck asked.

Paul's brick-like jaw moved up and down. "That was part of the deal, to commune with it or whatever. I told her she shouldn't, but she just laughed at me. She was nice enough about it, but she wasn't about to listen to me." He glanced away. "I was just her husband. She only listened to Sheila."

"She came out here in the midst of the storm this morning. It was freezing."

Paul looked at Chuck. "You have to understand, going out in the storm was no big deal for her. That's the sort of thing we did all the time. I know they'll say it was an accident. They'll do their review and file their report, but . . ." A tear escaped the corner of his eye and ran down his cheek.

"But," Chuck finished for him, "you're suspicious enough to come out here on your own, even though you should be in town right now, contacting family, talking with the authorities."

"That's what I've been doing all day. Megan's parents are on their way. They'll get here late tonight. We'll go to the mortuary together tomorrow. Lots of others are coming in, too. Megan's brother and sister, and one of her cousins. But I had this little window of time, before dark, to come out here and see for myself what happened."

"You brought a gun with you."

"I was regular army. I'm still a reservist." He swung his rifle back and forth. "So I brought this along. My good old .30-06. And I'm glad I did." He stopped the gun, its barrel aimed at Chuck's shins. "It's your turn now."

"You might want to set your safety before you hear what I have to say," Chuck warned. "Or, at least, keep your finger away from the trigger." He drew a breath. "Sheila Bender is my mother."

Paul's mouth fell open. "What did you just say?"

"To repeat: I think you and I are on the same side."

Paul's eyes grew flinty. "Explain."

Chuck spread his hands. "I'd heard Megan was working for Sheila and figured Sheila might be using her somehow. That's what my mother does."

"Spoken like someone who would know."

"I've got a lot of experience on that front."

"Why'd you come back out here, after you found Megan this morning?"

Chuck could think of no good reason to bring the homeless man into the discussion. He said, "I agree with you that the park authorities will see your wife's death as an accident. That's what they'll want to determine. An accident ruling will remove the park from having to deal with the real question: whether the collapse, in fact, was caused by the seismic truck."

"Do you think there might be any evidence proving as much?"

"That's what I came out here to try to find out," Chuck lied, "if you'd just be kind enough to put away your gun."

Paul slung his rifle over his shoulder. They began their search with the fallen block of sandstone beneath which Chuck and Janelle had found Megan's body.

The block lay deep in afternoon shadow below the bluffs, returned to its resting place after the removal of Megan's body. The bloodstained soil at the base of the boulder was barely visible in the end-of-the-day gloom.

Paul faced the boulder, his chin to his chest. "Death was part of everything Megan and I did," he said softly. "It was part of her job—first ascents, canyon traverses, exposed climbs—all while taking pictures of herself tricked out in her sponsors' latest clothes and gear. Other pro outdoor athletes face the same thing. We've lost a lot of friends along the way. Too many."

He squeezed the back of his neck with his beefy hand.

"But it was me who was supposed to go first. We joked about that. She'd take all the risks, day after day, and then at some point I'd get sent off to the Middle East with the reserves and get myself blown to smithereens."

He looked at Chuck.

"There was a part of me that was really happy with what she was getting from Sheila. Your mother was mostly good for her, I think. Megan had taken to dwelling on all the people we've lost. But your mom helped her see beyond her sadness. That's why I went along with Megan's telling everyone around town they had to give Sheila a try. And why I didn't work very hard at keeping her from going out on the arch."

He pressed his knuckles to his teeth and sobbed once, a harsh release of anguish from deep in his chest, then pivoted abruptly away from the boulder.

"Let's do a quick site survey, why don't we?" Chuck suggested gently, using the archaeological term for what he had in mind now that he'd committed to investigating the site of the collapse with Paul.

They walked together along the line of fallen blocks. The jagged boulders lay in the wet soil where they'd come to rest, brush and grass crushed beneath them. Several of the boulders had smashed into one another as they struck the earth, shattering into smaller shards that lay scattered like shrapnel across the ground.

Chuck sniffed the air at the south end of the line of boulders and straightened in surprise. "Smell that?"

Paul inhaled through his nose, his nostrils flared. "Smells like a hot spring."

"It's sulfur." Chuck strode to the final boulder in the line. The odor of rotten eggs grew stronger with each step. The chunk of stone, twice the size of a refrigerator, rose as high as his head. Black streaks of desert varnish striped the side of the block facing him.

The gaseous smell permeated the air, overwhelming the scent of drying sage wafting from the flat in the wake of the storm.

He rounded the boulder ahead of Paul, stepping over pieces of sandstone littering the earth. On the far side of the block, he came to what until this morning had been the top of the arch. The former upper surface of the span, now facing sideways, was worn and weathered and covered with orange and green lichen.

He stared at the stone in shocked silence.

In the middle of the sandstone block was a perfect circle, an inch across, drilled into the surface of the stone.

23

Chuck drew a startled breath. He leaned forward, studying the drilled hole up close. The hole, clearly manmade, was two inches deep. He slid the tip of his finger around the hole's outer edge. The edge was sharp and unworn, indicating the hole had been drilled in the very recent past.

Paul rounded the boulder and stood at Chuck's side. He, too, gaped at the hole drilled in the stone.

"I knew it," he growled. He shucked his gun from his shoulder and turned away from the block, his eyes sweeping the surrounding sandstone promontories, rifle clutched in his hands.

Chuck told him, "Whoever did this is long gone."

"I'll kill them," Paul said through gritted teeth, his knuckles white where they wrapped around the gun's polished wood stock.

"I don't think it's as simple as it looks." Chuck withdrew his finger from the drill hole and sniffed it. "Whew," he exclaimed, grimacing.

He held up his finger to Paul. Green residue stained its tip.

Paul swiped the edge of the hole with his finger and smelled it. "Ugh," he said, gagging. "What the hell?"

"It's Pyrodex. An improved version of black powder. A lot of my hunter friends are using it these days, so I'm pretty familiar with it."

"Oh, yeah. You're right," Paul said, his eyes lighting with recognition. "I've done some muzzleloader hunting." He examined his stained fingertip. "I didn't realize they were dying the stuff green, though."

"That's to make it stand out from traditional black powder. Pyrodex is fairly new. It isn't classified as a true explosive. It can be purchased in bulk without a permit and transported easily because it's far less flammable than black powder. But if you pack enough of it in a confined space and put an electrical charge to it, it can do some real damage. Pyrodex still contains sulfur, like black powder. That's the rotten-egg odor we're smelling." Chuck wiped his finger on his pant leg and pointed at the hole. "But there's a problem. We're smelling *unexploded* Pyrodex."

"You mean, someone was set to blow up the arch, but it never went off?"

"That's what it would seem like."

"There must have been another hole, another placement, that exploded and took down the arch."

"The smell of exploded powder would be much stronger, burnt and acrid. But there's none of that anywhere along all the fallen blocks."

"It would have dissipated by now, wouldn't it? The storm would have washed it away."

"There was no smell of spent blasting powder this morning, either, right after the collapse. And there was no concussive wave through the campground from an explosion. Just the rumble of the arch as it fell, preceded by the thumps from the seismic truck."

"What are you saying?"

"As best I can tell," Chuck said, "someone was all set to blow up the arch, but the thumper truck beat them to it."

Janelle ran to Chuck when he walked down the campground driveway, returning to the trailer as night descended on Devil's Garden.

She wrapped him in a tight embrace in the middle of the drive. "You're all right," she said.

"I didn't mean to worry you," he apologized, stroking her hair. "I didn't think I'd be so late."

They hugged in front of Frank and Nora's motor home. In the gathering darkness, the interior of the couple's coach glowed with warm electric light. Nora stood at the stove in the compact kitchen, behind the RV's open living room. Frank sat in an easy chair in front of Nora, facing the driver and passenger seats and the coach's windshield, observing Chuck and Janelle through the tinted glass.

Janelle stepped back. "It's not that you're late. There was a gunshot. I'm almost sure that's what it was."

Chuck stiffened. He should have realized the sound of the shot from Paul's rifle, like the rumble of the falling arch, would carry to the campground. "That's right. I heard it, too." He drew Janelle by the hand toward the trailer, out of sight of Frank's prying eyes.

"I was going to come after you," Janelle said. "I talked with the other campers about it. They heard it, too. We all met up outside. They were pretty shaken up, especially the guy back there in the RV, Frank. He was really nervous—although I get the sense he's that way about pretty much everything. We waited for another gunshot. When there wasn't one, Frank said maybe it was just some deer hunter working the edge of the park."

"That could have been it, I guess."

"Did you get a lot of work done?"

"I accomplished more than I expected."

After rechecking all the fallen blocks and finding no other drill holes or any further sign of explosives, Chuck had exchanged contact information with Paul and they had split up, Paul heading west to the highway, Chuck returning to the campground via Devil's Garden Trail.

He held Janelle's hand as they walked to the trailer. "This has been a brutal day."

"I'm glad it's over," Janelle agreed. "Dinner's waiting for you. The girls and I already ate. Pasta, again."

"No wonder Rosie came up with the name she did for the cat. Speaking of which, has Fredo destroyed anything else?"

"Not yet. The girls have been all over her. They're arguing about who gets to sleep with her tonight."

"She should sleep in a box. Better yet, she should stay outside in a box."

"Try telling that to the girls. She cleaned up pretty well. It's clear she wasn't on her own for long. A few days at most, I'd bet."

"Did you find out if she belongs to anyone in the campground?"

"The girls carried her around to everyone this afternoon. Nothing."

"You saw what she did to our seat cushion," Chuck said. He smiled. "None of the old folks would claim her if she'd done anything like that to one of their million-dollar rigs."

Janelle returned Chuck's smile. She leaned her shoulder into him, knocking him off balance. "If that was the case, they wouldn't have just abandoned her, they'd have thrown her off a cliff." She pulled him to her side. "I told the girls about the homeless guy who helped Harold. They're convinced the cat belongs to him."

"Maybe they're right." Chuck drew a breath. "I assume you told them Harold died."

Janelle nodded. "They took the news surprisingly well. Rosie said, 'Well, he *was* really old.'"

"How do the other campers seem to be taking it?"

"Better than I would have expected. Kind of the same as Rosie, actually."

"I don't really blame them. The guy came across as quite a jerk."

"He was a mean one, all right. I talked to Nora about it. She said things like that happen when people get 'old and tippy,' as she put it. She told me Martha couldn't face coming back to her and Harold's motor home, so she's spending the night in town. The group will stay another couple of days, to make sure Martha's okay, before they head back south."

Chuck glanced at the motor coach owned by Harold and Martha, its windows dark. "What about that thing?"

"Somebody'll come get it, I guess."

"Maybe we can move in. Leave our trailer to Fredo and her slashing claws."

Janelle sat across from Chuck at the dinette in the trailer two hours later.

"I can't stop thinking about the homeless man," she said.

It was long after dark. Rosie had won the right to keep Fredo in bed with her for the night, arguing for first dibs over Carmelita based on the fact that it was she who'd found the cat.

Janelle looked through the picture window above the table. "He's out there all alone somewhere."

"By his own choice," Chuck said.

"I wouldn't say that. The look in his eyes was heartbreaking. He was so scared, but he was still trying to do the right thing. You saw how he was dressed, how skinny he was. The life he's living right now can't be by choice."

"I just meant that he's out here in the park of his own choosing, based on whatever his mind is telling him. Assuming that's the case, I don't see where there's much we can do for him."

"He looked like he was starving."

Rosie said from her bunk, "We should bring him some food."

Janelle said, "You're supposed to be going to sleep."

Rosie lay on her back with Pasta Alfredo nestled in the crook of her arm. "I'm never going to sleep tonight. Not one wink." She stroked the cat's head. "I'm going to pet Fredo all night long."

Chuck eyed the small refrigerator set in the cabinetry next to the bunk beds. He recalled the flash of movement he'd spotted atop the ridge earlier in the day—movement that definitely had been made by something larger than a cat.

"Actually," he said to Rosie, "we could do that, I suppose."

24

"Do what?" Rosie asked from her bunk bed.

"We could do what you said," Chuck explained. "We could bring the hungry man some food."

Janelle tucked a lock of hair behind her ear. "You almost sound like you're talking about doing it right now, tonight."

Chuck peered out the window at the stars high in the sky, the night crystalline after the passage of the storm. "Well, why not?"

"You can't be serious," Janelle said.

"We've got, what, three containers of leftover pasta in the fridge? We could leave one for him on top of the ridge. I think I saw him up there earlier. I'm sure he'd find it."

"We could do it tomorrow morning."

"You're the one who said he looked like he was starving. I agree. We've all got headlamps. We could walk up there right now. It'd be a neat thing to do under the stars, and a good way to end the day—with an act of goodwill for someone who performed an act of goodwill of his own—after everything that's happened."

"Yeah, yeah, yeah!" Rosie cheered. "I want to come along. Can I? Can I?"

Carmelita drew back the curtain to the upper bunk. "I'll come," she said.

Chuck teased her. "You'll take any excuse to spend time climbing around on rocks, won't you?"

"No," she corrected him. "I bet I can get a great picture of the stars for my story."

"You mean, that online thingy you and your friends do back and forth together on your phones?"

"Yeah," she said. "That." She hopped to the floor and said to Rosie, "While we're up there, we can say a prayer for the people who died."

While he'd eaten his dinner, Chuck had teamed with Janelle in sharing more details of the day's dual tragedies with the girls—Megan's fatal plunge along with the collapsing arch, followed by Harold's death in the ambulance after his fall from the ladder.

Carmelita continued, using the Spanglish names she and Rosie had adopted for Janelle's Mexican-immigrant parents. "*Grandpapá* and *Grandmamá* would like it if we did that."

Turning her back, Carmelita tugged her tie-dye T-shirt over her head and began pulling on the clothes she'd worn for the day.

Rosie sat up, her bare feet dangling off the edge of her bed. "This'll be fun," she said. "Scary, but fun." She put her hand on Pasta Alfredo, at her side, and looked down the aisle at Chuck. "Can we bring Fredo along to protect us?"

"She might run off," Chuck said. His eyes went to the torn dinette cushion. "We can't leave her in here, though."

Janelle said, "How about the truck? What more can she do to it?"

Chuck grinned. The seats of the aging Bender Archaeological crew cab were torn and tattered, and covered with worn blankets. "*Buena idea.*"

"I can't believe we're doing this," Janelle said to Chuck ten minutes later. They were halfway up the ridge, the girls a few steps ahead of them, their headlamps lighting matching circles of rock at their feet. "I can't believe how cold it is out here, either."

The night was significantly cooler than Chuck had anticipated, the temperature already well below freezing. He ascended the stone ramp with his hands in his jacket pockets. "Wait till we get to the top," he urged Janelle. "You'll be amazed."

Tucked beneath his elbow, Chuck toted a clear plastic container of leftover pasta and sautéed vegetables. The girls' pockets were filled with hard candies for the homeless man as well.

Reaching the top of the ridge, the girls shone their headlamps back down at Chuck and Janelle, blinding them as they completed the climb.

Chuck shielded his eyes with his hand. "What can you see from up there?"

The girls turned away. The beams of their headlamps tracked to and fro.

"Woja camolies!" Rosie exclaimed. "It's so beautiful!"

"Camolies?" Janelle asked, reaching the top of the ridge with Chuck.

"It's a kind of food," Rosie explained. "A pretend kind. I made it up because we're leaving food up here for the hungry man."

Carmelita swept the beam of her headlamp in a circle, then tilted her head back, launching the beam at the stars.

"There are so many of them," she said, pointing at the pinpricks of white crowding the sky overhead.

"There sure are." Chuck looked up at the night sky with her. "Southern Utah is one of the few places in the country you can see the stars this well pretty much every night of the year. The sky is clear here most of the time, and there aren't any lights from big cities to drown them out."

"It blows me away," Carmelita said, her fogged breath floating through the light of her headlamp.

The beam of Rosie's headlamp bounced up and down as she nodded. "It blows me away, too."

Chuck recited for his own benefit, as well as that of the girls, "'Now the night flows back, the mighty stillness embraces and includes me; I can see the stars again and the world of starlight.'"

He paused for a beat, allowing the darkness to swallow the sound of his voice, before continuing. "I think that's how it goes. It's what Ed Abbey wrote about looking at the night sky when he lived in a trailer out here a long time ago, just like we're doing now."

"Who was he?" Rosie asked.

"He was a park ranger in Arches. He wrote about how important it is to preserve places like this."

"I can see why," Rosie said. "He did a good job."

"I'll say. He's been dead for a long time, but the words he wrote are still helping."

Carmelita took out her phone, aimed it at the sky, and clicked several photos. "Go back a little and face sideways," she said to Rosie. "I want to get a picture of your light shining across the rock."

Rosie positioned herself as instructed. "Like this?"

"Lower your head a little, so the rock is brighter."

Rosie angled her head downward.

"Perfect." Carmelita took a string of pictures, flipping her phone from vertical to horizontal and zooming in and out.

The view from the ridgetop was everything Chuck had hoped. The moon hadn't yet risen, giving full reign to the inverted bowl of stars overhead. The dull gray glow of Moab's lights, rising from the Colorado River bottoms to the south, smudged only the low horizon of the otherwise starry black sky. Venus twinkled just above the western horizon, bright as a distant streetlight. Below the shining planet, the uplift of Entrada sandstone at the heart of the park sawtoothed the skyline. At the foot of the ridge opposite the campground, the park road was a dim ribbon of black winding through the desert.

Turning away from the road, Chuck peered down the sloping rock ramp at the campground. The elderly campers' motor homes lined the driveway in two orderly rows. Rooftop security lights illuminated circles of pavement and dirt around several of the RVs. Yellow light shone from the coaches' picture windows, punctuated by flashes of blue from televisions playing inside.

Janelle pressed herself against Chuck's side, burrowing beneath his arm. "You're right, it's beautiful up here. But it's freezing."

He pulled her to him, tucking his arm around her shoulders. "It's worth it, though, isn't it?"

"Por seguro. Totalmente."

He aimed his headlamp down the top of the ridge, in the direction of the stone plug behind which Rosie had found Pasta Alfredo—or, more likely, where Fredo had allowed herself to be found. The ridgetop was deserted. He and Janelle strolled toward the low pinnacle. Janelle's headlamp flickered across the stone ridge as they walked.

"I can see why people go out on the arches," she said. "I feel like I'm almost weightless up here, on solid rock. I can only imagine how it must feel way out in the middle of one of the arches, surrounded by nothing but air."

The girls trailed Chuck and Janelle along the ridge. Chuck set the pasta on a rock shelf at the base of the stone hoodoo. The girls stacked the candies from their pockets on top of the container.

"This will make him happy," Rosie said, her headlamp directed at their charitable donation.

"Do you think he'll come get it?" Carmelita asked Chuck.

He swung his headlamp around them, piercing the darkness. "He will if he's hungry enough."

Rosie said, "I bet he's cold. We should have brought him a coat."

"If he takes the food, maybe we can get him one in town and leave it for him."

Carmelita asked, "What if he doesn't take the food?"

"I'd say that's pretty likely," Chuck said. "Sanford, the ranger I'm working with, thinks the guy will have hightailed it a long ways from here by now. I'll come back first thing in the morning and bring the food back down to camp if he doesn't show up and take it. We don't want any birds or animals getting into it."

He faced away from the stone projection. "Line up with me, would you?" he asked the girls and Janelle.

They stood with their backs to the pinnacle, facing the spine of the ridge.

"Now for something completely cool," he told them. "Turn off your headlamps."

Rosie fumbled for the on-off switch on the lamp strapped to her forehead. Her light continued to shine. "I can't make it work."

"Here you go." Chuck reached to turn off her light. He switched off his own, as did Janelle and Carmelita.

Inky blackness enveloped the four of them.

"Oooo!" Rosie exclaimed.

Carmelita said, "It's like the stars are so close they're going to come down and hit us on the head."

"Wave your hand in front of your eyes before they adjust to the darkness," Chuck said.

Rosie chortled. "I can't even see it!"

"This is *so* sweet," said Carmelita.

Chuck's expanding pupils registered the rock ridge stretched ahead of them, a runway leading to the stars beyond. The reverberation of a vehicle engine in the far distance was the only sound of humanity in the still night, presumably coming from the highway outside the park to the west.

But the engine noise grew louder, closer, until headlights appeared, climbing out of Courthouse Wash on the park road, headed for Devil's Garden.

Chuck shivered. The park was closed overnight, and the road with it.

Who, then, was driving out here tonight, under the cover of darkness?

25

As the vehicle approached, Chuck led Janelle and girls along the ridge to where the spine of stone fell away to the trailhead parking lot at the end of the park road.

The sound of the engine increased as it drew nearer, revealing itself as the steady gas-engine purr of a passenger vehicle rather than the deeper diesel-engine growl of a work truck.

"Who's that?" Rosie asked as the car passed along the base of the ridge below.

"That's what I want to know," Chuck replied.

"Maybe it's a ghost," said Rosie.

"Ooo-*ooo*-ooo!" Carmelita hooted, imitating a spectral being.

Rosie pressed herself to Chuck's side. "That's scary, Carm."

"That's the idea," said Carmelita.

Imitating her sister, but many decibels louder, Rosie called out, "Ooo-*ooo*-ooo!"

"That should do it," Chuck said. "If there were any ghosts around here, I'm sure you just scared them off."

The car eased across the parking lot to Devil's Garden Trailhead parking lot, its headlights reflecting off the trail sign at the far side of the paved area.

Chuck said, "Let's stay quiet and see if we can tell who it is."

"Yeah, yeah, yeah!" whispered Rosie. "We'll be spies!"

"Shhh!" Carmelita warned her.

They watched in silence as the car rolled to a stop in front of the sign. The vehicle's headlights winked out and its engine died. The front door opened and shut, and the shadowy figure of the driver stood next to the vehicle. No one exited the passenger side of the car.

In the starlight, Chuck could make out nothing more than the shadowy shapes of the driver and vehicle in the otherwise empty lot. Whoever was below had to have permission to be here—most likely a park employee, approved by Sanford to have come out here tonight. But why?

The bright beam of a powerful flashlight shot across the desert from the side of the car. Chuck ducked, drawing Rosie to the surface of the rock with him. Carmelita and Janelle crouched, too.

Chuck clasped Rosie against him, willing her to silence. The beam of the flashlight easily would reach the top of the ridge, illuminating them from the parking lot below, if directed their way.

Instead, the flashlight lit the trailhead sign in front of the car. The chirp of the vehicle locking reached the ridge, after which the driver set out past the sign and up the trail.

Chuck held his breath beside Janelle and the girls until the driver disappeared between the low stone walls bounding the path fifty yards north of the trailhead, the driver's location revealed by the flashlight flickering between the walls of stone.

"Time to get back down to the trailer." Chuck rose, pulling Rosie up with him. "It's getting late."

"Awww," she whined. "I want to find out who that is."

"It's a ghost," Carmelita said.

"Do you really think so, Carm?"

"Could be."

"Ooo-*ooo*-ooo!" Rosie said softly.

Both girls giggled.

"Chuck's right," Janelle said. "Time for bed."

They turned their headlamps back on.

"I'm *never* going to sleep tonight now, for sure," Rosie said as they walked back along the spine of the ridge. "I'll be too freaked out."

"Yeah, right," Carmelita said. "You always fall asleep in, like, two seconds."

"I do not. I don't sleep lots of times."

"Name just one time."

"Christmas Eve. I never sleep then."

"Suuuuure," Carmelita said.

Rosie's headlamp beam bobbled as she reared back and punched Carmelita's upper arm.

"Ow!" Carmelita cried.

"Rosie!" Janelle admonished. "Carm!"

"What are you yelling at me for?" Carmelita rubbed her arm. "I didn't do any—"

"Would you look at that." Chuck aimed his headlamp at the stone plug rising from the top of the ridge ahead of them.

The shelf at the base of the pinnacle, where they'd left the pasta and candies, was empty.

"Amazing!" Rosie scurried to the sandstone plug. Chuck jogged with Janelle and Carmelita to keep up.

"It's gone!" Rosie said when they reached the rock shelf. "He took the food."

She directed her headlamp past the low pinnacle. Her light revealed the rolling undulations of the ridge, but no sign of the homeless man.

"You're welcome!" Rosie called into the darkness.

"Quiet," Chuck implored her. *"Por favor."* He glanced over his shoulder at Devil's Garden Trail. The beam of the driver's flashlight continued to flicker between the walls of the corridor, still heading away from the trailhead. "We've done our good deed for the night," he said. "Let's head on down."

Carmelita and Rosie led the way off the ridge. Chuck and

Janelle fell back. "Permission to check on the vehicle," Chuck said softly.

He couldn't see her roll her eyes in the darkness, but the tone of her answer assured him she'd done so. "I figured you'd be asking."

"The arch, the two deaths, the homeless guy—there's too much going on that's making me uneasy right now. The park is supposed to be closed. I want to know who's out here tonight."

She descended a few steps in silence. "Okay, permission granted," she said, finally. "I want to know what's going on, too. I'll stick with the girls while you do your night stalker thing."

Chuck left his family in the brightly lit trailer, crept past the line of motor homes, and waited at the campground entrance until his eyes adjusted to the darkness. A hundred feet ahead, the vehicle was an indistinct black rectangle parked on the pavement. The beam of the flashlight flickered between the walls of the sandstone corridor, signaling the driver's imminent arrival back at the trailhead.

Chuck cursed beneath his breath. No more than fifteen minutes had passed since the car had arrived at the parking lot. Why was the driver coming back so soon? Chuck sprinted across the parking area and reached the car just as the bobbing flashlight emerged from the corridor.

The beam of light flashed across the vehicle. Chuck ducked behind its rear bumper. The light returned to the trail, and Chuck rose and studied the car. It was a mid-size sport utility vehicle, its color impossible to determine in the darkness. He leaned around the SUV, surveying its side. Whatever its color, the paint was smooth and uniform; no National Park Service emblem was affixed to its side.

Chuck rounded the vehicle and, cupping his hands to his eyes, peered inside.

He saw only blackness.

He put his finger to the on-off switch on his headlamp. The driver was fifty feet away, traversing the final stretch of trail to the parking lot through waist-high sage.

Chuck had only a few seconds. He kept his eyes on the blackness inside the car, took a deep breath, and clicked on his headlamp. The interior of the car filled with light.

He blinked, his eyes adjusting to the sudden brightness. The SUV had velour seats, tan in color. The dashboard was a matching light brown. The passenger seat was empty, as was the footwell in front of it.

Chuck swung the beam of his headlamp along the dashboard. It, too, was clear of any revelatory objects.

He reached for the switch to his headlamp, ready to turn off his light and escape into the darkness of the desert. But he froze with his finger on the switch, his eyes on an item dangling above the car's dashboard.

Hanging from the rearview mirror was a miniature Native American dreamcatcher. Chuck aimed his headlamp at it.

Like all dreamcatchers, the one in the SUV consisted of a webbed wooden hoop strung with thin fiber to resemble a spider's web with a tiny hole at its center. Feathers hung from the sides and bottom of the hoop, completing the object.

Dreamcatchers were believed to capture dreams floating through the night air. Good dreams escaped through the small hole at the center of the circular web, while bad dreams were trapped in the web until the first rays of the morning sun struck and destroyed them. Navajo artisans produced exquisite dreamcatchers with sanded red-willow hoops in perfect circles, elaborate webs woven with natural fibers, and beaded cords that hung from the hoops, leading to dangling raven and magpie feathers.

The dreamcatcher on the SUV mirror was obviously Navajo, its red-willow hoop tugged into a precise three-inch circle by the strands of its intricately woven web. The cords leading to the hanging feathers were beaded with tiny pellets in a range of colors, and the black feathers that dangled from the cords were those of a raven, the trickster bird of *Diné* lore.

The flashlight captured Chuck in its powerful beam. He dropped to his stomach beside the car, flicked off his own headlamp, and scrambled away from the SUV, diving into the brush at the edge of the parking lot just as the flashlight-wielding driver reached the trailhead and swung the light across the pavement.

Chuck lay in the brush while the beam of light roved to and fro.

Why, he asked himself as he corralled his stuttering breaths, was he hiding?

Ducking for cover had been a reflexive maneuver, as had his initial decision to investigate the unknown car in the wake of today's deaths. The driver of the SUV presumably had every right to be here in Devil's Garden, whereas—other than a vague sense of protecting his family—Chuck had no equal and opposite right to be spying.

He kept his head down, hoping the driver of the car was as concerned about Chuck's presence in the parking lot as Chuck was about the driver's presence.

Sure enough, the flashlight winked out. The sound of footsteps reached Chuck as the driver strode to the SUV through the sudden darkness. The front door opened and closed, the engine started, and the SUV backed from its parking place. Chuck lay still as the car's headlights swept across the brush where he hid. The car swung past him, crossed the empty lot, and departed on the park road toward town, disappearing behind the sandstone ridge.

Chuck stood and slapped dirt from his pants and jacket. The driver had to be either Sanford or Elsie in their private vehicle. What were the odds anyone else would be capable of gaining unaccompanied access into the closed park tonight *and* have a finely crafted Navajo dreamcatcher hanging from the rearview mirror of their car?

Answer: slim to none.

Which led Chuck to the next, far more intriguing question.

Why had Sanford or Elsie driven all the way out here and hiked away from the parking lot on Devil's Garden Trail tonight, only to return to the trailhead after walking such a short distance?

26

A brisk knock sounded on the trailer door early the next morning.

"Char-lie," Sheila trilled from outside. "Are you in there?"

Chuck groaned and rolled to face Janelle in the bed at the back of the camper.

Janelle said to him softly, mimicking Sheila's birdlike chirrup, "Rise and shine, *Char-lie*. Your mother's all yours." She put her lips to his ear and whispered, "But if she tries any more of that innuendo crap with the girls, I'll throw her out on her ear."

Chuck slid out of bed, walked barefooted to the front of the trailer, and opened the door. Sheila climbed the stairs past him.

"Grandma!" Rosie cheered from where she lay on the lower bunk with Fredo perched on her chest.

"Good morning, sweetums," Sheila said from the entryway.

Carmelita's upper bunk curtain was drawn, hiding her from view.

Janelle sat up in the bed at the back of the trailer. "Good morning, Sheila," she said, tucking the bedsheets around her. "Welcome to our home away from home."

Sheila glanced around the camper. "Cute little place you've got here." Addressing Chuck in the doorway behind her, she said, "Reminds me of some of the trailers you and I lived in."

"This is a lot nicer than any of those," Chuck replied.

Her eyes went to the shredded dinette seat cushion. "If you say so."

Janelle slipped out of bed and into the bathroom, her clothes held to her chest.

In place of yesterday's gossamer dress, today Sheila wore a heavy-corded sweater-dress that reached to her knees, with purple leggings below. Over her ivory sweater-dress she wore a short-waisted black down coat. She took off the coat and extended it behind her to Chuck.

"Who's that you've got there with you, Rosie?" She released the coat into Chuck's hands without looking back at him and walked up the aisle to pet Fredo. The cat yowled and pawed at Sheila's outstretched fingers.

"Yikes!" She jerked back her hand.

Fredo folded herself against Rosie's chest, her yellow eyes fixed on Sheila.

"There, there, Fredo." Rosie scratched Fredo's ears. "It's all right. It's just Grandma."

Straightening beside the bunk beds, Sheila shook her hand briskly in the air. "Cats and I never have gotten along."

Carmelita pulled back the upper bunk curtain and stared eye-to-eye with Sheila. "Hi," she said softly.

"Hi, *Grandma*," Sheila directed, emphasizing the second word.

"Um. Hi, *Grandma*," Carmelita said, mimicking Sheila's emphasis.

Chuck caught a flash of anger in Sheila's eyes as she spun away from the bunk beds. She bent over the dinette table to peer out the picture window. "It's a wonderful day out there," she said, her back to the girls.

Chuck checked the clock above the stove. Seven forty-five. No seismic thumps rolled through the campground from outside the park boundary. "It's a nice start to the day, anyway."

"I greet the rising sun every morning on my yoga mat with an upward-facing dog," she announced, turning from the window. "There's no better way to begin the day."

"Good for you," Chuck said. The old Sheila rarely had gotten out of bed before noon.

Rosie tickled Fredo's chin. "Pasta Alfredo is facing up right now, too. But she's a cat, not a dog."

"That's an odd name for a cat, or any pet for that matter," Sheila said. "Why did you give her an Italian name when you're Hispanic or Latino or Latina or whatever?"

"Latinx," Carmelita said from the upper bunk.

"La-what?"

"Latinx. That's what we are. With an *x*."

"I don't get it," Sheila said.

Carmelita raised her phone to her mouth. "Hey, you," she said.

"Yes, you?" the phone's search engine replied in the British-accented male voice Carmelita had programmed into it.

"What's the difference between Latinx, with an *x*, and Latino, with an *o*?"

Her phone responded in its British voice, "Latinx, ending with the letter *x*, is the accepted gender-neutral identifier for people of Latin American heritage, used primarily in the United States. Alternative term: *Hispanic*."

Carmelita waved her phone at Sheila. "Got it?"

Sheila's back went stiff. She exhaled sharply.

Chuck smiled and shook his head. "Am I married to a Hispanic woman, a Latino woman, or a Latinx woman?"

Janelle stepped out of the bathroom, now dressed. "I kind of like Latinx."

"It's totally rad," Carmelita confirmed.

Chuck grinned at the two of them. "Latinx it is. I'm not sure I'll ever be able to keep up with all the new phrases out there, though. Like *LGBTQ*. I'm still not sure what all those letters stand for." He looked to Carmelita for help. "I mean, I know *gay*. And *bi*. And the *T* stands for *transvestite*, I know that one."

"Trans*gender*," Carmelita corrected him. "Or better yet, just *trans*."

"How do you know all this? Are you thirteen or thirty-three?"

Janelle pointed at the phone in Carmelita's hand. "That thing knows all."

"Which is what worries the hell out of me." Chuck glanced at Rosie. "The *heck* out of me. Which is what worries the heck out of me."

"That's all right," Rosie told him. "You can cuss in front of me. I'm eleven."

Sheila turned her attention from Carmelita to Rosie, crooning, "Aren't you the sweetest thing." She stroked Rosie's round calf, beneath the sheet at the foot of the lower bunk, her hand well clear of Fredo's claws. A hint of brittleness entered her voice, her eyes fixed on Rosie's chubby figure. "You know, sweetie, a little hot yoga, to sweat off some pounds, certainly wouldn't do you any harm. Maybe you should ask your mother about getting into a children's class."

Chuck gritted his teeth. "Out," he said curtly to Sheila, pointing at the door. "Outside. Now. I'll get dressed and meet you." He held Sheila's puffy coat out to her.

Sheila marched past him, accepting the coat with a rigidly outthrust hand. He pulled the door closed after her and turned back into the trailer. Striding up the aisle, he changed out of his pajama bottoms and T-shirt into jeans, a fresh T-shirt, and a fleece top.

"Keep her out there," Janelle warned him when he returned to the doorway.

He put on his jacket and ball cap. "I'll try."

"No, you'll do better than that," Janelle insisted. "Keep . . . her . . . outside."

"You got it, *jefe*."

* * *

Sheila waited beside the Bender Archaeological pickup truck.

The November sky was clear and the morning sun warm despite the early hour, as if yesterday's ice storm had never happened. The tangy scent of the drying desert floated through the campground.

"Let's take a stroll, shall we?" Sheila suggested when Chuck reached her.

They walked through the campground past the motor homes.

"You're a different person these days," Chuck said to his mother. "The same in some ways, but different in lots of others."

"I'll take that as a compliment," she replied, "whether you meant it that way or not. Because, yes. Yes, I am."

"I did mean it as a compliment." Chuck paused. "Sort of."

"But . . . ?" Sheila urged as they walked.

He bit his lower lip. In all the years of his upbringing, he'd chosen in the interest of survival to remain silent rather than confront his mother. The tactic had worked. He *had* survived, and gone on to live a decent, if lonely, life in the years that followed.

But he no longer was lonely. His life with Janelle and the girls was full to overflowing, in the best way imaginable. Since meeting up with Sheila again yesterday, however, a sudden shadow had enveloped him and his family, as dark as the room at the back of his mother's apartment.

Why had Sheila denied knowing Megan yesterday? And how did Sheila's denial play into the death of the woman who'd been her fixer and apparent acolyte?

He stopped in the middle of the drive.

If he'd learned anything from Janelle and her stand-up ways over the last four years, it was that, when called for, there was value in confrontation.

Sheila turned to him.

"When we came to see you yesterday," Chuck said, "you already knew Megan had died."

The morning sun shone full on Sheila's pinched face. She licked her lips, shellacked in red, the tip of her tongue darting from one corner of her thin mouth to the other. "Of course I did," she said. "Megan was a wonderful young woman. I heard the news just before you arrived. It had nothing to do with you, so I didn't see anything to be gained by discussing it."

"Not even when I asked you about it?"

"Not even then."

"You had to have known how close we were to where it happened."

"I knew nothing of the sort." Sheila waved a hand at the sandstone bluffs bounding the campground. "I have no idea where I am right now. For all I know, you were miles and miles from where the arch fell, in some whole other part of the park."

Chuck resumed walking. According to Paul, Sheila had directed Megan to Landscape Arch because of its proximity to the O&G Seismic thumper truck outside the park's northern boundary. No doubt Sheila knew far more about her whereabouts in the park than she was letting on.

She fell into step beside him. A handful of paved parking spots fronted the driveway just inside the campground entrance, providing overflow parking for campers' extra vehicles. Only one of the spots was occupied, by a sleek European-model SUV.

"Nice wheels," Chuck commented as they passed the car, noting that the rearview mirror had nothing hanging from it.

"It gets me where I need to go," Sheila replied.

"What brings you out here this morning?"

She took her phone from her jacket pocket and checked it. "You'll know soon enough," she said, putting the phone away.

They reached the entrance to the campground, the trailhead parking lot before them. White park-service vehicles occupied a handful of the slots—sedans topped with emergency lights, pickup trucks with brown National Park Service arrowhead emblems on their doors, and Sanford's truck with its chief ranger stripes. The vehicles were empty and the trail leading away from the parking lot was deserted.

Chuck lifted his cap and ran his fingers through his close-cropped hair. He was glad to see how early Sanford and the investigation team had set out for the arch. What would they make of the hole drilled in the top of the span? And of the unexploded Pyrodex?

No private tourist cars or RVs were parked among the government vehicles.

"Looks like the road is still closed to visitors," Chuck noted to Sheila, pulling his cap back down over his eyes.

"It is."

"How'd you get through?"

"I know people who know people. I explained to the ranger who I was. She let me by."

A car engine sounded in the distance, approaching along the final stretch of the road.

"Right on time," Sheila said.

27

A bright red pickup truck appeared from behind the sandstone ridge. The O&G Seismic logo was stenciled on the truck's doors.

"Ohhh," Sheila said, raising her eyebrows.

George Epson steered the truck past the investigation team's vehicles to a parking spot near the campground entrance. He nodded coolly to Chuck and Sheila as he climbed out. In place of the grease-stained overalls he'd worn yesterday, he sported classic day-hiker's garb—loose pants, a long-sleeved cotton shirt, and a broad-brimmed canvas hat. He'd shaved much of his beard, leaving a manicured strip from sideburn to sideburn just wide enough to cover his jaw. He'd trimmed his mustache, too. Where yesterday the thatch of hair beneath his nose had sprouted all directions, now it cut straight across his upper lip, meeting his thinned beard close on either side of his mouth.

Chuck studied the freshly primped O&G manager. Someone from the company's media department clearly had gotten to him; the public relations effort by O&G Seismic already was in full swing.

Chuck crossed the pavement to George. "What are you doing here?"

George pulled a daypack from the back of his truck and threw it over his shoulder. "Sanford asked for my help."

"*Your* help? This is all your fault."

George replied calmly, "No one knows what caused the arch to collapse. That's the purpose of this morning's investigation."

"Everybody knows what caused it to fall: you did."

"I wasn't with the geological assessment truck yesterday morning. I was at the maintenance yard in town."

"Sanford told me you're the regional operations manager for O&G. That means the thumper truck was doing its thing under your orders."

"The company's geologists determine where the truck performs its quantification assessments. I have no say in its coordinate directives."

"You've been practicing that response, haven't you, George? Nice togs you're wearing today, too. You're all set for the television cameras. I have to hand it to your bosses. They've got themselves quite the little toady in you."

George squared his shoulders. His eyes shot sparks but he maintained his civil tone. "Sanford asked me to join his team."

"Because your bosses forced him to."

George's face turned bright red. "I don't have to listen to this," he growled.

"Careful there," Chuck said. "Remember what I'm sure your media minders have been telling you, that you have to keep your cool no matter what."

George rocked back on his heels and clamped his mouth shut.

"Let's keep our focus on what happened yesterday, why don't we?" Chuck continued. "An innocent person was killed beneath Landscape Arch. Maybe not directly at your hand, but close enough. You shouldn't forget that."

George slumped and his face grew pale.

Sheila, having approached to Chuck's side, said to George, "You owe me an apology."

The O&G manager touched the brim of his canvas hat to her in welcome. "Hello, Sheila."

Chuck stepped back, his mouth falling open. "Wait a minute. The two of you know each other?"

"Of course we do," said Sheila.

"Yes," George admitted, adding, "Moab's a small town."

Sheila narrowed her eyes. "You needn't be ashamed of having availed yourself of my services, George—at Megan's recommendation, I might add."

Chuck stared at the manager and his mother, recalling the O&G Seismic mug Sheila had pulled from her kitchen cabinet. "Just how incestuous is Moab, anyway?"

George aimed a finger at Sheila. "It wasn't incestuous at all until she showed up."

Sheila turned to Chuck. "Aren't you going to defend me, Charlie?"

"I'd say you're fully capable of defending yourself."

She lifted an eyebrow. "True." She turned to George. "You and your geo truck cost me a lot of money yesterday."

"Money?"

"You heard what I said. I don't appreciate the role you played in Megan's demise."

George's face twisted. "Only because of the money you'll lose."

"Yes, because of that," Sheila replied primly. "Megan was very important to me."

"You mean, she was important to your bottom line."

"Precisely. And now, in a puff of smoke, she's gone."

"Something tells me you'll be just fine."

Sheila flattened her red lips. "That's right, I will be. No thanks to you."

The O&G manager dipped his head, his neck stiff. "If you'll excuse me, some of us want to learn what actually happened out there."

He set off up the trail.

Sheila watched George depart. "It's nice to see he's finally cleaned up his act. I've been telling him to do that for weeks."

"You . . . you . . ." Chuck stammered.

Another car engine sounded, approaching on the far side of the ridge.

"There we are," Sheila said. "It's about time."

A mini SUV, sky blue with sparkling chrome rims, entered the parking lot. The car, Frank and Nora's pull-behind vehicle, had been parked in front of the couple's motor home last night.

Sheila raised a hand in greeting as the mini SUV rolled across the pavement toward her and Chuck. Nora was driving, with Martha in the passenger seat. Nora returned Sheila's wave, while Martha sat unmoving, staring through the windshield.

The car stopped beside Sheila. The driver's side window opened, and Nora gushed, "Thank you so much for being here."

"I'll never *not* be here for you," Sheila replied.

Martha climbed out of the passenger seat, rounded the car, and collapsed, sobbing, into Sheila's arms.

28

"There, now." Sheila soothed Martha, holding her close. "I've got you. I'm here with you now."

Martha's sobs eased. Sheila took a tissue from the pocket of her down coat, handed it to Martha, and walked with her down the drive to Harold and Martha's motor home, an arm wrapped around her waist. The two women stood beside the coach, facing the site of Harold's fatal fall, Martha's head on Sheila's shoulder.

Sheila removed her arm from around Martha and massaged the back of Martha's neck. Martha stepped away and entered the motor home. Sheila followed, closing the door behind them.

Nora said to Chuck from inside the car, her hands on the wheel, "Your mother is a gem. An absolute lifesaver." She drove on into the campground, parked in front of the motor home she shared with Frank, and disappeared inside.

Chuck shook his head to himself as he walked back through the campground. George was a client of his mother. Martha and Nora were, too, it appeared. Who *wasn't* a client of hers?

A flicker of movement high on the rock ridge between the campground and park road caught his eye. He looked up to see a man standing atop the ridge. As Chuck watched, the man ducked behind the point of stone where Rosie had found Pasta Alfredo, and where Chuck and his family had left the container of pasta last night.

Chuck ran to the base of the ridge and strode up the sloped stone ramp. He reached the crown of the ridge and stood with his hands on his hips, taking deep breaths.

The homeless man sat fifty feet away, facing Chuck, his back to the stone pinnacle. The pasta container rested on the stone beside him. The man was dressed in the same ragged clothes he'd worn when he'd come to Harold's aid yesterday. He cradled a calico house cat in his lap. The man made no attempt to conceal himself, but he didn't look directly at Chuck, either.

Chuck approached along the top of the ridge. "Hey, there," he said between deep breaths when he reached the homeless man.

The man bowed his head, his face to the cat in his arms. The calico was skinny, with bald spots showing between matted tufts of fur.

"Thanks for letting me join you up here," Chuck said.

The man stroked the house cat with his thin fingers, saying nothing.

"Would you like to tell me your name?" Chuck asked. "Mine's Chuck. But I bet you already know that."

The man spoke a single word, his head still bent over the calico. "Glen."

Easing himself to a sitting position next to Glen, Chuck rested his hands on his raised knees, his back to the stone hoodoo, and glanced sideways. The portion of Glen's face not covered by his beard was dark brown and scorched by the sun.

Chuck stared out across the desert. "How'd you like the pasta?"

Glen scratched the cat's ears.

"I realize you showed yourself to me up here for a reason. What is it you know that you want me to know? What do you want to tell me?"

Glen said nothing.

"Thanks for helping Harold, the man who fell from the ladder," Chuck said. "You sure got there fast."

177

Glen's body spasmed. The calico leapt from his arms and scurried from sight behind the point of rock. Glen scrabbled crab-like away from Chuck, the seat of his pants sliding on the rough stone surface. He eyed Chuck from several feet away, his gaze centered on Chuck's chest.

"What is it? What'd I say?" Chuck asked.

Glen spun and sat with his back to Chuck.

"I take it you don't want to be thanked for what you did," Chuck said. "But why did you let me see you just now? Why didn't you run off when I came up here?"

Glen slowly raised his hand and extended a trembling finger west, toward toppled Landscape Arch.

"Right," Chuck said. "I followed your tracks to the arch yesterday. But I'm betting you already know that, don't you?"

Glen shifted until he sat facing Chuck. He glanced Chuck's direction and away.

Chuck decided the glance was a "yes."

"Did you go to the arch for a specific reason?"

Again, Glen glanced at Chuck. *Yes.*

"Did the reason you went to the arch have to do with me?"

Glen looked out across the desert. *No.*

Chuck frowned. Glen had hiked off-trail across the desert to the site of the toppled arch sometime after the rangers and first responders had returned from the site with Megan's body.

"Did it have to do with the rangers and what they did or didn't find out there?"

Glen turned his face to Chuck. This time, he held Chuck's gaze for a full second, his dark brown eyes blazing, before looking down at the bare rock between them.

"Okay," Chuck said. "Now we're getting somewhere."

Glen knew something about what had happened at the site of the collapsed arch—but what?

Rosie broke into Chuck's train of thought.

"Chuuu-uck!" she called out from the campground below, breaking his name into two syllables.

Pushing himself to his feet, Chuck walked to the rounded edge of the ridge. Rosie stood in the campground drive below, her hand to her forehead, her head swiveling.

"Up here!" Chuck called to her.

She peered up at him on the ridge. "*Mamá* says to come," she yelled. "It's time for breakfast."

"I'll be right down," Chuck told her. "Just a few more minutes."

But when he turned back to the stone pinnacle, only the pasta container remained. Glen was gone.

PART THREE

"The idea of wilderness needs no defense, it only needs defenders."

—Edward Abbey, *The Journey Home*

29

Chuck didn't chase after Glen. If and when he wanted Chuck to find him again, Glen would make it happen.

Chuck retrieved the empty pasta container and descended the ridge to the trailer. Inside, the girls sat at the dinette table, bowls of cereal in front of them. Fredo rested on the tabletop between the girls' bowls. Chuck was tempted to question the health aspects of allowing the cat to lay on the dining table while the girls ate, but he knew how far he'd get if he voiced his concerns.

Chuck caught Janelle's eye as she rinsed her bowl in the sink. "Could I talk to you for a minute?" he asked, tilting his head toward the door.

She dried her hands and grabbed her jacket.

Outside, she asked, "Where's your mother?"

Chuck led her past the trailer and crew cab to the campground driveway. "You're not going to believe it." He described Martha's return in Nora's car, and the fact that Sheila was now looking after Harold's widow. "The two of them are in Martha's RV," he finished.

He and Janelle walked toward the back of the campground.

"There's more," he said. He explained that he'd tracked the homeless man to the collapsed arch the previous day, and admitted to having been forced by Paul's well-placed gunshot to meet and speak with Megan's widower yesterday evening.

Janelle spun Chuck by the elbow to face her. "You should have told me right away," she said, her fingers digging into his arm.

"I didn't want to worry you."

"I'm not worried. I'm pissed off."

"I'm telling you now."

She raised a finger and opened her mouth to respond, but he inserted quickly, "There's one more thing."

She paused, her finger suspended in the air. He described his encounter with Glen on top of the ridge a few minutes ago. She lowered her hand as he spoke.

"You say he was silent," she noted when Chuck finished. "But he told you his name."

"That was the only word he spoke."

"Which proves he's at least capable of speaking."

"I think he's frightened."

"Maybe he's scared speechless." Janelle squeezed the bridge of her nose with her thumb and forefinger. "Too many coincidences. I'm not buying it. It's all interrelated somehow, it's gotta be—the seismic truck, Megan's death, Harold's accident, the trigger-happy guy you just told me about, and now, Glen." She lowered her hand and asked, "You know the one thing that's the continuing thread through every last bit of this?"

Chuck nodded but let Janelle provide the answer.

"Your mother."

Chuck kept an eye out of the trailer window as he and the girls ate cereal at the dinette table, Pasta Alfredo now in Rosie's lap. When he caught sight of Sanford and the investigation team members returning to their vehicles in the parking lot outside the campground, he threw on his jacket and jogged to meet them.

He reached Sanford as the chief ranger arrived at his truck. The half-dozen park staffers trailing Sanford dropped their packs to the pavement and stood together at the trailhead, drinking from water bottles. The members of the investigation team wore traditional park-service garb—green slacks and jackets over gray button-up shirts—though in a bow to comfort, their headwear consisted of ball caps rather than the National Park Service's time-honored Smokey Bear hats made of stiff straw. George stood among the uniformed team members.

Chuck pointed across the pavement at the O&G Seismic manager in his natty hiker's garb and demanded of Sanford, "What the hell are you doing including him in your investigation?"

"He knows more about seismology than the rest of us put together."

"You're letting the fox guard the henhouse."

"George knows his stuff," the chief ranger contended. "He feels terrible about what happened. His expertise was critical to us this morning."

"You mean, he was critical in covering up any role O&G played in the collapse."

"That's enough, Chuck," Sanford warned.

"Fine," Chuck snapped. He turned his back on George. "What *did* you manage to find out there?"

"That's none of your business. You're supposed to be focusing on the pictograph."

"I should tell you: I returned to the site of the collapse yesterday—that is, to the scene of the crime."

Sanford drew himself to full height, still inches shorter than Chuck. "How many times do I have to tell you? We're not talking about a crime here."

"If that's the case, then why don't you tell me what you and your team—and George, of course—made of the drill hole and blasting powder in the arch?"

Sanford's eyes bulged. "Drill hole? What the hell are you talking about?"

"I'm talking about the hole in the fallen block at the far south end of the line of fallen rocks. It's an inch around and two inches deep. Perfectly cylindrical. It was filled with blasting powder before the arch fell; there are still remnants of the powder around its edge. It's on the side facing east, away from the flat—the side that, until yesterday, was the top of the arch."

"I have no idea what you're talking about."

"You couldn't have missed it," Chuck insisted. "It's head-high, plain as day, right there in the rock in front of you."

"We didn't miss a thing. I'm sure of it. We certainly wouldn't have missed anything as obvious as that. We surveyed the entire length of the collapse, block by block."

"That can't possibly be right."

Sanford scowled. "Let me ask you this: If you found this supposed drill hole in the arch yesterday, as you say, then why didn't you tell me about it right away? Why didn't you take a picture of it with your phone and send it to me as soon as you saw it?"

"I . . ." When Chuck had come across the hole yesterday, he'd been focused on Paul Johnson—and Paul's .30-06. By the time Chuck left the arch and headed back to camp, his thoughts had been so tangled that the notion of checking in with Sanford hadn't occurred to him.

Or, Chuck asked himself, had his subconscious been at work? Was Sanford not to be trusted? The fact that the chief ranger denied the existence of the impossible-to-miss drill hole certainly added a layer of suspicion. But why would Sanford have reason to deny the hole's existence?

Chuck glanced over his shoulder at George. Was that it? Sanford's defense of the O&G manager was open and unabashed. But why would either of the men have wanted to blow up the arch? Moreover, how could all the other members of the investigation team have missed seeing the drill hole, too—or, how could Sanford possibly convince every last one of them to lie and say they hadn't seen it?

Chuck scratched his ear. Sanford was waiting for his answer. All he could come up with was, "Um."

"You know what, Chuck?" Sanford said. "I think you're imagining things; you're seeing things that aren't real. Besides which, you had no right to go back to the arch, which has nothing to do with why you're here."

"Wrong!" Chuck exploded. "The arch has *everything* to do with why I'm here. You and I both know George and his goddamn seismic people are the ones who brought it down, given the unexploded drill hole you so obviously missed. The seismic work is precisely the sort of thing you've hired me to try to stop, for Elsie and her people and everybody else who cares about the destruction of public lands."

"Quiet," Sanford snarled. He glanced across the parking lot at George and the other members of the investigation team. "The contract is just between you and me at this point."

Chuck dropped his voice but made no attempt to hide his anger. "You've brought the real culprit right into the middle of your so-called investigation," he hissed. "And you didn't even look hard enough to see the drill hole." He threw up his hands in disgust. "You have to go back out there right now, this instant."

"We didn't miss a thing out there." Sanford folded his arms on top of his round stomach and looked Chuck up and down.

Chuck glared back at the chief ranger, his arms stiff at his sides. Then he blinked, his arms loosening.

The fact was, Sanford and the investigation team could not have missed the drill hole in the toppled arch, and Sanford could not possibly convince all the team members to deny the hole's existence, either—which meant the chief ranger might well be telling the truth about not having seen the drill hole.

If that was the case, could it be Chuck himself who was

mistaken? Was the hole in the arch, in fact, natural?

He knew full well that hard pebbles, when rocked in a circular motion by passing winds over the course of years, commonly gouged cylindrical holes in soft sandstone.

Was that the sort of hole he'd seen in the fallen block yesterday? Had he gotten so caught up in Paul's conspiracy theories that he'd incorrectly convinced himself the hole was manmade? And had he further convinced himself the sulfurous green residue in the hole was blasting powder, when it simply had been common, bright green, highly odorous juniper pollen?

There was only one way to find out for sure. He had to return to the site of the collapsed arch for another look, and it would be best to do so right away, before park visitors were allowed back into Devil's Garden—perhaps as soon as the investigation team cleared out of the trailhead parking lot.

Sanford lifted his chin. "You know," he said, his eyes glinting, "for coming as highly recommended as you did, I'm really beginning to wonder about you."

"I'm way past wondering about you," Chuck spat back, masking his uncertainty about the hole in the toppled arch. "I'm fully and entirely suspicious about whose side you're really on."

Sanford turned away from Chuck and strode across the pavement to George and the other investigation team members. Chuck observed the chief ranger's gait. Was it Sanford who'd driven here in the SUV last night and ventured up Devil's Garden Trail with the flashlight? Chuck shook his head in frustration. He had no way of knowing; he'd been flat on his stomach, hidden in the brush, when the driver had returned to the parked car.

Chuck left the trailhead parking lot and reentered the campground. The German camper who'd lasted out yesterday's storm in his pint-sized rental car exited the communal bathroom as

Chuck passed it.

"*Hallo,*" the camper greeted Chuck.

They walked together toward their respective campsites.

"You are right," the German said in his heavy accent. "The weather, it is very much better today."

"Like I said, it's the desert," Chuck replied, wanting only to get away from the man.

The German camper was ruggedly handsome, taller than Chuck and wider at the shoulders. His cascading blond hair matched his flaxen beard.

"I am so liking it here in the desert." He grinned. "Though yesterday, okay, not so much."

"There aren't many better places in the world," Chuck agreed.

"I can see why the writer Edward Abbey made this place his home."

Chuck pivoted and ogled the German. "You know who Ed Abbey is?"

"Of course. He is the reason I am here. I know it is late in the season and it is cold and I have only a small tent. But Edward Abbey suffered much more during the time when he was here. It was during summer. The temperatures was very hot."

"He was a tough one, that's for sure," Chuck said.

"Much more tough than John Wayne," the German agreed.

"Ed Abbey was a real person. John Wayne was an actor who killed Indians in old Western movies."

"Those type of Western films is very popular where I come from, in *Deutschland.*"

"What about Ed Abbey?"

"He is more and more popular also in my country. I am a part of the Green Party. We know about him very much. We try to be like him. And so I wanted to come here, where he is."

Chuck put his fist to his chest and intoned, "*Desert Solitaire.*"

The camper smiled, his mustache lifting at the sides of his

mouth, and put his fist to his chest, too. "*Das ist* right. *Wüste Solitär.*"

Chuck held out his fist to the German. "You came to the right place."

"*Ja,*" the German said. "Even after yesterday." He bumped Chuck's knuckles with his own and walked on down the drive, headed for his campsite.

Chuck stared after the German camper. Another Abbey fan, just like Sanford.

Or was the chief ranger faking it?

30

The girls waved at Chuck from inside the trailer, their faces to the window above the dinette table. He returned their waves as he approached.

Sheila had yet to reemerge from Martha's motor home. She likely would be out and about soon enough, however. If Chuck returned to the site of the toppled arch alone, he'd be leaving Janelle and the girls on their own in the campground—directly in Sheila's line of fire, without him to run interference.

He opened the trailer door and stuck his head inside. "Who wants to help me track down some bad guys?"

Rosie raised her hand and bounced in her seat at the table. "I do, I do!"

"Carm?"

Carmelita moaned. "Do I have to?"

"Careful you don't get too excited."

Rosie giggled, earning a stormy squint from her sister.

"How about you?" Chuck called to Janelle.

She poked her head from the bathroom, toothbrush in hand. "It'll be good to get away from here," she said without referring to Sheila by name.

"What about Pasta Alfredo?" Rosie asked.

Fredo lifted her head from the table.

"You're staying put," Chuck told the cat. "This time, though, you'll be relaxing in your new home."

An hour later, Chuck lifted his ball cap and wiped nervous perspiration from his forehead. He resettled the hat on his head as he hiked with Janelle, Carmelita, and Rosie through the final passageway to the collapsed arch.

The trailhead parking lot had been empty of the investigation team members and their vehicles when he, Janelle, and the girls had passed through it, and the trail was free of other hikers, too.

Chuck was alone with his family, approaching the place where, barely twelve hours ago, he'd been shot at and nearly killed.

"I bet Fredo's mad," Rosie said, hiking a step behind him.

"She laid right down when we put her in her new box," Chuck assured her from his lead position.

He'd emptied one of his plastic gear totes and cut breathing holes in its lid with a utility knife, then lined the box with the fleece blanket from Rosie's bed, set the cat inside, and snapped the lid over her. As they left the trailer, Fredo had rested on the blanket with her head on her paws, eyeing them through the semi-transparent side of the box.

"I'm going to take her for a walk when we get back," Rosie said.

"Maybe we can figure out some sort of leash for her so she won't run off." Chuck paused. "Though if she *were* to run off . . ."

"Hush," Janelle cautioned from the back of the line, a smile in her voice.

"Yeah, hush!" Rosie exclaimed. "Fredo's ours and we love her."

Chuck slowed and peered ahead as they neared the end of the cliff-walled passage and the opening beyond. The girls and Janelle bunched behind him. Like Chuck, Rosie wore a pile jacket, jeans, and hiking boots. Carmelita, meanwhile, had selected an outfit for the hike that befitted her new standing as a teenager: a turquoise, form-fitting neoprene running top, black climbing tights that hugged her skinny legs, and neon-pink trail-running shoes.

Ahead, the mid-morning sun set the swaths of ricegrass in the flat aglow. Chuck led his family out of the passage and across the opening. Other than a collared lizard scurrying up the trail ahead of him, he saw no signs of movement in the flat or on the surrounding bluffs. Still, the hairs on the back of his neck prickled. Were they really alone out here?

He picked up his pace, prompting Janelle to call from the back of the line, "Are we on a hike or a run?"

He slowed.

Carmelita muttered, "I could have gone on a run on my own if you hadn't made me come out here with you."

A number of retorts occurred to Chuck. He compressed his lips to keep himself from giving voice to any of them.

They passed the wooden viewpoint fence and made their way along the line of fallen blocks. The southernmost chunk of toppled sandstone rested on a low rise. Chuck climbed the slope to it, noting that the soil at the block's base was tracked with boot prints from the investigation team. The tracks circled the block, eradicating those made by Chuck and Paul yesterday evening.

Chuck trailed the ill-defined prints of the team members around the boulder, pressing his hand to the cool surface of the stone for balance. He stepped away from the far side of the block and checked its face.

The drill hole was gone.

Rosie, Carmelita, and Janelle rounded the rock and examined the east-facing side of the boulder with Chuck, who stared at the block in shocked silence.

"What are we looking at?" Rosie asked.

Carmelita smacked her chewing gum. "A rock."

"I bet you could climb it, Carm," Rosie said.

Carmelita eyed the block, which rose higher than the girls'

heads. "I bet you could, too."

"Goody," said Rosie. "Let's try!"

"Sorry, we're not here for that," Janelle said.

"What are we here for, then?" Carmelita asked.

"Oh, I just remembered," Rosie said. Her voice dropped to a conspiratorial whisper. "Bad guys!"

The girls turned slow circles, scanning the bluffs around them, their forefingers outstretched as pistols.

Chuck stepped forward and ran his hand across the face of the rock. Someone had gouged a depression in the side of the block, obliterating the drill hole. In the hole's place, the newly chiseled depression resembled a spot on the boulder where another tumbling chunk of stone had struck the face of the block when the arch had fractured and tumbled in pieces to the ground. Palm-sized shards of sandstone, newly hacked from the side of the boulder, lay on the ground at the base of the block. Chuck picked up the pieces one by one and studied them. None of the shards showed any sign of the circular drill hole; whoever had hacked into the side of the rock had taken away all the incriminating pieces.

Chuck put each of the shards to his nose. The remaining pieces of rock were clean, giving off no scent of Pyrodex. He pivoted, searching the ground for any sign of the blasting powder that might have scattered across the soil when the block fell in the midst of the storm. Nothing. If any residual powder had reached the earth, the precipitation from the storm—or, perhaps, whoever had obliterated the drill hole—had cleared it away.

Whichever the case, all evidence of the drill hole and powder was gone.

Chuck said to Carmelita, "You're right. It's just a rock. It looks like we walked all the way out here for nothing."

She jutted her chin. "Well, *yeah.*"

Rosie said, "You told us we were chasing after bad guys."

"We're chasing after something some bad guys *did*."

Chuck faced the chiseled spot on the fallen boulder, a finger to his lips. Destroying the drill hole in the soft sandstone would have been a simple matter—a few blows followed by the disposal of any shards of stone bearing evidence of the hole.

Had Paul, Megan's widower, returned overnight to remove evidence of the drill hole and blast residue from the block? That would mean Paul almost certainly had drilled the blast hole in the arch in the first place. And *that* would explain why Megan's widower had come to the arch, armed, mere hours after his wife's death: to get rid of the hole and blasting powder.

Except Chuck had shown up, interrupting Paul's attempt to do so.

Any identifiable tracks left by the obliterator of the drill hole would be mixed in with those of the investigation team members earlier this morning. Logic, however, said the destroyer of the hole, whether Paul or someone else, had entered the park from the highway to the west, and perhaps left identifiable tracks in the process.

Chuck pointed at the stone ramp down which Paul had descended from the bluff after firing his rifle yesterday. "Let's head up there. We can get a sense of what it was like when the arch fell."

Rosie asked, "Will there be any kitties up on top?"

"I doubt it. I bet the lost cats prefer to stay close to the campground. But the view from up where the arch fell should be pretty cool. We might even be able to see all the way west to the highway."

Rosie kneaded her hands, eyeing the stone ramp. "Goody." She crossed the sandy soil to the base of the bluff and ascended, the soles of her hiking boots gripping the gritty stone surface. Chuck stayed close behind her. Janelle and Carmelita trailed a few steps back.

Atop the bluff, Rosie strode to the protruding shoulder of stone from which Landscape Arch had extended. She rested her hand on the rock. "Is this where the arch was?"

Chuck placed his hand on the stone surface above hers. "Yep. Until yesterday morning."

She rubbed the rock. "It's sad, isn't it?"

He looked out at the empty space between the bluffs. "It's really sad."

"Awww." Rosie reached higher, placing her hand over his.

Carmelita arrived at the shoulder of stone. "You guys are such nerds," she said, even as she gazed across the opening with a look of sadness in her eyes.

Chuck leaned around the stone shoulder to observe the point where the arch had cracked and fallen to the flat below. The end of the shoulder was cleanly sheered, showing no signs of irregular fracturing from the force of an explosion.

He set off across the sculpted sandstone uplift toward the highway. How far would he have to go before he encountered a stretch of sand between here and the road—and in it, he hoped, a set of potentially identifiable tracks?

"Where are you headed?" Janelle called from where she stood behind him with the girls.

He turned to her. "Oh, um, I was just looking around."

"You always want to see what's over the next hill, don't you?"

"We all do, don't we?" He caught Rosie's eye. "Let's make sure there aren't any kitties hiding up here. How about it?"

"Yeppers!" she agreed.

She charged past him. Fifty yards away, leading Chuck by a few steps across the rolling sandstone, she scurried over a slanted rise of rock and plunged from sight, her agonized screech splitting the air.

31

Chuck dashed over the sandstone rise. Rosie lay on her side at the foot of a three-foot drop-off, curled on the flat bottom of a shallow pothole.

"Oww, oww, oww!" She grasped her ankle, her hands wrapped around the top of her hiking boot. Her breaths came in sharp gasps. "I fell! It hurts, it hurts, it hurts!"

The round cavity in the stone, hidden on the far side of the low rock dome, was waist deep and a dozen feet across, its surface a mixture of dried dirt and sand. Chuck hopped into the depression and settled at Rosie's side. He stroked her shoulder, unsure what to do next.

"It hurts so bad," Rosie said, tears squeezing from the corners of her closed eyes.

Janelle and Carmelita appeared at the top of the rise.

"*¡Rosalita mía!*" Janelle slid into the pothole next to Rosie. "*¡Pobrecita!* You poor thing." She probed Rosie's head and neck with her fingers. "Do you hurt anywhere other than your leg?"

Rosie massaged her ankle and chanted, her face contorted with pain, "Just here, just here, just here."

"*Bueno,*" Janelle said, turning her attention to Rosie's injury.

Rosie rolled to her back and lifted herself on her elbows, watching as Janelle prodded her lower leg.

"It's already swelling some," Janelle reported.

She gripped the sides of Rosie's boot with both hands and squeezed. Rosie moaned weakly.

"I can't be certain just with palpation, but I don't think it's broken," Janelle said, releasing Rosie's leg. "We'll need to take off the boot to allow for the edema."

Chuck put his hand on top of his hat and squinted up at the sun, high overhead in the clear blue sky. The day was comfortably warm but not hot, the campground less than a mile away. "The sooner we get her back to camp and get some ice on her ankle, the better," he said. Bending down, he massaged Rosie's chin with his finger. "How about a piggyback ride? Think you can handle that?"

She sat up straight and scrubbed her eyes with her fists. "Okay," she whimpered. "That'd be fun."

Janelle took off Rosie's boot. Dropping his daypack, Chuck pulled Rosie to a standing position and helped her onto his back. She wrapped her arms around his neck and he stood up, lifting her into the air and tucking his hands beneath her legs.

"Oof," he exclaimed. "You're not a little kid anymore, are you?"

"Nope, I'm a big kid," Rosie said, no longer whimpering. She released her grip around his neck long enough to slap him on the shoulder. "Giddyup, pony man!"

"I'm glad to see you're already feeling better." Janelle cocked an eyebrow at Chuck. "Are you sure you don't want to rethink this?"

"I'm pretty sure I can handle it."

Janelle reached for Chuck's daypack, but Carmelita dropped into the pothole and grabbed the pack first.

"I got it," she said, slinging Chuck's pack over her shoulder atop her own daypack.

"Thanks for helping, Carm," Rosie said.

As Carmelita turned away, Chuck spotted a prideful glow spreading across her cheeks.

Carmelita led the way up and out of the cavity. Chuck turned to follow. Ahead of him, a couple hundred feet from where he stood in the bottom of the depression, the sheered shoulder of stone that had supported Landscape Arch poked into the air.

He looked down, gauging how best to scramble out of the bowl with Rosie on his back. In front of his feet, the track of a smooth-soled walking shoe was imprinted in the dried soil. He swung Rosie in an abrupt circle, studying the round bottom of the hole.

"Yee-haw!" Rosie hollered as they spun, tightening her grip around Chuck's neck.

Chuck hoisted her a few inches higher on his back. The loose soil at the bottom of the depression was gouged by the lugged prints of his and Janelle's hiking boots and the rubber knobs on the soles of Carmelita's running shoes. He returned to examining the single remaining print of the walking shoe. The footprint was average in size. It had not been made by the lugged hiking boots Paul had been wearing yesterday afternoon, nor by Glen's worn running shoes.

The print was pressed more than half an inch into the sandy dirt. Whoever made it had done so when the soil in the bottom of the pothole was saturated and soft—no doubt during yesterday's storm.

Chuck glanced up. The line of sight from the pothole to the arch was clear and uninterrupted.

He considered the comparison he'd made yesterday between Paul Johnson and Ed Abbey's infamously crazed character, George Washington Hayduke.

Could Paul have come to the site of the collapsed arch wearing different shoes during the storm yesterday? Was the widower, in fact, his wife's murderer?

Chuck eyed the rock stump in the distance.

Even if Paul had been here during the storm, however, and even if he had drilled the hole in the arch and filled the hole with blasting powder, the explosion had not gone off.

Paul wasn't a killer—though he may well have intended to be one.

Chuck closed his eyes, perplexed.

Other than Paul, who else might have been here yesterday during the storm? What, exactly, had they been up to? And, most important, what role, if any, had their actions played in Megan's death?

"Come *on*," Carmelita demanded, looking down at Chuck from the top of the hole.

Chuck opened his eyes. "Ready?"

"I was born ready."

"Just like your mother."

Carmelita took Chuck's hand, helping him clamber out of the depression with Rosie on his back. He cast a longing look toward the highway and any additional tracks waiting to be discovered, then followed Carmelita and Janelle back across the uplift and down the sloping stone ramp to Devil's Garden Trail.

Somehow, he managed to carry Rosie to the campground. He staggered down the campground drive, nearing the trailer.

The German camper hustled over from his campsite. "May I help?"

"Sure," Chuck said wearily. "Thanks."

The German lifted Rosie from Chuck's back and settled her against his chest, cradling her in his arms as effortlessly as if she were Fredo.

Rosie stared with a look of rapture at the blond-bearded camper's face as he toted her down the drive and past the trailer. At Janelle's direction, the German lowered Rosie to the bench seat of the picnic table at the back of the campsite, her back to the tabletop.

"Thank you," Rosie effused, gazing into the man's electric-blue eyes.

"I am happy of service," the German said, bowing.

As he departed, the girls exchanged googly-eyed glances.

"He's *luscious*," Rosie whispered to Carmelita, her tongue lolling from her mouth.

The girls dissolved into fits of laughter.

Janelle said in Chuck's ear, "See what I mean? Rosie's teen years are going to be the end of us."

Chuck put his hands to his lower back. "I'm about at my end right now." He turned to the girls and groaned, massaging his back muscles with his fingers.

"*Lo siento*," Rosie apologized, swallowing her laughter. She swung her uninjured right leg back and forth beneath the bench.

"No apology necessary. It's me, not you," Chuck said. "Your old man's getting old."

"And gray," Carmelita said, her lips curved in a teasing half-smile, as she dropped his daypack on the table.

Chuck glowered at her, his eyes twinkling. "Thanks for reminding me."

"You're welcome, old man."

He slumped to a seat on the bench next to Rosie and lowered his head to hide his smile.

Janelle crouched, checking Rosie's injured ankle. "Not much more swelling," she reported. "Want to try putting some weight on it?"

Rosie recoiled. "Do I have to?"

"Of course not, *m'hija*."

"Okay, then. I'll try."

Rosie pushed herself to a standing position and balanced on her right leg. Janelle supported her as she took a hopping step with her left foot, landing with her weight again on her right.

"You're doing great," Janelle encouraged.

"I'm walking!" Rosie crowed.

Chuck sat up and rested his elbows on the tabletop behind him.

Rosie took another hopping step toward the trailer with Janelle at her side.

"We need to get Fredo out of her box. I bet she has to piss like a racehorse," Rosie said to Carmelita.

At the same instant, Sheila appeared around the corner of the camper. "My, my," she said to Rosie. "You're a regular ball of fire, aren't you?"

Chuck's mother no longer wore her down coat over her corded sweater-dress, which ended above her knees, her purple leggings covering her lower legs.

Clinging to Janelle's arm, Rosie lifted her injured ankle a few inches, obviously waiting for Sheila to comment on her misfortune. Instead, Sheila turned her attention to Carmelita.

"You're just like me," Chuck's mother said, pointing at Carmelita's snug running tights. "We're twins." Sheila hoisted the hem of her dress, revealing her purple-swathed thighs.

Carmelita gawked, open-mouthed, at Sheila.

"You and me," Chuck's mother said conspiratorially, "we know the kinds of curves we have to show to get what we want from—"

"*No*," Janelle cut in, her eyes icy. She stepped in front of Sheila. "There'll be no more of that."

Sheila dropped the hem of her sweater-dress back to her knees. "Well, well, well." She put her fingers to her lips, observing Janelle through slitted eyes. "Mother bear speaks."

"I'll do more than speak if I have to."

Sheila waved her hands in front of her and stepped backward, her thin brows raised in mock fear. "Oh, gosh, I'm so frightened."

Chuck shot to his feet and stepped between Janelle and Sheila, facing his mother. "You should be."

"No, Charlie," Sheila said. "You're the one who should be scared." She aimed a bony finger past him at Janelle. "You've got a tiger by the tail with that one."

"Actually," Chuck said, "I see her more as a mountain lion." Reaching behind him, he brushed Janelle's fingers with his own. Then he held out his hand to Sheila, indicating the way back past the trailer and out of the campsite. "After you."

"Are you *really* asking me to leave?" she huffed.

"No. I'm telling you to leave." He took her by the elbow and turned her away from Janelle and the girls. "Let's go, Mother."

32

Chuck led Sheila past the trailer. He released her arm and they walked together up the drive and out of the campground.

"I have to say, I'm impressed." Sheila broke the silence between them when they were halfway across the empty expanse of the Devil's Garden Trailhead parking lot. "I don't remember the last time you stood up to me."

"Try never," Chuck said.

A blustery midday breeze blew across the pavement from the west.

"That'd be about right." Sheila wrapped her arms around her waist as she walked beside him, her sweater-dress pressed to her thighs by the wind. "Believe it or not, it was your refusal to ever confront me that led me to really give some thought to all the mistakes I made when I raised you."

"You *didn't* raise me, not really. I just kept my head down. That's what seemed to make the most sense."

"If it's any consolation, after Derrick left me in California, I realized I'd treated you the way I'd allowed all the men in my life to treat me—like dirt. Maybe it was the example my mother set, letting my father shove her around. Whatever the reason, I'm not proud of it, Charlie. But there it is, the unvarnished truth."

"As you see it."

"Yes, as I see it. It took me far too long, but I finally figured out how to turn the mistakes I'd made with you into assets with every new man who entered my life, and that's exactly what I've done, from then until now."

"Assets?"

"I reached a turning point in my life with the guy who came along after Derrick," Sheila said. "His name was Manolo, a big bear of a man with mean, slapping hands. I threw him out, told him never to come back, just as I'd done with countless others before him. This time was different, though. I looked at myself in the mirror—black eye, bruised cheek, smeared makeup—and I decided that was it. No more. I'm ashamed to admit it, but the thought crossed my mind of how simple it had been to keep you in your place while you were growing up, without my even having to think about it. I figured, why not try the same thing with the next guy who came along?"

They stopped at the far end of the parking lot. Sagebrush rustled in the breezy gusts. A raven cawed from a distant bluff, its cry hoarse and grating.

Chuck stared out across the desert. "There always was a next boyfriend with you, wasn't there?"

"And there always will be, I expect. But it's different now."

He turned to her. "Different how?"

"I proved to myself that men are easy." Sheila repeated the words: "Men . . . are . . . *easy*. They're so incredibly simple-minded. They're driven by their insecurities, just as I always had been. I'd just never allowed myself to see them that way before." She curled her hand into a fist in front of her. "From then on, with every man I met, I took control from the very first minute. Just like that, everything changed." She shook her fist at the rustling sage branches.

"Was that when you took up fortune telling?"

"I told you: I don't tell fortunes. I see for people. The two are very different. I don't pretend to be clairvoyant. Rather, I help people on their personal journeys through life."

"Paul, Megan's husband, told me you've turned yourself into an environmentalist, too."

"Moab has a way of doing that to a person." She paused. "You met Paul?"

"He met me, more like."

Sheila sighed. "He's a good man, even if he didn't entirely appreciate all I was doing for Megan."

"Paul told me you sent Megan there. He said you directed her to go out on the arch every morning, just as the thumper truck started its work."

"Actually, it was more of a mutual idea between us," Sheila said. "She wanted to do all she could. She was insistent. She left her phone behind and didn't take any pictures. She wanted to avoid any problems with her sponsors, who might not have fully approved. But she reported what she was doing on her news-feed to her followers, without revealing her exact location, like a secret she was sharing. It was really working, too. Her numbers were way up, in just the first week."

"Until yesterday."

When Sheila said nothing, Chuck pressed her. "Sanford told me Megan was your best friend."

"We were business partners. Plus, I was doing all I could to help her."

He flicked his hand. "The seeing thing."

"You can be as rude as you want, Charlie. It doesn't matter to me. The 'seeing thing,' as you call it, has been very good for me."

"You started doing it in California, right?"

Sheila nodded. "Southern Californians are the most insecure people on the planet. They spend every penny they have seeking reassurance, on drugs, Botox, personal trainers—or on anyone willing to tell them what they should do with their lives. I began seeing for women at first. Then, more and more, I saw for men, too. I told them what they wanted to hear, what they needed to hear. I made a little money at it, but the competition was fierce. In LA, seers are as common as convertibles. I needed new territory. Moab fit the bill—plenty of newcomers with money, most of them environmentalist types unfamiliar with seeing. When I showed up here, hardly anyone even knew what a seer was. But they were ready for me, whether they knew it or not."

"Is that how you know Nora?"

"Of course. Nora was the first of her group to come to me. Martha and the others followed. They're a tight-knit bunch. That'll be a big help to Martha in the days ahead. She tells me she doesn't have much left in the way of family."

"They seem to have created their own sort of family among themselves."

"I have no doubt they'll do a good job of supporting her."

"You know Sanford, too. How'd you come to meet him?"

"Through his wife, Elsie."

Chuck tilted his head forward. So far, everything Sheila had said matched with what he knew.

"She's a fine person," Sheila went on. "Like everyone, though, she's had some hard times. I'm doing everything I can to help her."

Chuck kicked a pebble off the pavement, sending it tumbling into the dirt at the edge of the parking lot. Sanford had spoken of how hard it had been for Elsie to leave her family in northern Arizona and follow him around Utah from park to park. It couldn't have been easy for her to start a new life with each move, as her husband climbed the National Park Service administrative ranks.

"Sanford came to see me at Elsie's urging," Sheila said. "It certainly wasn't his idea."

That, too, fit with what the chief ranger had told Chuck.

"There's a lot of pain in him," Sheila continued, "but he wouldn't open himself to me. It happens sometimes. All men are easy, but some are easier than others." She shrugged. "At least it gave me the opportunity to convince him to give you the contract."

Chuck's jaw dropped. "You did *what*?"

"I suggested you for the contract, for the map thingy, the one in the cave."

He gaped at her. "Elsie said you knew about the pictograph. But I had no idea you had anything to do with the contract. Sanford never said anything about that when I told him it would give me a chance to see you again."

She patted his arm. "Calm down, Charlie. Everything I do is completely confidential."

"But I don't get it. You said Sanford refused to open himself to you."

Sheila put a finger to her bright red lips. "It was Elsie who first told me about the cave painting. She said her plan was to use it to wake up the politicians in Salt Lake City. After she told me about the painting, I told Sanford you were just the person to do the work she said was needed. Next thing you know, you've got yourself a nice contract, and I've got myself the chance to meet my grandbabies."

Chuck kicked another piece of gravel off the asphalt, harder this time, shooting it into the bushes lining the parking area. He squeezed his lips together. Janelle was right: Sheila was the single continuous thread running through everything, since the minute he'd arrived in the park—and long before that as well, if her claim to have gotten him the contract was to be believed.

"They're not babies," Chuck said. "And they're not your—" He bit his lip. What were the girls to Sheila, if not her grand-daughters?

"I don't care what you think Carmelita and Rosie are to me, Charlie. But you have to believe me when I say I have only your best interests at heart. And theirs." She took him by the elbow, turned him to her, and looked him in the eye. "I couldn't be more proud of you, of who you've become."

Chuck's entire body quaked. The last thing he wanted was the blessing of this woman who'd shunned him his entire life, his mother in name only.

He yanked his arm from her grasp.

Her eyes tightened to pinpricks. She dropped her hand to her side, spun away from him, and strutted back across the empty parking lot.

Chuck nearly sank to the ground, his legs shaking. Should he forgive his mother? Did she deserve his absolution? Did she even want it?

Then he straightened. What was there to forgive? Her insinuations concerning Carmelita's tight-fitting clothing, and her not-so-veiled suggestion for Rosie to lose some weight deserved only his disgust.

Everything Sheila had said to him just now had been an act, no different than the seer nonsense she spouted to her clients. She'd simply offered the answers she knew Chuck wanted to hear, nothing more. She might think of herself as a different person these days, but she hadn't changed a bit. She was still the same self-absorbed woman who had raised him—the woman who had shown him by example who he didn't want to be.

He trailed Sheila across the pavement and back into the campground. Her sweater-dress flapped at her legs as she strode ahead of him to Martha's motor home. She entered without knocking, closing the door behind her.

Janelle met Chuck outside their trailer.

"Thanks for getting Sheila away from Carm and Rosie," she said. "How'd it go with her?"

"Everything she said confirmed to me she's still the enemy of all that's good and right in the world."

"That sounds pretty harsh."

"You had to be there."

"I'm glad I wasn't, actually."

Leashed by a length of nylon cord fashioned by Chuck, Pasta Alfredo lay in the sand behind the trailer as Chuck, Janelle, and the girls ate lunch at the picnic table, shaded by the piñon branches overhead.

Chuck finished his sandwich and rested his forearms on the edge of the table, his eyelids drooping.

Janelle nudged him. "Sorry to be the bearer of bad news, but you've got a schedule to keep if we're ever going to get back to Durango."

He shook himself and stood up. As usual, Janelle was right. It was time he got back to work on the contract his mother had won for him.

Forty-five minutes later, he set his gear pack on the ground at the mouth of the hidden cavern, withdrew a two-foot length of rebar he'd stowed in the pack's main pouch, and drove the iron rod into the sand outside the cave, setting the site's datum point—the first step in the process of creating a precisely measured grid emanating from the mouth of the cavern.

According to the directives of the contract he'd signed with Sanford, he would complete the grid measurements and use them to create a digital map of the cavern's external setting. He also would measure and photograph the pictograph inside the cavern, segment by segment. Ultimately, he would use ArchaeoComplete software to stitch the photographs together and generate a three-dimensional graphic representation of the pictograph and cavern, including the cave's setting, for use in the publicity effort aimed at regaining protection for the national monuments.

He looped his measuring tape over the iron rod and measured distances outside the cave from the newly determined center point of the site, working from compass point to compass point around the hidden opening. That task complete, he lay on his back and squirmed into the cavern while clutching the measuring tape to his chest. Inside, he reached past his head and extended the measuring tape to the far wall of the grotto. He rolled to his side, craning his neck to check where the tape met the base of the wall—and gasped at what he saw in front of him at floor level.

33

Chuck's headlamp illuminated a partial depiction he hadn't yet seen. In it, three human figures ascended from a cupped object half-obscured by the sandy floor of the chamber. The three humans were Ancestral Puebloan, Fremont, and Mogollon. The figures rose together toward a blazing sun, floating above a landscape of sandstone ridges and deep canyons.

Spinning his body to face the rear of the cavern, Chuck scooped sand away from the bottom of the far wall. Handful by handful, he revealed more of the cupped object from which the human figures emerged. The object turned out to be a stone-walled kiva—one of the thousands of sunken ceremonial rooms constructed for spiritual use by the ancient peoples at the height of their societies. Every kiva featured a small hole in the center of its floor known as a *sipapu* from which, according to contemporary interpretations, the ancient peoples believed the first of their kind had emerged from the underworld deep beneath the Earth's surface.

Chuck uncovered the kiva and lay back from the wall, gazing in wonder at the scene of the three figures rising from the rock-lined ceremonial chamber. A tiny black dot denoted the sipapu in the chamber's floor. The painting clearly represented the emergence story of the ancient cultures. The fact that it showed representatives of each of the three societies emerging together from the kiva was, in a word, astounding.

The Southwest archaeological community believed that, while trading regularly with one another, the various ancient groups mostly had lived and developed separately from each other over the several centuries of their existence. In contrast, modern indigenous groups—direct descendants of the ancient ones—had worked closely together in recent years to win the initial establishment of the national monuments. The modern tribes continued their close collaboration now, in their fight to return the monuments to their original size. In the light of Chuck's headlamp, the painting of the creation story, plus the other paintings in the cavern depicting peaceful coexistence between the ancient cultures, indicated the same collaborative spirit may well have existed between the ancient societies to a significantly greater degree than modern anthropologists currently believed.

Chuck spun the outer ring on his headlamp, narrowing its beam until it illuminated only the newly uncovered depiction of the ancient creation story, with the three distinct human figures rising peacefully from the kiva one after the other. As he eyed the figures, the doubts he harbored about Sanford's publicity plan gave way to hope. The creation story, rendered here by artists from the three distinct ancient artistic traditions, was the final piece of the puzzle. The exquisite pictograph in the cavern might have the power to change the way Utahns perceived the southern half of their state, tipping the balance from exploitation to preservation. Chuck's job was to create as precise and detailed a digital representation of the cavern and pictograph as possible, for use by Elsie and her fellow tribal members in the fight to protect their sacred ancestral lands.

He set back to work. By the time he left the cave, having recorded the last of the necessary measurements inside, the eastern sky was purple with evening.

He shouldered his pack, pushed his way through the sage branches and out of the hidden opening, and hiked along the base of the wall to the notch leading to the loop trail. A mile to the southeast, the three sandstone bluffs that bounded the north side of the campground rose against the darkening sky in a trio of successive waves, their vertical west walls lit by the setting sun.

Chuck's knees and lower back ached. Hunger pangs growled in his stomach; he was famished after his long afternoon of work. Rather than return through the notch to the trail and follow the loop path's circuitous route back to the trailhead, he could save nearly a mile of walking by cutting straight back to camp across the backcountry-access area open to off-trail hiking north of the campground.

Turning away from the notch and the trail beyond it, he set out across the desert, the three matching bluffs beckoning him in the distance. After half a mile, he descended into a steep dirt-walled arroyo. He climbed out the other side, kicking the toes of his boots into the loose soil for traction, and continued toward the campground. He wended his way past the outstretched branches of gnarled junipers and rough-barked piñons, detouring around patches of biological soil crust along the way.

The late-day desert was quiet, the breeze having abated with the onset of evening, the wrens and ravens settled in trees and stone crevices for the coming night.

He reached the bluffs north of the campground, their west-facing walls marking the end of the sagebrush flat that extended eastward from the trailhead parking lot. He passed the nearest of the three walls, the soles of his boots digging into the loose sand at its base. The wall of the middle bluff loomed ahead, orange in the last rays of the falling sun.

He froze in mid-stride at the sound of someone sobbing uncontrollably.

"Oh, Jesus, no," a man's voice cried from the base of the middle bluff. "Please, please, no."

Chuck sprinted ahead. He came upon Sanford in his park-service uniform kneeling in the sand at the foot of the middle bluff's west wall. The chief ranger clutched the body of a man in his arms. The man lay on his back, his legs splayed on the ground, his arms limp at his sides. The chief ranger rocked the man's upper body back and forth, weeping.

Chuck slowed and edged forward until he drew close enough to recognize the man in Sanford's arms. Glen.

Glen was dressed in his worn shirt and khaki slacks. His head lolled from the crook of Sanford's arm, his eyes open but unseeing.

"Sanford," Chuck said softly as he approached.

The chief ranger did not look up. He continued to rock Glen's torso, moaning, his head down.

"Sanford," Chuck repeated, louder, as he came to a stop beside the pair.

Glen's neck was bent horrifically to one side, obviously snapped. A contusion purpled his temple. The sand next to his body was gouged where he had plummeted from the clifftop above, fatally striking the ground headfirst.

Sanford looked up at Chuck. The waning sunlight illuminated bottomless grief in the chief ranger's eyes. Tears rolled down his cheeks, gathering in his beard. He turned his face away and bent once more over Glen's prostrate form.

Chuck laid a hand on Sanford's shoulder. "This young man is, was, named Glen. He told me so."

"I know," Sanford said. "Elsie and I chose it. This is our son."

34

Chuck rocked back on his heels. "I'm sorry, Sanford. I'm so sorry."

Sanford's sobs subsided.

"What . . . what happened?" Chuck asked.

Sanford slid Glen's body to the ground. "It doesn't really matter. Not anymore." The chief ranger took a deep wracking breath. "He's at peace. Finally."

Chuck peered around them. Broken rays of sun filtered through the limbs of piñons flanking the bluff. Beyond the trees, the open desert spread to the west, aflame in the last of the day's sunlight. He squinted up at the vertical wall of stone. "How . . . ?" he ventured.

Sanford raked his nose with his forearm. His words came haltingly, his gaze fixed on his son's body.

"Glen has been . . . troubled. For a long time. He was diagnosed with schizophrenia not long after he turned nineteen, more than three years ago. Voices spoke to him in his head. He hardly ate. He was convinced his mother and I were his enemies. We kept him with us as long as we could. But he stole from us. He had terrible fits of anger. He destroyed our home . . . his home . . . more than once. Finally, a few weeks ago, he threatened Elsie with a kitchen knife. He didn't know what he was doing, of course, but that was it for me. I'd had enough. I wanted to have him arrested. I believed we could get him into the medical system that way, through a court order. He finally would have gotten the help he needed. But Elsie wouldn't hear of it."

Sanford glanced at Chuck and continued his story.

"We told him he couldn't stay with us anymore. We were heartbroken, of course. We convinced him to carry a phone. We called him every day. We'd leave a message when he didn't answer, which was most of the time. We let him know we loved him. The few times he did answer, he didn't say anything, but we knew he was there, listening, and we'd take turns talking to him. He hiked out here on his own. I'd talked to him about how Ed Abbey had found his life's purpose in Arches. One of the times when I left a message on Glen's phone, I told him I'd spotted him out here and that I was happy for him, that I thought being out here would be good for him. We had the locator beacon activated on his phone. He probably knew about it. We tracked his every move."

The chief ranger leaned back and pointed at the top of the wall.

"He stayed up there on the bluff most of the time. He'd sneak into the campground at night. I'm sure that's where he got his water. I imagine he went through the trash for food scraps, too. He was surviving, against all odds."

Chuck said, "The homeless people you talked about, the ones you described as living in national parks near big cities . . ."

"There's no such thing," Sanford admitted. His eyes went to his son's body. "Just Glen."

"He had a kind heart."

"Like his mother," the chief ranger agreed. "But," he asked, looking up at Chuck, "how do you know that? How do you know his name?"

"I met him on the ridge on the south side of the campground."

"Ahh." Sanford nodded through his tears. "The locator beacon showed him going over that way every couple days or so.

He'd work his way around, out of sight of the campground, and spend a few hours up there, then return here to the bluff. We couldn't figure out why."

"There are stray cats up there."

"That makes sense." Sanford laid his hand on Glen's still chest. "My son," he murmured. Then he said to Chuck, "Glen loved animals, from when he was little. Hamsters, turtles, dogs, chickens. Elsie and I could barely keep up."

"Why did he do this to himself?" Chuck wondered aloud. "You said he was surviving, getting by."

"He called me an hour ago, but he hung up before I could answer. He'd never called before, not once in all the weeks since he came out here. He must have known I'd come as soon as I saw his number."

"Do you think he was signaling you?"

"He must have wanted me to find him—his body, that is. That's the only thing I can think of."

"What did you see when you got here?"

"I tracked him by his phone beacon. I went up on the bluff, but he wasn't there. I went to the edge of the cliff to see if I could spot him somewhere. When I looked down . . ." Sanford patted Glen's arm. Then he grasped his son's shoulder with both hands and shook it, rocking Glen's upper body. "Glen," he cried. "Glen."

"I'm so sorry," Chuck repeated.

He stepped back, his eyes tracking to the top of the wall. Why had Glen chosen right now, this evening, to kill himself?

When Chuck had sat with Glen yesterday, the young man had seemed fully alive. He had told Chuck his name, and had pointed with purposeful intent toward the toppled arch. Glen had hiked across the desert to the site of the collapsed span. He had come to Harold's aid when the elderly camper had fallen from the ladder—a life-affirming gesture if ever there was one. Yet now, only a day later, Glen was dead, an apparent suicide.

* * *

A puff of air stirred at the foot of the bluff, carrying with it the first hint of the evening chill. Chuck turned his face to the slight breeze, gazing through the trees at the open desert beyond.

Three people now had died here in Devil's Garden in the last forty-eight hours. Each death, on its own, came with a seemingly rational explanation. But what were the odds of all three deaths here, in just the last two days?

He took out his phone. "I'll call 911."

"No," said Sanford. "Not yet. I want to call Elsie first. I know she'll want to be with him before anyone else. She'll want to offer him her blessing, to send him on his way. Glen is our only child."

"Okay." Chuck replaced his phone. "I need to check in with Janelle in camp. How about if I meet Elsie at the parking lot and walk her out here? Then you can stay with Glen."

"I'd appreciate that," Sanford said. Still kneeling over his son's body, he pulled his phone from the nylon pouch at his waist.

Chuck rounded the base of the wall, passing from Sanford's sight as he headed for the campground. As he walked, an invisible hand, chillingly cold, settled on the back of his neck.

What had Glen been attempting to communicate yesterday when he had pointed at the collapsed arch from the ridge above the campground? Why had he hiked to the site of the toppled span? And what had led to his plunge from the cliff this evening?

Chuck put his fingers to the back of his neck and squeezed, dispelling the sinister iciness. He needed answers.

Turning away from the campground, he trod through the deep sand to the point where the two stone bluffs nearest the campground came together. A cleft between the flanking bluffs rose at a low angle away from the sand. Chuck ascended the fissure without difficulty, his hands to the facing rock walls, his boots wedged for traction.

Leaving the cleft where it widened, he climbed to the top of the middle bluff, five stories above the desert floor. He walked west, toward the setting sun. Thirty feet back from the edge of the vertical wall at the end of the bluff, he came to a jutting prow of sandstone. The prow served as a roof, sheltering a waist-high space protected from the weather on three sides. The space extended ten feet beneath the overhang. A dusty sleeping bag lay on a foam pad under the stone roof. Plastic gallon jugs of water lined the rear of the space in an orderly row, along with cans of vegetables and tinned meat. A hand-operated can opener, a plastic plate, and metal spoon and fork rested on a rock shelf at the back of the space. A solar phone charger sat next to the dishes.

Chuck peered west from Glen's makeshift camp, shading his eyes from the orb of the sun perched above the western horizon. From where he stood, the sweeping view of the desert, cut by shallow washes and flanked by stone promontories, was spectacular. He could not convince himself that Glen, troubled though he was, would have chosen this tremendous setting and this magnificent evening to end his life.

Chuck walked to the edge of the cliff. Below, at the base of the bluff, Sanford knelt over Glen's body. The chief ranger held out his phone, jabbing at its face.

Two small spots of yellow, wedged in a shallow crevice atop the cliff, caught Chuck's eye. He squatted and studied the spots. They were crumbs from some sort of baked good. The fact that they had yet to be gobbled up by a mouse or passing bird indicated they had fallen into the crevice only a short time ago.

Chuck frowned. Why, in the midst of the mental storm that surely would have preceded Glen's decision to kill himself, would he have paused to eat?

35

Chuck retreated from the cliff and descended the cleft between the flanking bluffs. The sun set as he jogged toward the campground. The temperature dropped several degrees the instant the warming rays of the sun disappeared.

He increased his pace to a run as he neared the trailer, and breathed a sigh of relief when he caught sight of Janelle and Rosie through the camper's picture window. Janelle stood at the stove, while Rosie sat at the dinette table.

He left his pack in the bed of the pickup and entered the trailer. "You're here," he said to Janelle, who stood before a sizzling skillet, spatula in hand.

She smiled as she looked up at him. "Where else would we be? Us womenfolk have to make sure we have dinner ready for our man when he gets home from his hard day of work."

"We're making fajitas," Rosie announced. She sat at the dinette table, a cutting board before her, slicing a green pepper into strips with a small knife. "All except Carmelita. She's laaaaazy."

Carmelita reclined on the bed at the back of the trailer in stockinged feet, her head propped on pillows, an oversized paperback open on her stomach. She turned a page, offering no response.

"Your sister is reading a real book instead of her phone," Chuck said to Rosie. "You've got to give it up to her for that."

Carmelita exhaled forcefully, the sound carrying to the front of the trailer, her face still hidden behind her book.

"I'm learning how to chop things," Rosie said. The tip of her tongue showed between her lips as she worked. "I'm being real careful, just like *Mamá* showed me."

"Good for you," Chuck said. "Where's Pasta Alfredo?"

Rosie tipped her head toward the rear of the trailer. Carmelita lifted her book to reveal the cat curled on her chest.

Rosie said, "Me and Fredo are still best friends, but I'm busy right now."

Chuck took a deep breath and released it. He had no choice but to break the atmosphere of warmth inside the camper; he needed to let Janelle and the girls know about Glen's death, and about his offer to escort Elsie to her son's body.

"I'm afraid I have some sad news," he told them. "Remember the homeless man we left food for, up on the ridge last night? He died this afternoon."

Janelle set the spatula on the counter and turned to Chuck. "He *what*?"

"No!" Rosie cried, dropping her knife to the cutting board. "You said he was nice. You said he helped the old man who fell from the ladder."

On the bed, Carmelita closed her book over her finger and looked at Chuck with questioning eyes.

Chuck explained that he'd come across Sanford with Glen's body, that Glen was the son of the chief ranger and Elsie, and that Elsie was on her way to bless her son before Sanford summoned the authorities. "I'm going to escort her to him when she gets here in a few minutes," he finished.

"I'm so sad," Rosie said.

Janelle turned off the burner beneath the skillet. "Outside," she directed Chuck. "*Now*." She squeezed Rosie's shoulder. "I'll be right back, *m'hija*. It'll be all right."

Janelle slipped past Chuck and exited the trailer. At the dinette, Rosie sniffled, her head hanging over the cutting board.

Carmelita set her book and Fredo aside and slid off the end of the bed. She walked down the aisle, slipped onto the bench seat next to Rosie, and put her arm around her sister's slumped shoulders.

Chuck mouthed his thanks to Carmelita and left the trailer. He found Janelle pacing beside the picnic table behind the camper in the waning evening light.

"This is not normal," she said when he reached her, "and you damn well know it."

"I've got a lot of questions myself," Chuck said. "Although Glen *was* mentally ill. Sanford told me he'd been dealing with it for years."

"But what made him kill himself right now, tonight?" she asked, giving voice to the same question vexing Chuck. "That's three deaths in two days now."

"Maybe that's what set him off," Chuck reasoned. "He's been hanging around the campground. He must have known about Megan's death. I'll bet he found out Harold died, too. Maybe the combination of the two deaths was too much for him, and something inside him snapped."

"Death begets more death?" She shook her head. "I don't know. All I do know is, I don't like whatever it is that's going on in this place right now."

"What if we get out of here for the night? We'll drive into town and get a motel room. I'll meet Elsie when she gets here. We can leave as soon as I take her to Sanford."

Janelle pursed her lips. "I'm glad you're helping them."

"I'll be back as soon as I walk her out there."

He grabbed his jacket and set out. In the gathering evening gloom, the interiors of all the motor homes except Martha's glowed with electric light. Martha's RV was illuminated only by the light of a single candle flickering inside its front room.

Chuck stared through the tall windshield of the coach. In the shadowy interior, Martha sat on the far side of a built-in table behind the driver's seat, her lined face lit by the flame of the candle. Sheila sat at the U-shaped table with her back to Chuck, her long hair flowing down her back. A third person sat at the table, too, hidden by Sheila.

Chuck crept to the front of the motor home and peeked inside. The third person at the table, her face now visible beyond Sheila's shoulder, was Nora. The three women grasped hands across the tabletop, the candle centered between them.

A car engine sounded, approaching up the park road. Chuck ducked away from Martha's RV and jogged to the Devil's Garden parking area, arriving as an SUV rolled to a stop at the trailhead next to Sanford's truck in the otherwise empty lot. Chuck hurried over to the car. The Navajo dreamcatcher from last night hung from the rearview mirror, the colorfully beaded cords swaying beneath the webbed hoop.

Elsie climbed out of the SUV. She wore brown slacks, white canvas tennis shoes, and a lightweight jacket. Her black hair was tied loosely at the back of her neck.

Chuck scrutinized her. She'd driven out here to Devil's Garden last night, alone. Now, her son was dead.

Tears streaked Elsie's round cheeks, but her eyes held his, unwavering, as he expressed his condolences.

She thanked him and turned to the desert. "Glen loved the land around Moab," she said. "Sometimes I think he loved it too much. He told me once he thought the land wanted to swallow him up. But still he came out to this place."

"I'm so sorry," Chuck said. In the face of Elsie's grief, was it heartless of him to confront her? No, he decided. He owed it to Glen to learn the truth. "You came out here last night," he said, his voice gentle but probing.

"It was you," she said, facing him. "You were at my car last night."

"Yes, I was."

"What were you doing there?"

"I was checking on you. The park was closed, it was late, but still you showed up. My girls are staying here in the campground with me. It's my job to keep them safe."

"That's what I was trying to do, too."

"What do you mean?"

"I was trying to keep my child safe, the same as you."

"Did you think Glen was in danger?"

"Only to himself. After Megan's death and the death of the man yesterday, Sanford and I were worried. We decided I should drive out here. We thought he might come to me, his mother, if I was alone. He didn't answer when I called him on his phone, which was normal, so I left him a message. I hiked out a ways on the trail and waved my flashlight around, but he didn't come. When I walked back and saw you at my car, I thought for a second you were Glen. I was so excited. But I got enough of a look at you before you ducked out of sight to recognize that you were not him. I didn't know who you were, though, and I was frightened. So I got in my car and left."

"I didn't mean to scare you. I was scared myself."

"I wish it had been Glen instead of you last night. Then maybe . . . maybe . . ."

"Sanford said he thought it was good that Glen had come out here to Devil's Garden."

"Before he got sick, he loved what his father did. Glen was so proud. When he came out here to the park, both Sanford and I believed it would be good for him. That's what we hoped, anyway."

"Did he know about the pictograph?"

"We wanted to tell him. We thought just knowing about it, and the peace it shows between the ancient ones, would be helpful to him. But he had torn up our house more than once. He broke the window on the display case, ripped the rugs from the walls. We decided we should not tell him. The pictograph was too precious. Maybe we should have, though. Maybe it would've made a difference."

"From what Sanford said to me, it sounds as if you did everything you could for Glen."

Elsie's breath caught in her throat, but in accordance with Navajo custom, she did not cry. "And now, there is one more thing I must do for him. I must give him my blessing, as his mother, before they take him away."

They left the parking lot. Chuck set a steady pace ahead of Elsie up the path. From the junction at the start of the loop, he led her off the trail and across the desert toward the three bluffs lined together north of the campground, their tombstone-like walls now somber with evening shadow. The wall of the middle bluff reared above them as they neared it. Ahead of Elsie, Chuck rounded a piñon and came to an abrupt halt, staring.

Glen's lifeless body lay sprawled at the base of the cliff.

But Sanford was gone.

36

Chuck ran to Glen's body. He scanned the surrounding trees and brush for any sign of Sanford, but the chief ranger was nowhere to be seen.

Elsie fell to her knees in the sand beside her son's broken form. She caressed his pallid cheeks and stroked his matted hair.

Chuck said, "Sanford told me he would meet you here. Do you have any idea where he went?"

She shook her head.

Chuck whirled, his eyes searching. Nothing.

Why, knowing Elsie was on her way, would Sanford have left his son's side? After the three deaths in Devil's Garden, was the chief ranger in some sort of danger, too?

Or—Chuck's blood ran cold—was Sanford a threat himself?

The chief ranger had hidden the fact that Glen was his son. What more might he be hiding? What might he know about the circumstances surrounding Glen's death that he hadn't told Chuck—and what, of those unknown circumstances, might have driven him to leave Glen's body, knowing Elsie was on her way?

Chuck bit the inside of his cheek hard enough to draw blood. "I have to find Sanford."

"Go. Find him," Elsie replied, kneeling over Glen with her head bowed. Slender wrinkles mapped the back of her neck, like the thin lines of the pictograph in the cavern. "I will stay here with my son."

Chuck pulled his phone from his pocket. When he'd looked down at Sanford from the top of the cliff, the chief ranger had been tapping the face of his phone beside Glen's body, attempting to call Elsie.

Chuck checked his phone screen. Only a single wavering bar of service appeared.

He had his answer.

When Sanford had failed to get an adequate signal for his phone here, close against the base of the bluff, he no doubt had followed Chuck toward the campground, where a repeater tower bathed the campsites in strong coverage. Chuck and Elsie would have bypassed Sanford's route to the campground when they'd hiked to Glen's body from the trailhead.

But Sanford should have returned to Glen's body after completing his call to Elsie.

Chuck peered past the base of the bluff.

In Martha's motor home a few minutes ago, Martha and Nora had held hands around the candle with Sheila, their seer—and the common thread connecting all three deaths in Devil's Garden. If anyone knew Sanford's whereabouts right now, it was Chuck's mother.

Spinning away from Elsie, Chuck set out for Martha's RV at a sprint. The swath of desert through which he ran was dark with shadow. He tripped and sprawled to the ground, skinning his palms.

He shoved himself to his feet and kept running, slowing only when he neared the campground. He put a hand to his chest and drew gulping breaths while he took long strides through the trees. Lights glowed from the windows of the motor homes. Two people were speaking outside one of the coaches. Chuck angled toward the sound.

One of the two speakers was Sheila. ". . . will get you nowhere," she said. "You, of all people, should know that."

Chuck dropped to a crouch, listening.

Sanford's voice came next, hoarse with grief. "We trusted you. Elsie and I trusted you."

"It was you who sent him away," Sheila said.

"Only on your recommendation. Tough love, that's what you said he needed."

Chuck crept forward.

"You have to help Elsie," Sanford begged. "You have to come with me. She'll be there by now."

"I'll do no such thing," Sheila replied. "He was your problem to begin with, and he's your problem now."

"How can you do this to her?"

"I bear no responsibility. None whatsoever. You do—you and Elsie. It was your decision. There's no reason for you to deny it."

Chuck slipped through the shadows. A motor home loomed above him. Lights shone from the coach's side windows. The voices of Sheila and Sanford came from the campground driveway in front of the RV.

"Look at me," Sheila demanded. "You know full well what I'm talking about."

"I . . . I refuse to—"

"Don't lie to yourself, Sanford," she said, cutting him off. "Or to me. There's nothing further I can do for you. You need to leave me alone and get back to your son."

"To my son's body," Sanford said mournfully.

"Go to him. Leave me be," Sheila said, her voice sharp. "I've got more than enough to deal with here, with Frank."

Chuck stiffened. Frank?

He peered around the corner of the motor home in time to see Sheila walk up the campground drive, leaving Sanford standing alone in the near darkness. A few sites up the drive, a door opened and clicked shut.

Chuck scampered past the RV, ducking beneath its glowing windows. He straightened and strode to Sanford in the middle of the drive.

"I listened to you talking with Sheila," Chuck said, confronting the chief ranger. "It sounds like you disagree with her about who's responsible for Glen's death."

"No, Sheila's right," Sanford said. "Elsie and I are ultimately responsible. But your mother bears some responsibility, too. So does Megan."

Chuck's eyes widened. "Megan?"

37

"I haven't told you the whole story." Sanford drew a breath. "Glen fell in love with Megan. Or thought he did, inasmuch as he was capable of falling in love with anyone in his state of mind."

"But she was married."

"That didn't matter to Glen. He met her through Elsie. Megan knew Glen was ill, but she still went for walks with him, took him for coffee. She was just trying to be helpful, but he got it in his head she was doing those things because she loved him as much as he loved her. That was what led to the big argument, the night he threatened Elsie with the knife. We tried to explain to him how things really were, but he wouldn't hear of it. His mind wouldn't let him."

"You told me earlier Megan was Sheila's fixer."

Sanford nodded. "She was the reason Sheila got so popular so fast in Moab. Everybody in town liked Megan. When she told people they should go to Sheila, they lined right up. Megan was happy to do it, of course, because she worshipped your mother."

"She worshipped Sheila? Are you sure about that?"

"Absolutely. But she ended up doing too good a job, to the point where she started taking on some of the overflow herself."

"How do you know all this?"

"Whenever Megan came by to pick up Glen, she'd talk about it with Elsie. She couldn't bring it up with Paul. He didn't like how tight she'd gotten with Sheila. If he'd have found out Megan was dabbling in all that seeing stuff herself, I don't know what he'd have done."

Chuck pictured Paul with his gun, and the obliterated drill

hole in the arch. Was Sanford now, finally, telling the whole truth?

"Megan went along with Sheila about recommending that we kick Glen out of our house for his own good," the chief ranger said. "The two of them teamed up on us, I guess you could say. But in the end, Elsie and I are the ones who told him he had to leave."

"Did Glen ever threaten to kill himself?"

Sanford shook his head forcefully, his mustache sweeping back and forth in the half-light. "Never. Not once. He was addled, confused. He was angry a lot of the time. But he wasn't suicidal. Just the opposite, in fact. His schizophrenia manifested itself in visions of his own grandiosity. He thought he was better, smarter, more capable than other people. He was ill, yes, but he never showed us any indication that he wanted to harm himself." Sanford squeezed his eyes shut. "That's what makes what he did to himself so difficult to comprehend."

"What if he knew Megan had died? If he loved her, or thought he did, could her death have precipitated something in him?"

Sanford studied Chuck. "I suppose that's possible, but . . ." He looked at his feet. "I've been thinking about it since I . . . since . . ."

Chuck asked gently, "But you don't think it was very likely?"

Sanford raised his head, his eyes alight. "No, I don't. I know he was sick, but the whole idea of suicide . . . that wasn't Glen. That wasn't the son Elsie and I raised, and it definitely wasn't who he'd become through his illness. He thought more of himself, not less. I can't believe my son killed himself. I *don't* believe it."

"If it's any solace, I agree with you." Chuck held Sanford's gaze. "What about Frank?"

Sanford blinked at Chuck. Nervousness rose in his eyes. "Who?"

"Sheila told you just now that she had to deal with him."

Sanford drew a breath. "She did, didn't she?"

Chuck waited.

"I'm not sure what she was referring to," the chief ranger said, looking past Chuck's shoulder.

"You're not sure, or you won't say?"

"I . . . I don't know."

"That's all I'm going to get from you, isn't it?"

Sanford licked his lips. He didn't speak.

Chuck grunted, giving up. "Elsie is out at the bluff with Glen. She's waiting. You need to go to her, and you need to call 911. You can't put it off any longer."

"Okay," Sanford said without hesitation. He turned and set off up the campground drive, headed for the trailhead, putting his phone to his ear as he departed.

Chuck spun and hustled the opposite direction until he drew near enough to the trailer to catch sight through the window of Janelle and the girls eating dinner at the dinette table. They were safe.

He backtracked up the drive. The campground was quiet, the campers settled in their motor homes or at their picnic tables for the evening. The smell of burning charcoal and grilled meat hung in the air.

He pressed his thumbnail to his chin. After Sheila had left Sanford, which motor home door had opened and closed? The door to Martha's RV? Or to Frank and Nora's?

Sheila had said she had to deal with Frank.

Two sites beyond Martha's coach, Chuck came to Frank and Nora's RV. A curtain covered its windshield.

He strode to the side door of the motor home, triggering a motion-activated light above the doorframe. At his knock, a blind over the small window set in the door drew up and Nora's face appeared in the glass frame. The blind dropped back into place and the door opened.

"Chuck." Nora stood in the doorway, outlined by light from within. "Please, come in."

"Is Frank here?"

"Of course."

She stepped back, allowing Chuck to climb the stairs into the coach.

Pop-outs extended from both sides of the motor home, enlarging its front living room to apartment size. A suede leather sofa faced matching easy chairs in the expanded front room. Recessed ceiling lights illuminated a compact kitchen with cherry cabinets and a short granite countertop beyond the easy chairs at the back of the room.

"How about Sheila?" Chuck asked. "Is she here, too?"

Answering for Nora as he passed through the kitchen from the rear of the coach, Frank said, "I'm afraid Sheila isn't here."

Chuck took a seat on the sofa.

Frank wore a dress shirt buttoned over his bulbous belly, creased polyester slacks cinched with a wide leather belt, and leather slippers lined with fluffy white sheepskin. He sat on the edge of one of the easy chairs, his back to the kitchen. Nora, in loose slacks and a flowered blouse, retreated between the chairs to the back of the room and busied herself washing dishes at the kitchen sink.

Frank leaned forward in his chair, his elbows on his knees and his stomach lapping over his belt. "Sheila's not here, as I said."

Chuck sat forward, too. How, where, to begin? "I wanted to make sure you're doing okay after Harold's death."

Frank's brows drew together. "Who, me?"

"Nora told the ranger how upset you were after he fell. Justifiably so, it would seem. It was your ladder, after all."

Behind Frank, Nora rested her hands on the front of the sink.

"It was an accident, a terrible accident," Frank said. "A shock, to be sure. But Harold, well, he insisted on climbing the ladder before me. He was not someone easily dissuaded, I will say that."

"He'll be missed," Nora said. She reached into the sink, lifted a dripping dinner plate from the dishwater, and swabbed it with a washrag.

Frank sat back in his chair, pressed his palms together in front of his chest, and looked over his hands at Chuck. "It's Martha, of course, we're worried about—though I'm not sure I see it as your responsibility to be checking up on us old codgers."

"Sheila put me up to coming here, actually. I believe you know she's my mother. She's been so focused on Martha—and rightly so, as you say. But she's the sort who worries about everyone, as I believe you know as well."

Frank steepled his fingers and flexed them against one another. Appearing to choose his words with care, he said, "Your mother has been of great help to Nora and me."

Chuck waited.

Frank continued after a beat. "Our group was lucky to find her when we were staying in town. And now, she's really proving her value to Martha."

"Your group?" Chuck asked.

"Why, yes."

Nora picked up the conversation from the sink. "I was the first to learn of Sheila's services. As soon as I told the others, they wanted to meet her, too."

"How did you hear about her?" Chuck asked.

"That would have been through her young friend, Megan."

Chuck shook his head. "Another terrible accident."

"Oh, yes. Oh, yes," Nora warbled, her chin quivering. "Sheila told us about it. It's horrible, just horrid."

Frank sat up straight and put his hands on his knees. "You seem to have a lot of questions about these accidents."

"On my mother's behalf."

Frank inclined his bald head. "As you say."

Chuck held Frank's gaze. Frank stared back. Behind the thick lenses of his glasses, his eyes were dark and glinting. A steel-framed clock affixed to the wall beside him clicked off the seconds one by one.

Chuck looked past Frank at Nora, who wiped the kitchen counter with her washrag. She lifted the rag and shook it over the sink, sending yellow crumbs cascading into the dishwater.

38

Chuck pressed his hands together between his legs to keep them from shaking. The crumbs tumbling from Nora's washrag matched those in the crevice atop the cliff.

Nora wrung out the wet cloth.

Chuck hadn't pushed hard when he'd questioned Sanford in the wake of Glen's death. But he owed Frank and Nora no such consideration.

He began obliquely, addressing Frank in the easy chair opposite him. "My mother made the point that when two people die within hours of one another, in a place that probably hasn't seen a single death in a very long time, it's important to ask questions."

Frank's eyes, recessed deep in their sockets, constricted. "It's important for *the authorities* to ask questions, perhaps."

"Not when I suspect the authorities of being involved."

Frank visibly relaxed, shoulders dropping. "You do, do you?"

"To be perfectly honest, I have some concerns about the chief ranger, Sanford."

Frank rested his hands on the arms of his chair. "Ah-ha."

"And Sanford's son, Glen."

Frank nodded knowingly.

"You've met him?"

The man's fingers twisted around the arms of the chair. "Glen, Sanford's son? Um, I know *of* him, yes."

Nora set the washrag aside and plucked a dish towel from a wall hook. She dried her hands with it robotically, staring at the back of her husband's head.

"What do you know?" Chuck asked Frank.

"Why are you asking?"

"As I said, I have my concerns about Glen's father. I think you might share those concerns."

"I do."

"Because . . . ?" Chuck urged.

Frank's eyes darted around the room.

Nora spoke from the kitchen. "Tell him, Frank."

He twisted and looked over his shoulder at her. "Tell him what, exactly?"

"Isn't it clear enough to you? He already knows."

Frank sat still, facing Nora.

Chuck took his cue from her. "She's right, Frank. I know about Glen. I know he's dead."

Frank turned slowly until he again faced Chuck. "Yes," he said, his eyes hooded. "He is."

"You were there. I know you were with him."

"I was only trying to help," Frank said. "I brought him food—some pound cake Nora had baked. I held it out to him, trying to convince him to come away from the edge. But he jumped. There was nothing I could do."

Frank's explanation sounded stiff and prepared, as if he'd been readying himself for this moment.

"Why didn't you tell anyone?"

"It just happened a little while ago. I would have called it in, of course. But I saw his father coming. I wasn't sure what to do. I waited until he found Glen, then I came straight back here."

"How did you know him? How did you know where he was?"

Frank's eyes roved the room. "Sheila," he said eventually, looking at Chuck with obvious reluctance. "She knows everyone. Everything."

Nora folded the dish towel, laid it on the counter, and placed her hand on top of it.

Chuck asked, "She sent you to do what? To try to help him somehow?"

"That's right," Frank agreed, too quickly. His eyes went to his feet, his heels drawn to the foot of the chair, his leather slippers pressed against one another.

Chuck eyed the slippers, their sheepskin collars touching. They were for use inside the motor home. But what type of shoes did Frank wear outside?

The bare skin on top of Frank's head reflected the light shining from the ceiling above him. "Sheila believed I could serve as a mentor to the young man," he explained, still looking down, "given that I had the time available while we were staying in the campground."

Chuck scanned the room while Frank spoke. Two sets of shoes rested on a mat beside the doorway: a pair of women's sneakers, and a pair of men's leather walking shoes, flecked with dried mud. The walking shoes were of average size, with smooth rubber soles.

Chuck returned his attention to Frank. "I want to know about Megan."

Frank raised his head. "Megan?"

Nora drew open a narrow drawer beside the sink with a trembling hand. "Yes, dear," she said, her fingers on the drawer handle. "He wants to know about Megan."

Frank's face hardened. He lifted his arm from his chair, an abrupt movement, the back of his hand to his wife. "You will not speak again," he commanded without turning his head to her. "Not one more word."

Nora tightened her grip around the drawer handle, her knuckles turning white. The trembling in her hand ceased.

Frank again took hold of his chair, his fingertips digging into its padded arm. He said to Chuck, "We already spoke about her. She . . . she was Sheila's assistant. Her helper. She was an athlete. A runner."

"You knew Sheila sent her to the arch," Chuck said. It was a statement, not a question.

Fury flashed in Frank's eyes, hot and burning. "She never told me—" He swallowed the rest of his words. The anger in his eyes drained away, replaced by apprehension.

"That messed with your plans, didn't it?"

"I didn't kill her. That was never . . . that was not . . ." He sputtered to a stop.

Nora stared at the back of her husband's head.

Chuck said to Frank, "Sheila sent you to the arch, too, just like she did Megan. That's what my mother does these days. She directs. She plies the pliable—like you."

Chuck sat forward in his chair. *Sheila*. The daybed in her apartment, against the far wall of the darkened rear room; her promise in her voicemail message to fulfill all her seekers' physical desires; her boast to Chuck of receiving free rent for services she provided the owner of her condominium—who, she'd said, was more than willing to share.

Chuck shuddered. There was far more truth behind Sheila's lewd comments to Carmelita than he'd allowed himself to believe. His mother hadn't sold only her abilities as a seer to the retirees of Moab. To the owner of her condo and to seekers like Frank, she'd sold much more.

Frank held out his pudgy hands, imploring Chuck. "I only did what I was told."

"For your prostitute," Chuck shot back.

Behind Frank, Nora nodded. "That's right," she spat. "For your *whore*."

"I said *silence*!" Frank snapped without turning his head, his cheeks reddening.

"You thought I didn't know," Nora continued, addressing Frank's back. "But I knew all along."

She withdrew a snub-nosed pistol plated in gleaming stainless steel from the drawer beside the sink and wrapped both hands around it. Curling her finger over the trigger, she aimed the gun at the back of Frank's head.

"If you know what's good for you, Nora," Frank barked, still looking at Chuck, "you won't say another word. If you do, I'll—"

Nora's finger tightened around the trigger. The gun fired, sharp and piercing. Frank's forehead exploded outward. Bits of his skull sprayed across the carpet and he flopped face-first to the floor.

"You'll do *what*?" Nora demanded of her husband.

Red mist hung in the air above Frank's dead body.

Nora gripped the pistol in both hands. A wisp of blue smoke rose from the end of the gun's short barrel.

Chuck scrambled on hands and knees to the door of the motor home, wrenched the door open, and stumbled down the stairs and outside. Relieved when no gunshots rang out behind him, he charged past the motor home and sprinted for the trailer and his family.

Up and down the campground drive, motor home doors swung open and campers peered out. Janelle left the trailer with Carmelita and Rosie as Chuck approached at a run. Carmelita held Fredo against her chest. Rosie limped, clutching Janelle's arm.

Chuck met them in the middle of the driveway and hugged all three of them.

"What was—?" Janelle began, stepping back.

"Don't move," Nora commanded, cutting Janelle off as she strode down the drive toward them.

Chuck whirled to face her. She extended the pistol with one hand as she approached, the silver gun glinting in the last of the evening light.

39

Nora aimed the gun at Chuck's chest from a few feet away. Janelle stepped to his side, sheltering the girls behind her.

"I did what I had to do," Nora said. "You saw that. He threatened me. I had no choice."

Campers descended from their motor homes and approached from both directions. They halted twenty feet from Nora, Chuck, Janelle, and the girls—more than a dozen members of the RV group on one side, an equal number on the other. The German camper appeared behind the elderly campers.

Sheila and Martha approached from Martha's motor home. Martha joined the group of gathered campers, while Sheila shoved her way through the knot of people.

"What do you think you're doing?" she demanded of Nora.

Nora pivoted to Sheila, the gun extended in her hand.

Sheila froze, her eyes on the pistol. "That's the way it's going to be, is it?"

Nora turned, standing with Sheila on one side and Chuck, Janelle, and the girls on the other. She swept her gun back and forth between them.

"You're a fool, Nora," Sheila said. "You do whatever Frank tells you, like the meek little mouse you are."

"Not anymore," Nora said. Despite her lisp and Southern accent, newfound power in her voice lent conviction to her words. She lifted the gun. "Frank made me practice with this thing. He was so frightened a robber would break in on us. Practice, practice, practice. I hated every minute of it. But—" she toggled the pistol back and forth "—I can now say with certainty that practice does indeed make perfect."

Sheila glanced at Chuck.

He nodded to her, the slightest dip of his chin. Now, with his silent okay, Sheila would do what was required. As Nora's seer and confidant, she would step forward and take the gun from Nora's hand.

But his mother did no such thing. She stepped backward, away from Nora, returning to the group of gathered campers. Rather than join them, she kept reversing, parting the group around her. She spun and walked away, striding briskly up the driveway toward her car at the front of the campground.

Nora turned to Chuck, Janelle, and the girls. The look in her eyes was indiscernible in the evening gloom, but the shiny gun was plainly visible in her grip, trained on Chuck's sternum. The scent of expended gunpowder seeped from the mouth of the barrel, tinging the air.

Nora had fired the gun once with deadly effect. Chuck didn't doubt her willingness to fire it again.

He raised his hands to her. "Nora," he said. "There's no need for any more of this."

"I've had enough of men telling me what I need or don't need to do," she snarled.

Martha stepped to the front of the group of gathered campers. Holding out her hand to Nora, she ordered, "Give me that thing."

Nora spun with the gun to face Martha. "You, of all people," she hissed.

"This is not what we agreed to," Martha said. "For God's sake, Nora. There are children here."

"What *did* we agree to, then?" Nora demanded. "You got what you wanted. You're free and clear of your vile excuse of a husband."

"Not another word, Nora," Martha warned.

"That's what Frank said to me. Those exact words. That's why I killed him. He's dead, Martha. Frank's dead. And your Harold is just as—"

"No!" Martha cut in. Grief infused her voice. "I didn't . . . we didn't . . . I never wanted . . ."

"Oh, yes, you did," Nora rebuked Martha, her back to Chuck, Janelle, and the girls. "We both wanted our freedom, and you damn well know it."

Martha took a step toward Nora, her hands outstretched. "Sheila says I have to stay quiet. That's what she's been telling me, over and over. That's *all* she's been telling me. But I can't. I won't." She uttered a single final word: "Harold." Her shoulders shook with silent sobs.

Nora's body tensed. She steadied the pistol on Martha, her finger wrapped around the trigger. In the corner of his eye, Chuck caught sight of a flash of movement passing his head, accompanied by a screeching *yowl*.

Pasta Alfredo hurtled past him through the air and landed on Nora's back. Fredo dug her claws into Nora's gray hair, drawing back the woman's head. Nora's hand jerked and the gun fired, a white flash accompanied by an eardrum-searing blast.

Martha grabbed her thigh and crumpled to the ground. Carmelita bolted past Chuck and tackled Nora around the waist. Nora keeled forward, throwing out her hands. The gun flew free from Nora's grasp and skittered across the pavement as Carmelita drove her to the ground. Fredo leapt off Nora and ran into the shadows, trailing her rope leash. Carmelita put her knee on Nora's back, pressing the woman to the asphalt.

Chuck stepped forward. "I'll take her."

Carmelita clambered to her feet. Chuck pulled Nora to a standing position and secured her wrists behind her back with a firm grip.

Hurrying past Chuck and Nora, Janelle crouched beside

Martha, probing the woman's injured thigh with her fingers.

"She killed my Harold," Martha accused Nora through gritted teeth. Grimacing while Janelle performed her examination, Martha looked up at Chuck from where she sat on the driveway. "She pushed the ladder. I saw her, but I didn't want to believe it."

Nora leaned forward from Chuck's grasp until she loomed over Martha. "Yes, I killed him," she said. "As we both agreed. You know good and well what you told me yesterday, on the way back here from town."

Martha squeezed her eyes closed.

"Oh, no, you don't," Nora demanded. "No hiding."

Martha opened her eyes to slits, looking up at Nora.

"You said Harold was the meanest bastard who ever lived," Nora said, "and that Sheila had shown us what it was like to be our own women."

"But she went too far," Martha said. "She took our men from us. *You* took our men from us."

"Good riddance," Nora proclaimed. "I'll never, not for one minute, regret what I just did. I killed Frank in self-defense. The sniveling idiot. All the years I suffered with that man, and then he had the gall to . . . he had the gall to sleep with . . ." Nora eyed her fellow campers, circled around her and Martha. "Everyone here is my witness. I snapped, that's all. It was self-defense, as I said. And—" she gazed around her "—I was mistaken with what I said a minute ago about Harold. Martha doesn't know what she's talking about. Harold slipped on the ladder. He died. End of story."

Pasta Alfredo ambled back across the pavement from the edge of the driveway. Rosie scooped Fredo up and nuzzled the cat's fur with her chin, the rope leash trailing to the ground.

Carmelita untied the leash from Fredo's collar and turned to Chuck with the freed length of rope in her hands. "May I?"

Chuck grasped Nora's forearms behind her back while

Carmelita looped a climber's figure eight around the woman's thin wrists. Drawing the knot tight, Carmelita wrapped the remainder of the rope around the cinched figure eight and secured the dangling ends with a quick overhand knot.

From her sitting position, Martha said to Carmelita, "You saved my life."

"Pasta Alfredo did," Carmelita replied. "She knows how to fly. I just threw her."

Chuck looked up the driveway past Martha and the gathered campers. Sheila had vanished, swallowed by the encroaching darkness.

Carmelita grasped Nora's secured wrists. "I've got her," she assured Chuck.

The German camper worked his way through the crowd of onlookers and approached Carmelita. "Would you like if I help?" he asked her.

"Thanks, but I'm good," she said. "I tackled her once. I'll take her down again if I have to."

Chuck rested his hand on Carmelita's shoulder. "Spoken like a true Ortega."

"Like a true Bender, too," she said, looking at him with shining eyes.

A car engine started up, the sound coming from the campground entrance.

"Stop!" Sanford's cry came from the same direction, carrying over the rumble of the idling engine.

Chuck dropped his hand from Carmelita's shoulder. The chief ranger had returned to the campground, presumably upon hearing the gunshot that had taken Frank's life.

"We're good here," Carmelita said, her hands around Nora's roped wrists, the beefy German camper at her side.

Chuck left them, charging up the driveway.

40

Chuck approached Sheila's SUV at a run. Sanford stood in front of the vehicle, captured in the beams of the car's headlights, his pistol drawn and aimed at its windshield.

The engine died and Sheila left the vehicle.

"Calm down there, Sanford," she said, joining the chief ranger in the lights in front of the car. "I'm not going anywhere if you don't want me to."

Chuck slid to a stop in front of Sheila, his chest heaving. He vibrated with rage. "*You.*"

"You've got nothing on me, Charlie," she responded calmly.

"You told Frank to bomb Landscape Arch, timed for when the thumper truck began its work. You told him it was just a little monkeywrenching, to protect the environment. He had no idea what you really were up to."

Sheila lifted her chin. The beams of light struck the side of her head, slicing her face into defined planes of light and shadow. "I'm proud of what I had him do. He thought he'd dreamed up the idea of blowing up the arch himself on his hikes south of town, when he was trying—and, I might add, failing miserably—to lose weight on my orders. I fed him some lines about the environment and wilderness preservation. I told him he'd taken advantage of the world's resources his whole life, that he had to do what was right before he was too old and it was too late. It was all quite simple, really."

Chuck sucked deep breaths, his arms stiff at his sides. In the immediate aftermath of the arch collapse, when Frank had returned to the campground from toppled Landscape Arch, his fawning behavior toward Harold had been an act, played for Chuck and Janelle, and for his fellow campers as well.

"But Frank didn't do anything," Chuck said. "The explosion never went off. The thumps from the seismic truck caused the arch to fall. Either way, though, Megan ended up dead—" his voice trembled "—just as you wanted."

"Megan wanted a bigger cut," Sheila said bitterly, "then an even bigger one. When she started seeing clients on her own, I'd had enough. She got what she deserved."

"But there's no way you could have known for sure she'd be out on the arch when Frank blew it up."

Sheila tossed her head, her hair shimmering in the headlights. "Don't you see, Charlie? That's why I can talk about it as much as I want. I merely sent Megan out there at the same time as Frank and hoped for the best. If all I managed to do was put a scare into her, that would have been just fine. But I got much more than that." Her eyes went to Sanford's gun. "You can put that thing away now."

The pistol shook in the chief ranger's hand. "You got everything you wanted, didn't you?" he said to her.

"That I did."

"Only because of the way you used Frank," Chuck said.

She jutted her jaw. "You could say it was the other way around—that it was Frank who used me. After all, he was the one who put up the money. *He* paid *me*."

"The money doesn't matter," Chuck said. "You sent Frank to the arch. Megan's death is all your—"

He stopped in mid-sentence, his eyes on his mother, outlined in the headlights. In addition to Megan's death, there was Glen's death, too, and Frank's claim that Glen had leapt from the cliff. But Sanford was adamant that Glen never had shown signs that he was suicidal. Nor had Glen displayed any suicidal tendencies when Chuck had been with him on the ridge above the campground.

If Glen hadn't killed himself, however, that meant Frank had killed him instead. But why would Frank have done that?

He had drilled the hole in Landscape Arch and filled it with blasting powder, seeking to bring the arch down as directed by Sheila. But the seismic truck had beaten him to it, leaving the drill hole and powder residue behind as evidence. Chuck had discovered the hole and powder at the site of the collapsed arch—and he'd told only one other person, besides Janelle, about his discovery.

He turned to Sanford. "You, too."

Sanford shifted his feet, staring at the ground.

"The drill hole was there when you went to the site with your team," Chuck said. "You lied to me when you said you hadn't seen it. You knew you could convince the team, and Paul Johnson as well, that what they'd seen had been a naturally worn hole in the rock—as long as you made sure it was destroyed before anyone else saw it and studied it closely."

Sanford raised his head, his eyes clouded beneath his bushy eyebrows. "Yes."

The single word sent shock waves through Chuck. "You couldn't let the news of the attempted bombing of the arch reach the public, could you? You and Elsie were linked to Sheila. Everything you were working for on Elsie's behalf—the pictograph, the monuments—would have been ruined. You had to get rid of it, fast, before the park reopened." Chuck's eyes went to Sanford's holstered phone. "You got away from the others and made a call."

Sheila said to Sanford, "That's why I told you about Frank and his plans for the arch in the first place. Entrapment, I believe it's called."

Sanford's body sagged. He lowered his gun until it hung limp and unmoving from his hand.

Chuck said, "You called Sheila and told her about the hole, didn't you?"

Sheila's eyes gleamed. "Of course, he did." She addressed Sanford. "You didn't have Frank's number, but you knew he had to get back out there right away and destroy the drill hole—the evidence. You turned to me for help, and I gladly obliged."

Chuck curled his hands into fists. "Frank moved fast. He must have obliterated the hole and left just before I got back out there with Janelle and the girls."

The chief ranger's face fell. "I didn't have any choice," he pleaded, his voice breaking. "Elsie."

Chuck grabbed his sleeve. "Frank killed Glen, Sanford. He was up there on the cliff with him."

Sanford's eyes grew round. Blood drained from his face. "No. I don't believe it. Please, not that."

"Frank told me he offered food to Glen. He said Glen jumped. But you and I both know the truth. Glen never would have done that."

"Oh, dear God," Sanford moaned. "I protected Frank. Sheila told me what he was up to, but I kept quiet. I convinced myself he wouldn't go through with it. When I saw the hole, I didn't have any choice. I had to make sure it went away."

Chuck released Sanford's sleeve. "Glen went to the site of the collapsed arch yesterday. I tracked him there. Glen must have seen Frank coming back to the campground after it collapsed. Frank would have looped around to the campground, past Glen's hiding place up on the bluff. Glen must have grown suspicious. He went to the site of the collapse himself. He tried to tell me what he suspected by pointing at the arch. I'm sure that's why he called you, too, but he couldn't bring himself to say anything over the phone. I bet Frank saw Glen returning from the arch and realized Glen had found him out. He must have approached Glen at the edge of the cliff, with an offering of food. Glen never would have seen what was coming."

"Nooo!" Sanford howled, a cry of raw emotion. He shoved the gun in its holster and pressed both hands to his face.

Chuck exhaled heavily. Glen had scrabbled away from him atop the ridge, his fear obvious, when Chuck had thanked him for coming to Harold's aid so quickly after Harold fell from the ladder.

"I think Glen saw Nora shove the ladder with Harold on it, too," he said.

"Glen," Sanford cried through his fingers. "Oh, Glen." He bowed his head, sobbing. "What have I done?"

Sheila ignored the chief ranger. "Not bad, Charlie," she said. "You pretty much nailed it."

Chuck drew a sharp breath. "You know about Glen's death, too?"

"Of course," she said. "Frank was worried, on edge. He knew everything could be traced to him. When he spotted Glen coming back from the arch, he knew what he had to do. He called me for reassurance." She shrugged. "I had to consider Nora and what she'd done to Harold as well. Everything needed to be kept quiet. I merely agreed with Frank's plan." She put her hand on the chief ranger's arm. "Now, if you'll excuse me, Sanford." She edged him out of the headlights and away from the front of the car.

"You're not going anywhere," Chuck said. "Sanford's going to arrest you."

"Ha," she scoffed. "That's never going to happen."

Sanford stifled his sobs. "She's right." He dropped his hands, revealing his distraught face. "Glen's gone. Nothing will bring him back. If I press charges against your mother, the whole story will come out, but nothing will stick to her. She'll get off. And our chance to save the monuments—the one thing Elsie can do for Glen, for his legacy—will be lost in the headlines."

"What about Megan?" Chuck demanded. "What about *her* legacy?"

"Frank didn't kill her. Sheila didn't either."

Chuck groaned. "You're right," he said. "O&G Seismic killed Megan. George Epson killed her. He and his employees."

"They'll live with that for the rest of their lives. And that fact—as long as it remains unmuddied by what Frank and Sheila did—will play right into the campaign to save the monuments. Don't you see, Chuck? This is our chance, our *only* chance. For Elsie. For her people. For Glen."

Chuck's heart lodged in his throat. He shifted his gaze between Sheila, outlined in the light, and Sanford, hidden in the shadows.

"I guess that's it, then," Sheila said matter-of-factly. "I'm clean as a new day's dawn."

"You'll never work in Moab again," Chuck told her. "The rangers on Sanford's investigation team saw the drill hole and blast residue before Frank got rid of it. Now that it's gone, Sanford can insist it was natural. But there'll still be whispers around town. The truth will be out there, even if you can't legally be charged with anything."

"So what," Sheila said. "I'm ready to move on. There are lots more towns out there filled with people who'll pay me to tell them what they want to hear. Like I said, Charlie, people are easy—" she glanced at Sanford and her voice dropped a register "—and men are the easiest of them all."

She rounded the car, hitched her sweater-dress up her legs, and slid inside.

The engine started. Chuck stepped out of the way. Sirens sounded in the distance, headed for Devil's Garden, as his mother, the devil herself, drove past him and into the night.

ACKNOWLEDGMENTS

I would like to acknowledge the tireless work of nonprofit organizations, tribal entities, and individual citizens to protect and preserve our threatened national parks, national monuments, and public lands in Utah and across the West.

I owe a great debt to my early readers, John Peel, Kevin Graham, Margaret Mizushima, Chuck Greaves, and Andy Nettell, whose keen insights improved this book tremendously. I'm inspired by the intelligence, passion, and dedication of the team at Torrey House Press. Thank you, Kirsten Johanna Allen, Mark Bailey, Anne Terashima, Rachel Davis, and Kathleen Metcalf for all you do for me and the National Park Mystery Series, and for public lands conservation.

I appreciate the support for the National Park Mystery Series from independent booksellers, including my hometown Maria's Bookshop, Back of Beyond Books in Moab, the terrific member stores of the Mountains and Plains Independent Booksellers Association, and many more.

TERMS AND FURTHER READING

For plot purposes, this book simplifies and fictionalizes the historical makeup of, and interactions between, three cultures—Ancestral Puebloan, Fremont, and Mogollon—that populated portions of the American Southwest a thousand years ago.

As noted in the text, the term Ancestral Puebloan has replaced in recent years the term Anasazi for the ancient people who populated the Four Corners region, where Colorado, New Mexico, Arizona, and New Mexico meet.

The Fremont culture derives its name from the Fremont River, which flows through the heart of the culture's former homelands in central Utah. The river is named for early American explorer John Fremont.

The Mogollon culture, centered in southern New Mexico and Arizona, derives its name from the Mogollon Mountains, named for Spanish colonial Governor Don Juan Mogollon.

Among the best of the nonfiction books that offer historical and archaeological insight into the ancient cultures of the Southwest are *The Ancient Southwest: A Guide to Archaeological Sites* by Gregory McNamee with photos by Larry Lindahl, and *Ancient Ruins and Rock Art of the Southwest: An Archaeological Guide* by David Grant Noble.

In *The Lost World of the Old Ones* and *In Search of the Old Ones*, David Roberts provides a pair of personal accounts, separated by two decades, of a lifetime spent studying and exploring the archaeological wonders of the Southwest's ancient cultures.

ABOUT SCOTT GRAHAM

Scott Graham is the author of ten books, including the National Park Mystery Series from Torrey House Press, and *Extreme Kids,* winner of the National Outdoor Book Award. Graham is an avid outdoorsman who enjoys mountaineering, skiing, backpacking, mountain climbing, and whitewater rafting with his wife, who is an emergency physician, and their two sons. He lives in Durango, Colorado.

TORREY HOUSE PRESS

Voices for the Land

The economy is a wholly owned subsidiary of the environment, not the other way around.
—Senator Gaylord Nelson, founder of Earth Day

Torrey House Press is an independent nonprofit publisher promoting environmental conservation through literature. We believe that culture is changed through conversation and that lively, contemporary literature is the cutting edge of social change. We strive to identify exceptional writers, nurture their work, and engage the widest possible audience; to publish diverse voices with transformative stories that illuminate important facets of our ever-changing planet; to develop literary resources for the conservation movement, educating and entertaining readers, inspiring action.

Visit www.torreyhouse.org for reading group discussion guides, author interviews, and more.

As a 501(c)(3) nonprofit publisher, our work is made possible by the generous donations of readers like you. Join the Torrey House Press family and give today at www.torreyhouse.org/give.

This book was made possible with grants from Utah Humanities, Utah Division of Arts & Museums, Jeffrey S. and Helen H. Cardon Foundation, Barker Foundation, and Salt Lake County Zoo, Arts & Parks; donations from ATL Technology, Wasatch Advisors, BookBar, The King's English Bookshop, Jeff and Heather Adams, Robert and Camille Bailey Aagard, Curt and Nora Nichols, and Paula and Gary Evershed; generous donations from valued individual donors and subscribers; and support from the Torrey House Press board of directors.

Thank you for supporting Torrey House Press.

MESA VERDE VICTIM

A National Park Mystery
by Scott Graham

Coming June 2020 from Torrey House Press

TORREY HOUSE PRESS

SALT LAKE CITY • TORREY

PROLOGUE

Mesa Verde, Colorado
September 1891

A t first glance, the chamber looked coffin sized.

Joey Cannon breeched the hidden cavity at the bottom of the midden pile with the blade of his shovel. The heavily muscled sixteen-year-old stood neck deep in the crater he'd dug into the ancient trash heap over the last several hours, deepening and widening the hole by turns, tossing shovelfuls of soil, ash, and pebbles over his shoulder in long sooty arcs. Sweat streamed in runnels down his back. His palms were blistered, his forearms crying out for relief. Wafting from the clifftop above, the pungent scent of piñon and juniper trees bit his nostrils. It was long past nightfall, his kerosene lantern low on fuel and sputtering.

The hour was late, the minutes ticking past. He had until midnight, not a second longer, to unearth the rumored cache. If the artifacts waited, after centuries in hiding, as Gustaf Nordenskiold insisted, and if Joey reached them in time, he was to wrap them in cloth, stow them in his saddlebags, and set off for the train station thirty miles to the east, descending the rocky trail from the dig site, changing horses at the Mancos livery in the pre-dawn darkness, and galloping over Hesperus Divide to reach Durango by ten. There, he would add the treasures to the boxcar already loaded with objects gathered over the last two months by Gustaf. Joey would collect his reward from the Swedish explorer-scientist, and the train would chuff away to Denver, the artifacts bound ultimately for Stockholm.

Joey paused to wipe his brow with the sleeve of his coarse work shirt. He tucked the tail of the shirt into his canvas work pants and straightened his suspenders, thumbing them over his shoulders. He resettled his bandanna over his nose and mouth and resumed digging, intent on discovering the hidden cache in time—and thereby setting a new course for his life.

He'd toiled since childhood at his family's hardscrabble root-vegetable farm on the banks of the Mancos River. The farm was to him a place of endless tedium. Plant, irrigate, weed, repeat, year after monotonous year, with little time for formal schooling. Local girls ignored him, batting their eyes instead at the wealthy sons of ranchers and store owners. Soon enough, however, the girls would know their mistake. The money he'd already earned from Gustaf plus the sizable bonus the Swede pledged for the secret cache of treasures would enable Joey to buy a ticket to Denver and find a real job in the big city.

Gustaf—blond-haired, blue-eyed, in his early twenties—had stopped by the Cannon farm eight weeks ago. Seated on his handsome roan, he'd inquired of Joey's father in stilted English as to the availability of a laborer unafraid of hard work. Joey's father offered up his oldest son, and Joey rode away on the Swede's extra mount without a backward glance at his envious brothers and sisters, loping toward the green mesa looming nearly two thousand feet above the Mancos River.

In Gustaf's employ, Joey worked his way across the plateau with the other three members of the Swede's excavation team from one stone-and-mortar housing complex to the next. A prehistoric tribe had constructed the multi-story dwellings deep in canyons beneath overhanging cliffs over many centuries until, for unknown reasons, they deserted the mesa en masse, leaving an abundance of their worldly goods behind. With his fellow hired diggers, Joey gathered the tribe's abandoned possessions and packaged them in wooden crates lined with straw—finely crafted clay pots and mugs; clothing and jewelry including beaded turquoise necklaces, elk-bone breastplates, deerskin jackets, and turkey-feather shawls; arrowheads, knife blades, and hide scrapers flaked from obsidian; and spiritual fetishes and children's toys fashioned from wood and clay to resemble rabbits, ravens, great horned owls, and bighorn sheep. They removed human remains interred at the base of the abandoned complexes as well—perfectly preserved skulls, full skeletons, and infant corpses wrapped in blankets and tucked into reed baskets.

Gustaf rode back and forth between the plateau and his suite in Durango's Strater Hotel. He assessed the team's progress on his visits to the remote canyons that cut deep into the mesa top, and communicated by letter and telegram with his primary financier—his father, the famed baron and noted Arctic explorer Adolf Eric Nordenskiold—while in Durango.

Gustaf's arrest in his room at the hotel, accused by local authorities of the theft and attempted removal of cultural items from the United States, proved only a minor complication. The Swede's wealth and connections resulted in his release from detention after only a few hours. His succinct telegram home, the contents of which he shared with Joey, said it all: "Much Trouble Some Expense No Danger."

Still, Gustaf's arrest and detention, brief though it was, spurred the Scandinavian to move up his departure date for his return to Europe—and to single out Joey for a solitary mission in a heretofore unexplored canyon on the far west side of the plateau, culminating in tonight's hurried final dig.

Midnight was less than an hour away when the tip of Joey's shovel broke through a layer of dried mud and intertwined sticks, punching into the hidden chamber at the bottom of the midden pile. Joey twisted the shovel, ripping apart the thatched twigs to create a blade-wide opening into the void beneath his feet. He squatted and reached through the opening, his arm disappearing to his elbow. Sweeping his hand back and forth, he captured only air in his extended fingers. He lay on his stomach and extended the full length of his arm into the hole, finding the cavity deeper and more voluminous than he'd initially thought.

He grinned. This had to be the secret chamber Gustaf sought.

Joey's fingers struck something stone-like standing upright in the vault-like space. The unseen artifact toppled over with a quiet *clink*.

He withdrew his arm. The odor of must and decay seeped from the cavity. Thatched willow branches formed a ragged edge around the opening, sheered by his shovel blade. He gripped the ragged edge and tugged. A plate-sized portion of plaited sticks and dried mud came away in his hands. He tore off another section of thatched sticks and mud, enlarging the opening enough to shimmy through to the chamber below.

He directed his lantern into the opening. The toppled artifact lay on the dusty bottom of the chamber amid a dozen more of the objects standing upright on the floor of the dark space. He drew an exhilarated breath. The bonus and the new life it promised him were nearly within his grasp.

He set his lamp in the dirt and swung his feet into the opening, preparing to drop into the chamber. Clods of dirt tumbled past him, falling into the chamber, as someone slid into the neck-deep hole behind him. Before he could turn to see who it was, the sharpened blade of an ax struck the top of his head. The ax cleaved his skull, parting bone and brain matter in a single powerful blow.

The killer withdrew the ax from Joey's head with a slippery *snick*. Joey's body slumped sideways and lay twitching. The killer tugged Joey's feet from the opening and slipped into the cavity, crouching with his leather satchel over his shoulder and Joey's flickering lantern in his hand.

The lantern illuminated a room the size of a small crypt lined with the priceless artifacts sought by Gustaf—and others. The killer filled his satchel with the objects and hoisted himself out of the chamber. He lifted Joey's dead body to a sitting position and shoved. The teenager's body slithered through the opening and flopped backward to the floor of the cavity with a muted *thump*.

The killer wedged the plate-sized portions of plaited sticks back into place, resealing the chamber. He climbed out of the hole and set about refilling it with Joey's shovel. Dirt and ash poured down the sides of the depression and gathered atop the hidden crypt. The stick-and-mud thatching disappeared beneath the cascading debris as the killer transformed the secret cavity, shovelful by shovelful, into Joey's unmarked grave.

PART ONE

"People here have begun to oppose my excavation and work in a way that makes it desirable for me to soon leave this area."

—Explorer-scientist Gustaf Nordenskiold, after his 1891 arrest for trespassing and cultural theft in the Mesa Verde region

1

"I hate this, I hate this, I hate this!" twelve-year-old Rosie Ortega screeched as she descended on auto-belay to the base of the indoor rock-climbing wall. She squeezed her eyes shut, her hands gripping the rope affixed to the seat harness belted around her plump waist.

Chuck Bender wrapped her in a bear hug when she reached the padded floor of the rock gym. "You did fine up there," he assured her.

"No, I didn't," she cried, stomping her foot. Tears pooled in her eyes. She wriggled from Chuck's grasp and tore at the climbing rope knotted at her waist. "I barely got off the ground."

Other climbers in the gym averted their gazes as Chuck helped Rosie free herself from the rope.

"Carm's so good," Rosie blubbered, her lower lip trembling. She pressed her knuckles to the corners of her walnut brown eyes. "I *hate* her," she said to the floor.

"I heard that," fourteen-year-old Carmelita called from where she clung to molded-resin holds thirty feet overhead, working a 5.13a problem extending across the ceiling from the top of the wall.

Chuck craned his head to look up at her. "Your sister didn't mean it."

"Yes, I did," Rosie declared, her head still down. "Well, the good part, at least."

"That much would be right," Chuck said to her. He massaged the back of her neck, below the mane of curly black hair billowing from beneath her climbing helmet. "Your sister is good at this sport. Which is a problem for me, too."

Rosie turned her face to him, her watery eyes widening. "For you?"

"I've always been a rock climber for fun. Nowadays, though, climbing is a big-time athletic deal, with everybody making it into a massive competition—and like you said, it just so happens Carm's pretty darn good at it."

"Because she's so skinny," Rosie pouted.

"Just because," Chuck said. "But you and I have to remember we're doing it for the fun of it when we're playing around on the easy routes down low on the wall while Carm's way up on the 5.13 stuff, zipping around the ceiling like a spider monkey."

"I am *not* a monkey," Carmelita exclaimed from above. Her dark pony tail hung from the back of her head below her helmet. "That's racist."

Chuck smiled up at her. "I said you *climb* like one. Sheesh."

Carmelita lost her grip. Her rope caught her and she swung back and forth, dangling beneath the holds. "You're so culturally inappropriate," she admonished Chuck. She shook out her chalked hands as the auto-belay engaged and she descended, the rope automatically unspooling to lower her to the ground.

Chuck fixed her with a teasing grin when she reached the floor of the gym. "Let me get this straight. You're labeling me a culturally inappropriate white man even though I married a Latina woman and have been stepfather to her two hot-shot Latina daughters ever since?"

"*O . . . M . . . G,*" Carm pronounced breathily, her eyes large and round. "I can't believe you just called Rosie and me hot. That's so totally and completely *wrong.*"

"I didn't say hot. I said hot-shot."

Carmelita arched an eyebrow at him, the corner of her mouth twisted downward. "It still has the word hot in it."

He sighed but maintained his grin. "The two of you are

handsome. How's that?"

"Better," Carmelita said. "Still judgmental, though."

He spread his hands. "I can't win, can I?"

"Nope."

He glanced at his watch. "It's about time to head for home. Your *mamá* will be coming off her shift pretty soon. I need to get started on a culturally inappropriate dinner for us." He dipped his graying head at Carmelita. "How about tacos?"

She groaned. "You're awful."

"*Grrracias*," he said, giving the 'r' an extra-hard trill.

"You're . . . you're . . . incorrigible."

Chuck put his chalked hands to his stomach, leaving matching white prints on his gray T-shirt. "Got me." He pointed at her shiny black climbing tights. "The way you use such big words, you're getting to be too smart for your own britches, you know that?"

Carmelita's thigh-hugging tights rose to her burgundy top, which featured the Durango Climbing Team logo across its snug chest. The top was sleeveless and cut high across her midriff, baring her flat stomach and the smooth skin of her shoulders.

"That's my plan for world domination," she told him, "using my prodigious intelligence to rule the planet."

"Scary." Chuck reached behind her head and gave her pony tail a yank.

"Hey," she protested, ducking out of his reach. "You'll get my hair all chalky."

"*Lo siento*," he apologized, still grinning.

He crossed the mat to his soft-sided duffle. The navy bag rested on the floor next to Rosie's purple duffle and Carmelita's climbing team bag. He toweled the chalk off his hands, changed from his climbing shoes into his sneakers, and retrieved his phone. Its screen lit up with messages the instant he turned it on.

WHAT IS HAPPENING AT YOUR PLACE??? read the most recent message, from Alice Roberts, the elderly woman who lived next door to the rundown Victorian Chuck had picked up cheap in Durango's historic Avenues District a decade ago, five years before he married the girls' mother, Janelle, after a whirlwind romance.

He read the other texts in backward time order.

The second-most-recent: *If this is the phone of Chuck Bender, please contact the Durango Police Department immediately.*

Again, minutes earlier: *If this is the phone of Chuck Bender, please contact the Durango Police Department immediately.*

Ten minutes before that, an initial message from Alice: *Chuck are you there? Do you know anything about the sirens?*

He shoved his phone into the pocket of his climbing sweats, waved for the girls to follow him, and sprinted for the parking lot.

He sped south on Main Avenue behind the wheel of the big, blocky, Bender Archaeological crew-cab pickup truck. Carmelita sat in the front passenger seat, Rosie on the rear bench seat behind her. It was mid-afternoon, a Saturday in mid-October, the cloudless sky brilliant blue, the temperature in the low seventies, the leaves on the maples and poplars lining the four-lane thoroughfare through town rusty red and golden yellow.

"What's going on?" Carmelita demanded as Chuck blasted through a caution light well above the speed limit.

"We're about to find out," he said through gritted teeth.

Turning off Main into the Avenues, he slung the pickup around tight corners, left, right, left again.

"Woo-hoo!" Rosie cheered from the rear seat, flopping back and forth with the swerving truck.

Chuck rounded the final corner and roared onto their block. Several black-and-white Durango Police Department

SUVs crowded the street ahead. The vehicles were parked haphazardly in front of the house, their bar lights flashing.

Chuck slammed the truck to a stop in the middle of the street and hopped out, his thoughts on Janelle, *only* on Janelle.

She'd left at five that morning for a partial shift as a substitute paramedic with the Durango Fire and Rescue Department, taking the first half of a twenty-four-hour shift for a full-timer who needed the day off. Her fill-in stint wasn't due to end for another couple of hours—but what if she'd returned home for some reason while he and the girls were at the gym?

He charged up the sidewalk. A twenty-something female police officer in uniform blues, brass badge gleaming on her chest, stepped off the covered front porch of the house. Her right hand hovered near her pistol, holstered at her waist. "Slow down," she warned.

The officer's mocha skin and charcoal eyes, lined with black makeup, identified her as East Indian, an anomaly among Durango's mostly white citizenry interspersed with Latinos and Native Americans.

Chuck didn't slow. "This is my home." He aimed his chin at the one-and-a-half-story brick house behind the officer as he neared her. "My wife." He halted before her, his breaths coming in constricted gasps.

"You're Mr. Bender?"

"Yes."

"I.D."

"What?"

"I need to see some identification."

He slapped his hands to his sweats. "I left my wallet in my bag at the gym."

"You'll have to go get it."

"Not a chance," Chuck said, shoving his way past the officer.

"Oh, no, you don't," she said, following.

He yanked out his phone, its screen glowing with the texts from the police department, and waved it at her as he walked. "I came as soon as I saw these."

She huffed as she trailed him. When he neared the porch, she said, "Not that way. Around back."

Chuck changed course. He put his shoulder to the faded wooden gate at the side of the house, slamming it open and striding along the narrow passage between the house and head-high wooden side fence.

"What can you tell me?" Chuck demanded over his shoulder to the officer.

"I'm on perimeter," the officer said, jogging to keep up. "You'll have to talk to the others."

They reached the back of the house. A single-car garage filled one corner of the compact backyard. In the other corner, the gnarled branches of an apple tree extended over a raised-bed garden, fallow with the onset of fall.

Between the garage and garden, the gate leading through the fence to the back alley stood open. On the cracked pavement of the alley, framed by the open gate, lay a human body.

Red stains spotted a white sheet stretched over the dead body, which rested on its back. A sizable stomach pressed the sheet upward in the middle.

Chuck nearly collapsed, his legs growing weak—the body was not Janelle, with her slender frame.

He strode toward the gate, his eyes on the corpse, until a uniformed police officer stepped through the gate and swung it closed behind her, blocking his view.

The officer was Sandra Kingsley, tall and willowy and, like Chuck, in her mid-forties. Her sandy brown hair was cut straight across at her chin in an old-school bob. Her lips formed a compressed line. "It's okay, Chuck," she said as she reached him in the center of the yard. "It's not her."

He stopped. "Who, then?"

She hesitated. "I can't say."

"But you know," he said, voicing what he sensed from her hesitation.

She tipped her head forward, the brim of her police cap briefly hiding her green eyes.

"I know who it is, too, don't I?"

She nodded again, a slight dip of her dimpled chin. Her gaze moved past him to the house when another officer exited the back door. The officer was even younger than the female officer out front. Peach fuzz covered his upper lip and acne pocked his cheeks. A shock of auburn hair showed beneath the visor of his cap.

The boyish officer descended the three wooden steps from the rear of the house, the screen door swinging shut behind him. He hustled past Chuck and Sandra and on through the back gate.

Sandra said to Chuck, "Whatever happened appears to have started in your house."

"In my . . . in our . . . ?"

"In your study, to be exact." She fixed him with an unblinking gaze. "Did you have anything in there someone might have wanted?"

"What makes you ask?"

"It's a mess in there."

He waved a hand at the dead body in the alley behind the fence. "I'm an archaeologist. What could I possibly have that would be worth that?"

"You've made some big discoveries over the years, headline-making stuff. Everybody in town knows it."

"I never keep anything of value in my house. Ever."

"Someone thought otherwise, it would seem."

"Can I see?"

"You can't go inside." She paused, catching her lower lip between her teeth. "But I guess you could peek in the window. Maybe you'll spot something."

Chuck climbed the stairs to the back door. Gripping the doorframe, he leaned sideways and peered through the window into the small back room that served as his study. Inside the room, his scarred oak desk was swept clean. Spiral notebooks, photographs, and a desk lamp that normally sat on top of the desk were scattered across the hardwood floor. His laptop and monitor lay on the floor as well.

The drawers to his pair of four-drawer file cabinets opposite the desk were pulled open, their contents piled on the floor. Framed pictures of Janelle and the girls had been lifted from the walls and added to the pile.

Chuck straightened from the window. "Jesus," he said, returning to Sandra in the yard. "It's unbelievable in there."

"Somebody was looking for something."

"Obviously."

"And . . . ?"

He pursed his lips. "I have no idea."

"Think hard. It would appear somebody thought something in your study was worth killing over."

He pivoted at the strangled cry of "Chuck!" from Janelle as she rounded the rear corner of the house. She rushed to him. They embraced as Sandra looked on.

"Thank God, you're okay," Chuck said, stepping back.

Janelle wore her Durango Fire and Rescue uniform—navy blue shirt and black cargo pants with large side pockets. Her olive face was lightly made up, her long black hair corralled in a bun at the back of her neck. Her cheeks were sunken and sallow, and a damp sheen of perspiration shone on her forehead.

"Carm and Rosie are out front," she said. "The officer wouldn't let them come with me."

Chuck's eyes strayed to the back fence. "For good reason."

She followed his gaze. "I heard he's in the alley."

"*He?*"

Sandra lifted a finger in warning, but Janelle continued. "It's all over the Fire and Rescue radios. That's why Mark—" Janelle's shift supervisor, Mark Chapman "—sent me home." She took Chuck's hands in hers. Her voice shook. "It's Barney, Chuck. They're saying it's Barney."

Chuck's knees trembled. "*Barney?* That's insane. Are you sure?"

Barney Klema was a senior archaeologist for Southwest Archaeology Enterprises, one of several firms based in town that, like Chuck's one-man company, performed site surveys and digs throughout the archaeologically rich region surrounding Durango known as the Four Corners, where Colorado, New Mexico, Arizona, and Utah met.

Chuck had worked with Barney on a number of contracts over the years. More than just an occasional work partner, however, Barney was one of Chuck's few close friends, a big teddy bear of a guy, jovial and kind-hearted. In the years since Chuck had become a sudden husband to Janelle and dad to Carmelita and Rosie, he credited Barney's counsel with helping him tamp down the hot-headedness he'd displayed all too often during his years as a bachelor.

Barney and his wife, Audrey, had raised a son in Durango. Jason was in his twenties now, living and working in Denver.

"Barney doesn't have an enemy in the world," Chuck said.

"He couldn't," Janelle agreed. "Plus . . ." She glanced at Sandra, her voice trailing off.

Chuck knew what she was thinking. "Plus, Clarence," he finished for her. He turned to Sandra. "Assuming that really is

Barney Klema out there, I want you to know two things. First, to repeat: no one would ever want to hurt Barney. Everybody loves him, me included." He paused.

"Second?" Sandra asked.

"Second is that Clarence Ortega, Janelle's brother, has been doing a lot of work with Barney over the last few weeks."

Chuck spun back to Janelle, his eyes wide. "Have you talked to him? Is he okay?"

Janelle tapped her phone, a rectangle in the side pocket of her pants. "I called him. He's at his apartment. He's fine."

Chuck said to Sandra, "Barney's company, Southwest Archaeology Enterprises, has nabbed just about every contract in the area the last few months. They've taken on a number of new workers as a result. Clarence is one of them."

Sandra said to Janelle, "I'm sorry I can't confirm what you've heard. But any information your brother can provide will be helpful."

"Which means you haven't arrested anyone yet."

Sandra nodded but said, "I can't officially comment."

Janelle slapped a hand to her mouth. "I just remembered. Barney's wife, Audrey." She reached for her phone.

Sandra raised a hand to stop her. "We'll get someone over to the house. It's better to tell her in person." Then, to both Janelle and Chuck, "We'll need to do a round of questions with the two of you right away, before—"

"I'll take it from here, Kingsley," a male police officer broke in as he entered the yard through the gate from the alley. The officer closed the gate behind him. He was in his mid-thirties, as fit and trim as Chuck, but broader at the shoulders. A clipped brown mustache covered his upper lip. Prominent cheekbones and a squared-off jaw bounded his angular face.

The officer lifted a clear-plastic evidence bag as he approached Chuck and Janelle. A three-by-five-inch postcard, bent and crumpled, rested in the bottom of the ziplock bag. The officer flipped the bag so the creased front of the card faced them.

Chuck stared at the card and gasped.